BAD GAMBLE

Fiona Guthrie could see but one way to release herself from the debt she had contracted to the insufferably condescending Lord Peter Chalmsforth. She accepted the invitation of the Earl of Newlyn to match her skill against his in a high-stake game of piquet.

The infamous Earl was willing to wager the money Fiona needed if Fiona were willing to wager the intimate favors he desired.

Fiona was sure that the lessons at cardplay that her late father had given her would prevail against this odious man. But as she lost hand after hand as the night went on and on, the odds against her mounted . . .

. . . until she knew it would take more than skill or luck to save what she prized so much from the hands that she loathed above all. . . .

A DEBT
OF HONOUR

A DEBT
OF HONOUR

by
Diana Brown

A SIGNET BOOK

NAL PENGUIN INC.

Copyright © 1982 by Diana Brown

SIGNET TRADEMARK REG. U.S. PAT. OFF. AND FOREIGN COUNTRIES
REGISTERED TRADEMARK—MARCA REGISTRADA
HECHO EN CHICAGO, U.S.A.

SIGNET, SIGNET CLASSIC, MENTOR, ONYX, PLUME, MERIDIAN AND
NAL BOOKS are published by NAL Penguin Inc.,
1633 Broadway, New York, New York 10019

First Printing, March, 1982

4   5   6   7   8   9   10   11   12

PRINTED IN THE UNITED STATES OF AMERICA

To Clarissa —
who sparkles!

How, Liberty! Girl, can it be by thee nam'd
Equality too! hussy, art not asham'd?
Free and Equal indeed, while mankind thou
    enchainest
And over their hearts a proud Despot so
    reignest.

               —Robert Burns
    "To the beautiful Miss Eliza J—n
      On her principles of liberty
               and equality"

I didn't find it very inspiring apart from the illustrations to which, in obedience to an irrepressible urge, I applied some rather fascinating embellishments."

I

"Many happy returns of the day!"

Lord Peter Chalmsforth kissed his mother and gave her the long, slender box he had brought with him.

As he took his seat on the delicate Chippendale sofa in his mother's immaculate and tastefully furnished morning room, the first thing to meet his eye was a cumbersome, goosenecked vase decorating, or rather defacing a small, oak table in the corner. It was yellow, a particularly hideous shade of yellow, with an embossed design of nymphs, in an even more hideous puce. Apart from the unsightliness of the colour and design, the vase had a complete want of symmetry. It was perfectly awful and Lord Peter Chalmsforth could not understand how his mother, a woman of impeccable taste, had ever allowed such an abomination into her home.

"I do like the way you always remember me on your birthday, Peter," his mother was saying as she unwrapped the slim packet. "I know it is I who should be giving you a gift, but I do so enjoy receiving things from you as your choices are invariably perfect. Getting you a present, however, is an onerous task, for you have such very definite ideas I can never be sure that what I select will meet with your approval."

"As your firstborn I no doubt caused you more difficulty in coming into the world than did the others, so it is fitting that it is I who should remember you on this day. I can't, however, ever remember being dissatisfied with anything you have given me."

The low and relaxed quality of his voice bore the same languid elegance as his carriage and form. He sat carelessly, yet altogether gracefully, his long buckskin-encased, top-booted legs stretched before him, his nut-brown superfine coat fitting to perfection, his white starched cravat simply but impeccably tied.

"Do you remember the fob I gave you last year?" his

1

mother asked. "I considered it truly handsome but I have yet to see you wear it."

"Yes, that fob is an exquisite piece. I shall always treasure it for the beauty of its design quite apart from its value, but it is an age now since I have worn any such adornment."

"Your taste in dress is excellent, Peter, though there may be times when it is a little too severe for my liking." Lady Chalmsforth could not repress a slight sigh as she remembered her resplendently garbed husband who would never be seen without at least two waistcoats. Peter, as usual, wore only one and that without braid or ornament. Still, there was no denying that he presented a handsome figure and she could not repress a mother's flush of pride.

"While we're on the subject of taste, Mother, may I enquire where that yellow and puce monstrosity came from?"

"What yellow and puce monstrosity?" Lady Chalmsforth's voice was decidedly defensive as she assiduously busied herself with opening her present.

"What do you mean, 'What yellow and puce monstrosity'? Don't tell me that you have more than one of those eyesores! You may imagine you have tucked it away in the corner, but I am sure you are quite as aware as I that its singularly distasteful presence destroys the perfection of this room. It is truly awful and I'm quite sure that you know it. Now where on earth did it come from?" His distaste was obvious, yet there was a slight hint of humour behind the languor of his demand.

"Oh, Peter, I was afraid you would notice it. Dear Amanda Markham gave it to me quite a long time ago—her brother brought it back from Italy and she insisted on my having it, saying it simply *belonged* here. I had it in the yellow bedroom, but that did not satisfy her. I was forced to bring it down so that she would stop asking about it. I know it is ugly, but Amanda is one of my greatest friends and she means so well. If only"—Lady Chalmsforth paused and looked over at the object of their discourse before adding a trifle wistfully—"if only her taste weren't quite so . . . so . . . colourful. Couldn't you sit with your back to it, dear, as I do?"

"Wherever I sat I should still know it was there," her son responded caustically, and his mother sighed.

"I know you would, Peter. Sometimes I find your sensitivity to beauty quite awe-inspiring, but I fear it must make life difficult for you. We live, after all, in a rather vulgar world."

"True, but once aware of that vulgarity, must we let it intrude into our personal lives?"

Lady Chalmsforth, glad of an opportunity to change the subject, had drawn from the box her son had given her an ivory fan, intricately carved with a design of entwined lotus leaves.

"How exquisite!" she exclaimed as she opened the fan and held it at arm's length to fully admire its delicate carving, her pale hands spreading the blades of ivory to their utmost expanse. "How truly exquisite! I've seen nothing quite like it before. Where did you find it?"

"At an auction at Sotheby's a few weeks ago. I knew it was old by the design and the shading of the ivory—I suspect it may be Mongol by the carving. Probably some nabob brought it back, completely unaware of its worth. I have had it restrung so that it should be perfectly safe for you to carry it. Although the ivory is extensively wrought, I believe it will hold perfectly well."

"I shall save it for Fanny Sefton's ball—that is the place for its debut. It will be perfect with my cream silk. Thank you, dear, thank you so very much."

She smiled at her son with an affection he quite clearly returned. They were very much alike in appearance and character, though Lady Chalmsforth possessed more warmth of disposition than did her son, who was regarded by most habitués of London society as haughty and arrogant. Peter Chalmsforth was a private man, his circle of intimates was small and he chose to keep it so. No woman, save his mother, had ever entered that circle. It was not that he eschewed society, far from it, for as holder of an old and illustrious title he was aware of his obligations and he upheld them punctiliously if not with relish. His mother, on the other hand, delighted in the round of engagements that had consumed her time since her husband's death four years previously. Until that unfortunate event she had spent much of the year at Perrynchase, the Chalmsforth seat in Hampshire, but once alone she could no longer bear surroundings which only too clearly reminded her of her deceased spouse. She had returned to London to take up residence in her townhouse on Brook Street, only rarely allowing herself to be lured back to Hampshire by her son. Perrynchase needed a woman's touch, every visit confirmed that to be so, but that touch should no longer be hers.

Dear Peter! His mother looked across at him in affection—his fair hair, almost touching the collar of his coat, was worn longer than most, but then Peter had always set his own style, and those discerning grey eyes set in that long, intelligent face, with its Chalmsforth features which were to be found again and again in the paintings in the gallery at Perrynchase. Neither of her other sons had possessed his sharp intellect nor his grace, though she thought that Sarah, had she survived, would have been much like him. Would they remain as close, she wondered, when at last he did select a wife? When George, her second son, had married, she had seen little of him. Quite selfishly, she had been overjoyed when his wife had borne a daughter, though she knew they wanted a son. Now, since George's death in a carriage accident, she saw more of his widow, Kitty, though their relationship could not be described as a close one—she found Kitty far too calculating, too obsessed with her own worth with little concern for others, even for her daughter, Susan, who, at eight had taken the death of her father far more to heart than had her mother. Even Gerald, the youngest Chalmsforth, with his devil-may-care attitude toward life, had shown more emotion over his brother's loss than had Kitty, but then Lady Chalmsforth hastened to remind herself that she should not judge the depths of the feelings of others, for Peter was accounted by many to be devoid of emotion and only she knew the depths to which he suffered.

She had so wanted a daughter, but Sarah had not survived past her fifth birthday. At least she had a treasure in Susan, her grandchild, her only grandchild, a fact of which she was fond of reminding Peter.

Chalmsforth seemed to sense the topic that was about to be raised again on this, his thirtieth birthday, as his mother began, "So, Peter, you pass into another decade."

"Yes, Mother, and I am still unmarried," her son concluded, though without rancour.

He was quite as aware as his mother of the importance of producing an heir for a title and a heritage which had been theirs for two centuries during which the Chalmsforths, by a series of prudent marriages, had managed to align themselves with the foremost families of England. It was, in fact, said of them that they never married, rather they contracted alliances. By so doing they had accumulated land, wealth, and power to earn a position which could never be overlooked, and while it commanded regard and respect, it also invited no little envy. If Chalmsforth at times found this position irksome, few knew it, for he had early recognized the importance of upholding a birthright which, though he might not have chosen it, was nevertheless an obligation he could not nor would ever evade. It had been re-emphasized to him in a letter he had received at Eton while his mother was awaiting Gerald's birth. He had kept it, though he no longer had to read it to remember its words:

"My darling Peter," his mother had written, "if God chooses to take me from you at this time, this is my own farewell to you. I pray it will not be so but, should it be, I pray you to receive comfort from Him and from your own dear father. Never forget that you, my own dear son, are the eldest Chalmsforth. Persevere with your studies and always lead the life which your position must demand of you. Remember always our family name and honour. I trust you will ever look after your brother, George, your sister, Sarah, and this new baby, should he or she survive, which I pray God may grant."

Though young then and given to high-spirited, even rebellious behaviour, he had been much affected by his mother's letter, the contents of which had never been discussed between them, though the bond of intimacy it had formed at that time had never weakened. It had caused him to be protective of his younger brothers, often against their wishes and his own inclination, though George had never resented it as did Gerald, whose flippant, rambunctious, at times wild, animal spirits caused him to rebel at anything he construed as control.

Half to himself, Chalmsforth sighed. That he must marry, he knew, yet he was loathe to allow a woman into his life. He had never found one with whom he wished to be joined in the permanency of marriage. He was, however, by no means impervious to feminine charms. He had, since his Oxford days, engaged in a number of discreet affairs with cooperative beauties, yet they had remained merely occasional companions, never privy to the complexities of his character, sharing his bed but not his mind. He doubted there was any woman in whom he would choose to confide.

Chalmsforth had been at his most carefree while serving with Wellington in his Peninsular campaigns, for life with the army he had found surprisingly to his liking. He enjoyed the company of men, the lack of constraint of life on the march, the excitement of the campaign, and the intellectual challenge of outwitting an enemy. He had earned the respect of the men who served with him and under him by his unquestionable fairness and his dauntless courage, though there were those among them who felt his bravery to be nothing less than a death wish. But when his brother George had been killed, Chalmsforth had been forced to resign his commission and return to England. His return was essential, however, for though he had never had any qualms about George's inheriting the title should he be killed, his youngest brother, Gerald, was far too immature and impulsive to assume such responsibilities. His own direct participation at an end, he was forced to follow events in the continuing Napoleonic wars vicariously through friends still serving abroad. He put his energies and his intellect into the development of a book collection which was said to rival even that of the Duke of Roxburghe. Though the accumulation and preservation of the world's knowledge appealed to his intellect, it was a poor substitute for the campaign, and his frustrations were often worked off within the confines of Gentleman Jackson's boxing saloon, where many a worthy opponent, observing his languid attitude, had learned only too late the devastating power of his fists when he was determined to win. Book collecting and boxing, an odd combination, the accumulation of knowledge coupled with man's most primitive instinct, perhaps it was the incongruity that appealed to him. A wife had no place in either sphere yet a wife was a necessity.

"The Dowager Marchioness of Orbury visited me just this week," his mother was saying. "You know her son is anxious that his eldest daughter should marry into the right family, and there could be no doubt that she considered ours to be the one."

"Orbury's daughter? Which one is that?" Chalmsforth put the question without enthusiasm. Season after season he had been pursued by persistent parents of marriageable daughters. How he loathed their blatant efforts to entrap him. All of their daughters over the course of time melded into one picture of English womanhood, comely and shy, yet totally insipid, devoid of intelligence, conversation, or any original thought. None had held any attraction or allure for him.

"Come, Peter, you must remember Annabel Telford. She is such a beauty, she can't have escaped your attention."

"Annabel Telford?" he questioned without any particular interest. "Oh, yes, I know who you mean. She is the one they call the Iceberg. She is a beauty, true, but so distant. Yes . . ." He paused. Since marriage was inevitable, why postpone it any longer, and the Orbury girl might do as well as any other. "Her bloodlines are certainly impeccable and despite her rather ethereal aspect, judging by the performance of her forebears I suspect she may bear children well."

"Darling, don't talk about Annabel Telford's being cold. You hardly sound like a panting lover yourself."

"No, I hardly cast myself in that role. Were it not for the necessity of producing an heir, I must admit I would prefer to remain unmarried."

"Yet you seem to enjoy those—those ladies with whom you do form relationships. That little flibberty-gibbet of an opera singer last year, for instance, not marriage material, of course, but you must have held her in some favour to bestow on her that diamond necklace which she flaunts all over town. I must say, I wish it had not been quite so ostentatious."

"She chose it herself, and since she enjoys it that is all that matters. She gave me a great deal of pleasure at a time when I most needed it after leaving the army. She was worth every penny of it." Chalmsforth spoke frankly and without hesitation on a matter that many men would have never have dared broach to their mothers, yet so it had always been between them.

"But a wife can bring you even more pleasure than a mistress," his mother argued. "And children, too."

"The latter I grant you, the former I doubt. However, I daresay Annabel Telford will answer quite as well as any other. Her appearance is certainly in her favour and that distant manner may prove to be an advantage. Yes, I think she may do quite well. I shall call upon her and, unless anything untoward occurs to discourage me, I shall very likely pay my addresses to her. Does that set your mind at ease?" Chalmsforth stretched his long legs before him and directed a questioning gaze at his mother who, though she seemed pleased, did not appear to be entirely satisfied.

"That's good, dear, though I might wish for a little more passion, but that, I am quite sure, will come. The Dowager Marchioness tells me that Annabel is a simply splendid young lady and stands to inherit handsomely on her mother's side." His mother continued to look hesitant. "There is one other matter, though, that I should mention. . . ."

"Well, Mother, out with it. Not pigeon-toed, is she?"

"No, of course not, dear, it is not about Annabel Telford. Her toes, as far as I know, are perfectly proper. Of course, I haven't personally inspected them, but her carriage is nothing short of queenly. No, this does not concern Miss Telford. It's about Gerald."

Chalmsford groaned. He might have known. Gerald was in a scrape again and he would be required to get him out of it. If he hated intervening in his brother's affairs, Gerald, he knew, detested his intervention even more so. He had never intervened from choice, only from necessity, and, had he not done so, what might have been the outcome? There had been the little milliner Gerald had run off with at sixteen; he had caught up with them on the road to Gretna Green and had paid off the young woman after it was ascertained she was not, as she had sworn, with child. Then there had been the Newmarket scandal. A group of young bloods had been suspected of having interfered with the jockeys' weights in an important race. Gerald had been among them and, though Chalmsforth was convinced that his brother had not, himself, done anything wrong, still any involvement in such a scheme could not be honourable. As a member of the Jockey Club, Chalmsforth had offered to resign, but the other members would not hear of it. And only last year Gerald had been challenged to a duel by elderly Lord Blanding who had accused him of paying undue attentions to his much younger, very pretty, and very flirtatious wife. It had taken all Chalmsforth's ingenuity to forestall an event that could have produced nothing but sorrow for his brother and shame for the family, whatever had been the outcome.

"I fear Gerald has been acting a little unwisely again," his mother continued calmly.

"What do you mean, *again*, when did Gerald ever act in any other manner?" Chalmsforth could not keep the irritation from his voice.

"I know, dear, but he is still so young. You must remember that you are nine years his senior, and you cast some wild oats in your youth. I have to admit, though, that you were never the trouble that Gerald is, though your father was here to handle matters then."

Chalmsforth groaned again. He knew he was in for a long diatribe on Gerald's latest feats and, settling back in his seat, he resigned himself to the inevitable. Like it or not, he would never be able to divorce himself from his brother's peccadilloes for, under the terms of his father's will, he was his brother's legal guardian until he attained the age of twenty-five.

"Well, what has brother Gerald been up to now?" he asked with some asperity.

"I have reason to believe he is mixed up with some girl."

"Gerald is always mixed up with some girl," Chalmsforth riposted.

"I know, but this time it seems to be different. He moons around the house whenever he visits me, quoting poetry and acting in such a soulful manner. I was hoping that this time he might present me with some eligible young lady, for I firmly believe that the influence of the right woman could make all the difference to Gerald. It seems, however, that he was introduced to this young woman at Vauxhall and she is, it would appear, a friend of young Guthrie, whose reputation leaves much to be desired. I'm most apprehensive, Peter."

"Guthrie?" Chalmsforth questioned. "Guthrie? Yes, he's the young whipper-snapper always in over his head. There's been some talk of forcing him to resign from White's because he's been making rather a nuisance of himself there. Won't leave the tables alone and horribly in debt."

"Such a shame. I knew his mother, Ellen Berrington, quite well. We came out at the same time and were great friends for a time. She was such a beauty and had a not inconsiderable fortune. You've no idea the envy she aroused, for the gentlemen that season scarcely looked at anyone else when she was present. No one could believe it when she accepted Aaron Guthrie, for she could have had anyone—oh, I know he came of a good family, and of course he had that great house in Cambridgeshire, but not a sou, and he never could leave the cards alone, nor anything else on which he might gamble for that matter. I hardly saw anything of Ellen after she married. She stayed at Culross Abbey, immured in that alien countryside, so unlike her, for she was always so gay and she simply loved parties. They say he gambled away all of her fortune and most of his estate before he died and now, it would seem, their son is rapidly disposing of whatever remained. Such a pity! An old family, too, and that abbey of theirs is quite historically significant, built by the Cisterians, I believe Ellen told me, some time in the twelfth century. So much for history!" Lady Chalmsforth sighed. "I do wish Gerald would choose friends of a more stable disposition."

"Gerald chooses his friends as the whim strikes him," his brother commented dryly, forbearing to add that he felt his brother had the same instabilities as the friends he chose. Noticing his mother's worried frown, he quickly consoled, "I doubt there's anything to concern yourself with, Mother. The young woman is probably some passing fancy. Gerald knows he cannot marry outside his station in life. I made that quite plain to him over that last incident, not if he wants to gain his full inheritance, that is. Gerald may be incorrigible, and I admit he falls in and out of love with the rapidity of a finch in a blossom bush, but he's no fool," Chalmsforth argued with an assurance he, himself, did not fully share.

"I know, Peter. It's just that Gerald is such an impressionable young man. Someone like this young woman may make him forget everything. He seems so . . . so besotted. She may persuade him to do something he may regret—he may run off with her just as he did before."

"Run off with her he may, but marry her he won't, not if he knows what's good for him. I doubt he wants to live in poverty, or what he would consider poverty. Where is he now?"

"He's gone off to Cambridgeshire with young Guthrie, that's why I'm talking to you about it. He was in such high spirits when he came to say good-bye, I had the awful feeling that he was up to something. I can't help but wonder whether the young woman may not be with him."

"All the better if she is," Chalmsforth replied caustically. "Perhaps a wild escapade like that may serve to rid her from his system. If she accompanies him on such a caper, even Gerald must realize she is not the sort of woman he could ever consider marrying."

"But, you see, I think from what he says that, though she's a friend of Neill Guthrie's, she is from a respectable family—not like the other one. Gerald said, I believe, that her father is in the church."

"In the church! Well, he certainly raised a daughter with little regard for moral or religious scruples." Chalmsforth was indignant. "What is the church coming to, placing such men in the pulpit to instruct others how to live while they allow such reprehensible conduct in their own families!"

"You are right, of course, Peter, but you see, if she is a decent girl, no matter how wrong she may be, if Gerald compromises her, he cannot abandon her. It would reflect upon him, upon the Chalmsforth name, should she make it known. Gerald sometimes says things he does not mean—he may have promised her marriage, she may be of the opinion that since he is of age he can make whatever matrimonial plans he wishes without further consulting anyone."

"If that is the case, her thinking should certainly be set aright."

"I couldn't agree with you more, dear." His mother leaned across to place her hand over his. "Do you happen to be going to Newmarket to look over your horses, by any chance? Culross Abbey is, I believe, not far off the Newmarket road."

"Very well." Chalmsforth resigned himself to the inevitable. "I shall stop and see what is going on there, though without doubt it will make for an awkward situation. I'm no friend of young Guthrie's, and Gerald will know why I am there and resent my intrusion as he always does. My appearance might even serve to drive him into something rather than prevent it."

Lady Chalmsforth breathed a sigh of relief.

"I doubt that, dear. I know I can rely on you, for you are the soul of discretion."

The soul of discretion eased himself out of the delicate sofa and quite slowly and very deliberately walked over to the corner table. Picking up the goose-necked vase that had confronted him throughout his visit, he held it up as though to examine the forms depicted on it. Then, just as deliberately, he let it fall from his long fingers to smash into a myriad fragments at his feet.

"Thank you, Peter." His mother's satisfaction was obvious. "The servants have been so horribly careful in dusting it and since I could never bring myself to do such a thing, I thought I should never be rid of it."

"I shall convey my apologies to Lady Markham when next

I see her for the mayhem I have wrought upon her gift to you. In the meantime, please assure her I am replacing it with a Sèvres from my own collection, in the ungodly event that she should possess its mate."

II

"We're jam-packed, me lud." The corpulent landlord of the Bell at Haddenheath stood apologetically wiping his hands on his sturdy apron. "They're coming out of the rafters. No proper accommodation left, nothing at least that I'd dare to offer the likes of your lordship."

"Oh Lord," Chalmsforth groaned under his breath. It had been a wretched day, a wretched day drawing to an even more wretched close.

It had started with that long session with his new secretary, Nicholson, who never seemed to get anything quite right—how he missed Trevor, not that he had begrudged him the chance to advance, in fact Chalmsforth, himself, had obtained for him his new position with a close friend who had been appointed Ambassador to Holland. Trevor would do well there; he deserved to succeed and Chalmsforth knew that he would. Even though he believed that Nicholson would, with time, acquit himself quite as well in handling his affairs, nevertheless, knowing that he had to go chasing across the country because of one of Gerald's scrapes had put him in an ill humour. He had had little patience with Nicholson, snapping at him repeatedly until he realized that the young man was on the point of tears, at which point he had felt thoroughly ashamed, yet in no better humour.

He had tried to restrain his annoyance when, having instructed Nicholson to accept an invitation to dine with the Marquess of Orbury at the end of the week, he discovered that he would be obliged to forego dining with the Sublime Society of Beefsteaks.

"Oh, damn!" He had thrown Orbury's card aside in disgust. The Beefsteaks was an exclusive gathering with membership limited to twenty-four congenial souls who devoted their evenings together to good humour, good food, and good fellowship. He preferred the plain steak, baked potatoes, and

13

onions eaten in their convivial society to evenings at White's or Crockford's, where all attention was focussed on the gaming tables which held little allure for him. Certainly to give up donning the blue coat, buff waistcoat, and red cape of the Beefsteaks in favour of an evening with the Orburys, many of whom he preferred to give a wide berth, was cause for vexation.

"Am I to infer your lordship accepts all invitations from the Marquess of Orbury?" Nicholson, pencil raised over notepad, obviously anxious to learn all he could of his employer's rather complicated position in society, had fixed his owl-like gaze upon Chalmsforth.

"I suppose so, at least until I instruct you otherwise," Chalmsforth agreed with reluctance. Having promised his mother, he must at least make an effort to become acquainted with the family of the lady who seemed destined to be his future wife, though he did not look upon it with pleasure.

No, the day had begun badly and even the exhilaration of pacing his perfectly matched chestnuts on that fine autumn day with only his manservant for company, a man for whom he had more regard than many of his own station in life, had not dispelled his ill humour, for he knew he was on a mission for which he had no relish, one which could only estrange him further from his only surviving brother.

"Is there no other inn close by?" Chalmsforth demanded of the Bell's landlord.

"O'course, me lud. There's the Jolly Weaver over at Grasston, and the Brace of Pheasants at Butterfield, and the White Hart at Weston, and the——"

"Spare me the entire listing. Which one is closest?"

"Well, closest is the Running Horse at Cagford, but I wasn't even going to mention that for all the rooms there have been spoken for this past se'ennight."

"Then which of the others would you recommend?" Chalmsforth tried to restrain his impatience.

The landlord scratched his head. "None of 'em really, me lud, cos, same as me, I'm sure they're all full."

Chalmsforth looked beyond the inn's courtyard at the darkening, bleak countryside beyond, nothingness for miles as far as he could see.

"You must pardon the question, but what can have caused such a descent on what appears to be a less than lively corner of our realm?"

14

"Why, the fight o'course," the landlord replied proudly.

"The fight?"

"Between Bill Neate and Ned Turner, over at Cagford. Day after tomorrow is the big event but the toffs've been descending on us all week. Good for business, o'course, but oh, the demands they make, it fair wears a body out. The missus says. . . ."

But Chalmsforth did not wait to hear what the missus said. He felt cheered for the first time that day.

"Ah, the prizefight—so that's it!"

The prizefight, that must be why Gerald had come down to Culross Abbey with young Guthrie. Chalmsforth had heard about it at Gentleman Jackson's—the fight of the decade they were calling it, wagers were flying back and forth. Guthrie, with his penchant for plunging, would undoubtedly be involved, especially with the fight being so close to his own back door. They were saying that more than two hundred thousand pounds had been staked on the mill, and it was expected that fifteen thousand spectators would be on hand to watch the two men battle it out. Chalmsforth had not been enthusiastic about the fight—neither were fighters he particularly admired and the crush would be formidable—but now he was quite delighted. Apart from the fight's providing the probable reason for Gerald's journey, it would provide an excuse for his own presence in the area. He was certain that his mother's alarm was unnecessary; nevertheless, to calm her fears he would drop by the abbey in the morning before going on to Newmarket.

"Anything will do for the night, landlord, suitable or not."

Again, the landlord scratched his head. "I suppose I could move young Lord Sutton who just came in and give you his corner room, though it's not much."

"Don't move Lord Sutton, just give me whatever there is. And before it gets completely dark I'm going to stretch my legs. Did I not notice a fine old church as I entered the village?"

"You did, indeed, me lud." The landlord waxed enthusiastic that someone had noticed Haddenheath's most prized possession after the abbey. "We're right proud of St. Matthew's—dates back to Saxon days, they say, not that many who come through here realize that. It is well worth looking at, me lud, and if Mr. Robarts, the rector of our parish, is around, he'll have many an interesting tale to tell. No matter what you say, I'm going to get that corner room ready for you as best I can and I'm going to see that the missus prepares you some of her good jugged hare and suet pudding and serves the cherry brandy I keep for special occasions."

The church tower, Chalmsforth found, was indeed Saxon and amazingly well preserved, though it appeared to have been modified considerably by the Normans, for the semicircular stair turret and the triple window between the tower and the church interior were certainly of a later period.

In the churchyard, Chalmsforth paused before an elaborate gravestone of intricate design and lengthy inscription, and on examining it he found it was of recent origin, for it read:

> Here is entombed Lady Ellen Guthrie, daughter of Sir Frank Berrington, loving wife of Sir Aaron Guthrie, devoted mother. Her beauty, of exquisite brilliance, was unfaded when she fell. Her understanding was of such quickness and reach that her knowledge was instant. Her heart, warmed with universal benevolence to the highest degree of sensibility, had a ready tear for pity, glowed with friendship as with a sacred and inviolate fire. Her love, to those blest with it, was happiness. Her sentiments were correct, refined, elevated. Her manner, so cheerful, was elegant, winning, and amiable so that while she was admired, she was beloved, and, while she enlightened, she enlivened. She was the delight of the world in which she lived, she was formed for life, yet she was prepared for death, that gentle wafting to immortality, where she lives in eternity.

It was an unusually elaborate inscription; the beauty of the language caused Chalmsforth to reflect. It was, quite obviously, the tomb of Guthrie's mother, and would seem to indicate that she had been greatly loved and equally missed, yet, remembering his mother's comments on Sir Aaron Guthrie having run through his wife's fortune, Chalmsforth wondered, a trifle cynically, whether the elaborate marker had not been born of a guilty conscience. Beside the lady's stone was a plainer one marking her husband's resting place, simply inscribed with the facts of his birth and death. Other Guthrie gravesites dated back to the early part of the seventeenth century when it would appear they had come from the highlands of Scotland to settle in the flats of the fenland. They had obviously been a powerful clan.

With twilight falling it was difficult to appreciate the interior of the church, dark except for two candles burning close to the altar. Heavy Norman piers with elaborately carved capitals supported the arches and, as Chalmsforth paused to examine a curious stone in the form of a rose in the pillar above the nave he was suddenly aware that he was not alone. Turning he found himself confronted by a tall, thin gentleman, of hard, wiry frame and a shock of white hair.

"Ah, I see you've discovered our rose stone," he smiled.

"It is a curious carving. I was wondering whether it had particular significance. Allow me to introduce myself—I am Chalmsforth, Lord Peter Chalmsforth of Perrynchase in Hampshire, and you, I take it, must be Mr. Robarts, rector of Haddenheath."

The parson expressed surprise that his name was known to the visitor until Chalmsforth explained that the landlord of the Bell had recommended Mr. Robarts as an authority on the church.

"I suppose I should be. I have held this living for almost thirty years. I think I know every nook and cranny of St. Matthew's by now. The rose stone you are looking at conceals a cavity in which we found a covered wooden dish bound in linen cloth; inside was the embalmed remains of a human heart. There was no way of knowing to whom the heart belonged—perhaps it was a relic, but more likely it may have belonged to a member of the Guthrie family and was placed there in Cromwell's time." He smiled fleetingly. "There are those who insist that it is the heart of Mary Queen of Scots, who was executed not far from here at Fotheringay, but I doubt it can ever be proved. I have examined the Guthrie family papers but can find nothing of its history."

"The Guthries seem to be an important family in this part of the country. I was remarking the number of gravestones bearing that name in the churchyard."

"Indeed, they have been, though precious few now remain. Undoubtedly you have heard of Culross Abbey—it has been their seat since it was presented to the family by James the first. They came with him from Scotland and served him well. Of late, the family has fallen upon bad times. They have been forced to sell much of the estate, indeed, little remains to them except the great abbey itself. Young Sir Neill has inherited a difficult task and I'm afraid. . . ." Mr. Robarts paused doubtfully. "But possibly you know the family, my lord."

"I am barely acquainted with Sir Neill Guthrie. My younger brother knows him considerably better than myself and is, in fact, a guest at the abbey—I shall be calling there in the morning. I was on my way to Newmarket and thought to take this detour not realizing that a prizefight was being held. It seems that the world and his wife has descended upon you."

"Ah, yes!" Mr. Robarts sighed heavily. "If only they would flock to the church as they flock to a fight. I suppose we just don't provide enough excitement for them, at least that is what that fellow Wesley was saying and I'm beginning to think he might have had a point. Not that I would consider anything outside the established church, my lord," he added hastily. "Please don't misunderstand. Still, it seems we are not altogether answering the needs of our flock."

"You may be right. There's no doubt Wesley was a good man at heart and his original intent was not to move outside the church but to light a fire within, something that proved to be too difficult. I'm afraid my view of Wesley is not a popular one in the House, however."

They had reached the porch, where Chalmsforth paused to admire the carved oak doors and a stone font.

"Lovely, quite lovely," he murmured. "And most ancient."

"This is a truly historic part of our land—it is also a country of rabble-rousers and free spirits, I must add. Cromwell was born not far from here at Huntingdon, Tom Paine at Thetford, and, of course, we all remember from our history books that Hereford the Wake who fought so hard against William the Conqueror made his glorious stand at Ely. The low country produces an unconventional breed—wild spirits of the fens, I call them."

"And I dare say you consider we Hampshire men to be traditionalists since we come from the original Wessex, Saxon country. I must say, though, that Cambridgeshire, notwithstanding her heroes, could use some of Hampshire's woodlands. I cannot get used to the devilish dullness of these fens."

"Ah, but you would, my lord, if you lived here. They have a beauty quite their own, such skies, such cloud formations, and I defy you to reproduce the magnificent sunset with which we are blessed. And such wildlife we have would never be seen in Hampshire, coypu and otter, geese and snipe, and the streams abound in roach and perch. No, no, I am convinced that those who find the fens uninteresting only do so because they do not know them. Live here for a while and I defy you to continue to hold that opinion."

"I shall, I regret, have to take your word for that, Mr. Robarts, for my stay will not be long."

Again as they passed Lady Guthrie's marker, Chalmsforth paused.

"She must have been a remarkable woman."

"She was indeed," Mr. Robarts concurred heartily. "I never knew such a kind, generous, and beautiful soul. She is sorely missed."

"My mother knew her well, but that was prior to her marriage. She never returned to London after settling here."

"No. As I said, this country can enchant you, and she loved both the fens and the abbey. Indeed, I can say without doubt that they were the happiest couple I have ever known." Mr. Robarts' voice shook with emotion and he blew his nose on a voluminous handkerchief. "Sir Neill was still in short trousers, indeed she was a relatively young woman when she died, and four years later Sir Aaron followed her. Dear me, I wonder what will become of them."

Mr. Robarts was quite plainly grieving so that Chalmsforth did not enquire exactly whom he meant by *them*, the Guthrie family as a whole, he presumed. Mr. Robarts' version of Ellen Berrington's marriage differed from the account his mother had given, but coming, as it did, from Haddenheath's rector, who obviously had close ties to the Guthrie family, it was hardly surprising, though Chalmsforth was struck by the depth of his grief that went far beyond mere loyalty.

It was almost dark and Chalmsforth realized that he was very hungry and the innkeeper's wife's hare and suet pudding, which originally had had little appeal, would be most welcome.

"I wish I might suggest that you dine with me instead of at the Bell, but my daughter is not yet returned from London. It would give us great pleasure if you would stay here for a time."

"My future plans are uncertain, but I shall certainly make

19

a point of coming to hear your sermon on Sunday if I am in the vicinity of St. Matthew's. For now, I bid you good night."

Mr. Robarts beamed and, hurrying back to the rectory, he went over in his mind some finishing touches to his topic: the lure of temporal temptations.

III

Chalmsforth's first view of Culross Abbey was impressive. The abbey lay on the outskirts of the village yet was not readily visible from the road. Set in a wooded grove, surrounded by a profusion of beech, poplar, and elm, all sadly in need of trimming, it was an immense, cloistered building with an octagonal tower and large mullioned windows yet, as Chalmsforth drew closer, signs of neglect and dilapidation were everywhere. Dense foliage and weeds abounded across walks and walls, all in varying stages of decay. The abbey itself was in even worse condition; indeed he doubted there had been any upkeep on the monumental building since the oriel windows had been added in what must have been the Elizabethan period. By the time he had reached the magnificent but derelict front portal, Chalmsforth concluded that it would require a fortune to restore the great abbey to anything resembling its former grandeur.

The elderly servant who admitted him appeared to be all of one with the air of grand decay, which he now noted was as evident within as without in the worn hangings and panelled walls bereft of any decoration, though the majesty of the Elizabethan stone staircase in the great hall, with its intricately carved oak banister, was unmitigated.

The library, into which Chalmsforth was shown to await the two young gentlemen who, though it was close to noon, were still abed, was equally bare. Those furnishings he could distinguish in the gloom of the dark panelled room, for the autumn sun barely penetrated the heavy mullioned windowpanes, were shabby and threadbare. As an inveterate book collector, he felt an aroused curiosity as he crossed to the bookcases set into the walls; it would have been the perfect setting to discover a sixteenth-century Antwerp printing of Plantin's *Polyglot Bible* or perhaps an illuminated manuscript of a *Book of Hours*. But there was nothing, nothing of any rarity, only a few novels and a prayer book, a large family Bible which he took down to examine, otherwise the shelves were bare.

As he turned away in disappointment he became aware, for the first time, that he was not alone. At the end of the room, he saw the back of a young woman who was collecting together playing cards strewn across a green baise table and on the floor beneath it. Several empty port bottles were in evidence, one of which had overturned and left a dark red pool on the floor by an overturned chair. It looked for all the world as though a fight had taken place and blood had been drawn, but Chalmsforth concluded the scene was nothing more than the remnants of a long and wild card party.

The room's occupant was of slender build yet had an exceedingly well-proportioned figure. Although her dark hair was caught atop her head, its natural inclination could be seen in the wispy curls that clung to the nape of her neck. The grey cambric dress she wore, drab and unadorned, had obviously seen many a season, for the material had been turned more than once.

A servant, or perhaps a young housekeeper, Chalmsforth concluded, yet when she turned and, on catching sight of him, threw him a rueful smile, involuntarily he caught his breath. Despite her plain garb and lack of fashion, she was the most beautiful creature imaginable. Her complexion, pale and clear, was highlighted by the rose of her cheeks. Dark curls framed a lively oval face with a slender, straight nose and soft, curved lips parted to reveal even, white teeth, and her smile gave evidence of good humour as well as welcome. Yet it was her eyes which caught and held Chalmsforth, shimmering beneath thick, dark lashes, clear and deep, the shade of lilac—of the wild lilac that grew in such profusion at Perrynchase. No servant she, for when she spoke, her voice was well-modulated and mellifluous and most certainly that of a lady.

"Please do excuse this awful mess. The servants, I fear, have been remiss this morning in not clearing it. I am quite put out that they thought to show a visitor in here."

Chalmsforth bowed in some perplexity, realizing that it was, indeed, more than the prizefight which had drawn his brother to Culross, and that this must be the young woman of whom his mother had spoken, the one of whom Gerald was enamoured, for only too obvious reasons.

22

"I am very glad that they did, however, for it has given me the opportunity of meeting you. I am Chalmsforth, Lord Peter Chalmsforth. Finding myself in Haddenheath and having heard that my brother was staying at the abbey, I decided to call. I understand, however, that he is not yet up."

"No, Gerald is still abed and may, I fear, be there for some time. He retired quite late and was, I regret to say, rather in his cups. In fact he had to be helped upstairs and he kept me awake half the night with his singing."

She spoke directly, yet the candour of her words took Chalmsforth aback for they left little to construe of the relationship that must exist between herself and his brother. She had not the appearance of a brazen hussy, yet only a hussy would speak so freely.

"I regret that my brother's behaviour inconvenienced you," was all Chalmsforth could bring himself to reply.

"Oh, it didn't inconvenience me in the least, though his repertoire of songs may leave something to be desired, but I am quite used to gentlemen imbibing more than they should and acting rather foolishly afterward. Your brother is really quite charming."

She smiled at him, as though taking him into her confidence, somehow making it more difficult to respond. He had never before felt himself at such a loss in regulating his brother's imprudent behaviour and was unsure which direction to take, perhaps because of her disconcerting beauty coupled, as it was, with her clear and direct gaze. She was entirely guileless, yet how could an innocent young woman speak of his brother in terms of such intimacy.

"I'm afraid Gerald leads rather a wild life. It is, perhaps, advantageous that, as a younger son, he does not have unlimited funds at his disposal." He knew that his words were pompous and, galled by the glint of amusement in her eyes, he pointedly ran his eyes over her worn dress before continuing with some asperity, "My brother does not appear to have been overgenerous, however, with his entirely ample allowance."

"I am sure he is quite as generous as his means allow. I can assure you it is no pleasant thing to be constantly counting pennies. Is it you who holds his purse strings?" she enquired with an infuriating air of forthright innocence. He was glad her question gave him the opportunity to enlighten someone he now considered to be a threat to the family.

"Yes, as a matter of fact I do, and shall until he is twenty-five, an age he will not reach for some four years, and even then his inheritance will not be immense."

"Poor Gerald, what a shame! I know the difficulty of being forced to rely upon others, whether they be reasonable or not, and young men particularly must find it difficult to bear. I'm sure he would enjoy spending freely. Men are not used to being parsimonious as are women, but undoubtedly what he has will serve. Means which may be insignificant to a gentleman of your standing may seem quite sufficient to others."

"You sound as though you would act as a good guide in matters of finance." Chalmsforth's deliberately sarcastic tone went unnoticed by the lady, who replied quietly,

"Let me say I am used to making a penny serve where sixpence is required."

She was cool, he thought, cool and no fool. She was going to be more difficult to dismiss than had been the milliner. He remembered his mother's intimation that her father was in the church and felt his expression of concern on that establishment to the rector of St. Matthew's was, indeed, justified. Yet, perhaps, her father was not entirely at fault; perhaps, given her all too obvious attributes which must have long attracted attention and with her equally obvious mercenary strain, she had chosen to go astray. Given an unprincipled woman in search of financial gain, there was one way that he was certain would bring an end to the matter, a way which would serve to open Gerald's eyes to her hard and shallow nature though it would, in all probability, temporarily increase their fraternal difficulties. Chalmsforth, as his eyes dwelt for a moment on the young woman's soft and inviting lips, was forced to admit that he was not averse to the plan; almost involuntarily, he moved closer to her.

"May I say that with such an exquisite face and an equally splendid form you should never have to worry that delightful head of yours with such mundane matters. There must be many who would be all too willing to take those onerous burdens from your slender shoulders. I know that I, for one, should consider it an honour." He felt a certain discomfort in the hackneyed aspect of his approach, yet he had not expected her flush of embarrassment nor the sudden doubt and hesitation which flooded her eyes.

"I fail to see what my looks have to do with making ends meet," she replied defensively.

24

"But, ma'am, everything—your looks, your most evident charms have everything to do with your fortune. Exquisite creatures such as yourself are not put on earth to trouble their heads with, as you put it, making a penny serve where sixpence is required, but rather to act as muses to us poor mortals, to float through life with the finest of raiment and adornment, with, in fact, everything at their disposal."

Her embarrassment dissipated suddenly in amusement.

"What a silly picture you draw if you refer to me. I shall never float through life in such a manner."

"But you should," he replied earnestly, and taking her hands in his he forgot that the course he was pursuing was prompted by anything other than his own desire. "I rather think we should suit, don't you? Unlike my brother, I do have unlimited funds and have every inclination to be uncommonly generous with them to a lady of your appeal. Do you not think you might like me quite as well as Gerald?"

A dark flush overspread her cheeks and her blue eyes darkened.

"Sir, I do not know you. I think you must be under some terrible misapprehension——"

"May we not, perhaps, immediately rectify our lack of acquaintance," he interrupted, drawing her to him with the intention of planting a kiss of conquest upon her enticing lips, yet, as he gathered her in his arms he had not counted on the faint scent of lavender that clung to her, nor the irresistible warmth and magnetism of her body against his own and, where he had sought to conquer, he became conquered. Her initial resistance soon dissipated as he caressed her back and the nape of her neck until her lips beneath his own became soft and supple and warm and moist, and her stirrings of ardour gave every evidence of matching his own. What began as a kiss to seal an agreement became a passionate, fervent embrace from which he released her at last only with the utmost reluctance, murmuring, as he did so, "For but one night, ma'am, you may name your price."

The blow came suddenly, surprisingly swift and strong, catching him off guard, almost causing him to lose his balance. He felt something warm and wet on his cheek and realized that the ring she wore had lacerated his cheek, that she had drawn blood.

"My lord, I fear you are under some terrible misapprehension or else you have utterly taken leave of your senses. I hope, for your sake, it is the former. In either event, your conduct is reprehensible, utterly detestable." Her eyes flashed with anger as she spoke, her hands clenched at her sides as though to prevent herself from striking him again.

"I was not aware that you were of that opinion a moment ago," he retorted, while attempting, quite unsuccessfully, to staunch the flow of blood from his cheek.

She flushed. "You . . . you do that sort of thing in a very expert manner. Quite obviously you have had a great deal of practice. If anything in my conduct led you to believe I wished for your advances, I am heartily sorry—I know I do not always guard my tongue as I should. "Here." She handed him an embroidered lawn handkerchief which he took, being unable, momentarily, to find his own.

Chalmsforth was at a loss to understand where his technique, usually so successful, had failed. Never before had he known rejection from the opposite sex where he had been determined to succeed. Had she assumed the role of a wronged woman because she sought marriage with his brother? The fragrance of her handkerchief, which he held against his face, reminded him of her lithe body in his arms and he fought the irrepressible urge to hold her again.

He hesitated. Was it possible that she had already gone through a form of marriage with his brother, was that what permitted her to talk so freely of his nightly escapades? The thought that that might be so infuriated him beyond all measure.

"You realize, I trust, that my brother is not free to marry where he chooses, that he requires my permission until he attains the age of five and twenty. But perhaps he has omitted to mention this fact to you Miss . . . Miss. . . ." Suddenly he realized that he did not know her name, yet he resolved that should she proclaim herself to be his brother's wife nothing would induce him to call her by their family name.

"Your brother obviously would not take me into his confidence on such a matter, Lord Chalmsforth, but I feel for him if he has you to please in selecting a wife." She turned from him in anger just as the door to the library opened to admit a short, buxom, grey-haired lady, also most plainly attired, who directed a friendly smile at Chalmsforth.

"Goodness me, Fiona, I didn't realize we had yet another visitor."

"Yes, Aunt Agatha. Allow me to present Lord Chalmsforth, brother of Neill's friend, Mr. Gerald Chalmsforth. Lord Chalmsforth, my aunt, Miss Agatha Guthrie."

"Your aunt!" Chalmsforth abruptly recalled Mr. Robarts' reference to *them* the previous evening. He barely bowed to the elder lady before turning to demand, "Then you are . . . but you cannot be . . . Sir Neill is not married, surely?"

"No, he is not. I am his sister, Fiona Guthrie."

Chalmsforth floundered. "But I though . . . I was unaware that he had a sister. Miss Guthrie, you must forgive me, I. . . ."

But she ignored his commenced apology, turning with deliberation to her aunt.

"Our guest has met with a most unfortunate accident, Aunt. On the way here his horse kicked up a stone that lacerated his cheek. I shall find someone to dress the wound for him, but since this room has not yet been cleared, perhaps you could show him into the drawing room."

"I shall, indeed, and I shall dress that cut myself for it looks to have gone quite deep. I wonder whether we shouldn't send for the apothecary."

"Pray do not, Miss Guthrie." Chalmsforth was in a state of acute embarrassment. It was not a state to which he was accustomed, of which fact he was quite sure that the younger Miss Guthrie was clearly aware. "I assure you the cut is nothing. I heal rapidly."

"It is just as well," Fiona Guthrie averred. "It would be unfortunate, indeed, to have such an aristocratic face marred by so trivial an accident."

With that Fiona withdrew, leaving him to the solicitous ministrations of her aunt. Despite his staunch refusals, she insisted upon personally bathing his face, commenting all the while upon the variety of hazzards that lay in wait for the unwary traveller. As he endured, rather impatiently, the lady's continued palliatives, he thought wryly of his mother's parting words—he had hardly been the soul of discretion in this instance.

IV

Chalmsforth was not to see Fiona Guthrie again until dinner that evening.

He had been obliged to endure the sympathy and solicitude of the elder Miss Guthrie for more than an hour before Sir Neill Guthrie and his brother descended, by which time he felt unduly glad to see their stalwart, if still indisposed countenances. His welcome from Guthrie was cordial, moreso than from his brother, though both accepted without question his explanation of visiting the neighbourhood to see the prizefight. Guthrie insisted that he remove immediately to the abbey, and Chalmsforth, remembering his cramped quarters and rather unpalatable fare of the night before, but prompted more by the necessity of apologizing without delay to Miss Fiona Guthrie, allowed his luggage to be sent for and installed above in the family wing, the only wing of the great building kept open during the winter months.

Gerald outwardly tolerated Chalmsforth's sudden appearance at the abbey, but his annoyance at his brother's unexpected arrival was not entirely suppressed. Gerald had been enjoying a position of supremacy over his host, an impressionable young man rather junior in years to himself, and he had no wish to relinquish it to his elder brother, whose air of natural superiority and leadership invariably influenced those who met him. Men, but more importantly women, had an unfortunate way of disregarding him once they met Chalmsforth, and Gerald had no wish that the adoring glances of a certain young lady, to whom Guthrie had introduced him in London and with whom he had been devastatingly taken, should be transferred to his brother. She was expected to arrive momentarily and it was she, rather than the prizefight, that had induced him to journey into the depths of Cambridgeshire where he hoped, within the closer confines of the abbey, he might expect something more substantial than adoring glances. With Chalmsforth at hand, even if the lady were willing, further intimacies would be difficult, if not impossible—his brother always managed to ruin everything for him, Gerald fumed, wishing he could turn the tables.

Dinner, served early that evening in the large ancestral dining hall, was a simple but ample meal of mulligatawny soup, rump steak pie, and damson pudding, well served under Fiona's watchful eye. It was clearly she, rather than her brother who sat opposite her at the head of the table arguing with Gerald on the merits of piquet over whist, who took charge of everything, quietly and efficiently. She had changed into a simple but less faded gown of poplin that, Chalmsforth noticed, matched the distinctive lilac shade of her eyes. She treated him in a direct yet distant manner, her anger of the morning completely dissipated, yet contrarily Chalmsforth wished she would show him something other than polite indifference. It was an attitude to which he was unused, and in this particular instance he found it unendurable. He felt he would have preferred rancour, for the fact that she showed him every proper courtesy as a guest at their table made him feel as discomfitted as a schoolboy caught stealing apples, obliged to endure the perfect civility and hospitality of the orchard owner without having the opportunity to make good his wrongdoing. He had never been so ill at ease, yet, despite his discomfiture, he was unable to keep his eyes from constantly returning to his fair hostess.

That hostess, together with her aunt, withdrew once the meal was over, leaving the gentlemen to their port and speculation on the next day's fight. Once she had gone, however, Chalmsforth found it increasingly difficult to keep his attention on the respective merits of the two pugilists so hotly disputed by the others and, when neither showed any sign of stirring from the table for the rest of the evening, Chalmsforth purposefully rose to announce that it was time to rejoin the ladies.

"Oh, but they usually sit on their own in the evening," Guthrie protested. "I doubt that they want our company any more than we theirs. I thought we might have a hand of piquet, unless, Lord Chalmsforth, you are of Gerald's opinion that whist is the better game."

"I should find tea with the ladies preferable to either."

His tone, which brooked no opposition, caused Gerald to

cast an oblique glance at his brother before Guthrie led them to a small sitting room at the end of the immense hallway, lit only by a fire in the hearth and working candles.

Fiona, seated before the fire, was engaged with a piece of needlework. Her aunt had evidently been employed at a similar task but had dozed off to sleep and her needlework, on the point of sliding from her capacious lap, dropped to the floor as she started awake on the entrance of the gentlemen.

Fiona raised her eyebrows at their entrance, but no other sign remarked how unusual it was to have her brother join them when he had visitors. If knowing his preference for the card table accompanied by repeated rounds from the cellar must have led her to conclude that only the presence of their latest guest could have caused a change in that routine, she made no mention of it, only saying before resuming her work,

"Neill, do ring for more candles and more tea, this is quite cold."

Chalmsforth sat down, rather apart from the others but in a position where he could watch Fiona and close enough to engage her in conversation for, should the opportunity arise, he hoped to be able to apologize for his blunder of the morning. Fresh tea having been served, the young men soon resumed their discussion of the prizefight and once again Aunt Agatha began to doze.

"You must find such an immense place difficult in the winter months," Chalmsforth began. "These early monasteries and abbeys were never built for comfort, I fear, though I notice many changes have been made in this one. The panelling is some of the finest I have encountered anywhere, and the rose design in the ceiling of the dining hall is most unusual."

Fiona raised her head for a moment before returning to her work.

"Yes, it is, but because it blends so well with the grain of the wood few people notice the carving. You are most observant."

Chalmsforth was unaccountably delighted at her approbation, but again she made him feel like a schoolboy. No one before had ever caused him to seek approval, he had always accepted it as his due, and he was at a loss to understand his present state. He could only ascribe it to boyish infatuation, quite ridiculous at his age, which he judged would pass once he had tendered apologies for his conduct.

"I must admit that we have our problems when winter really sets in, for our weather is damp at the best of times, but in winter the cold winds from the North Sea blend with the damp to make a bitterness which invades even the snuggest homes, let alone a pile such as this. It is why Aunt Agatha and I spend much of our time in this small sitting room, and why we use only one wing of the abbey. Though it may not make for warmth, it does contain some of the worst draughts that whistle freely through the corridors on the eastern side."

"It is a marvellous place though, worth some discomfort."

"That is exactly what I tell Neill when he complains. It was founded in the twelfth century by monks of the Cisterian order who came here from Yorkshire. You may have noticed their first building, a dormitory, which still stands not far from the main gate. It has, of course, been changed over the years, but it has not been altered, a distinction I think you may understand."

"I do, and I suspect it is because no arbitrary change was made that a unity has been achieved which makes it grow in splendour. Houses, grand houses, are much like people, I think."

She looked up at him again and smiled. "Exactly! I have said so myself, though Neill laughs at me."

Chalmsforth leaned across to try to decipher the design she was embroidering, and read aloud that part visible to him.

"En ma fin est . . . let me see now, where does that come from? Perhaps the emblem might give me a clue. May I see it?"

She moved her hands to disclose the design of a phoenix in flames and the full motto: *En ma fin est mon commencement.*

"That, if I am not mistaken, is the emblem of Marie de Guise, mother of Mary Queen of Scots."

Fiona's eyes lit up in astonishment.

"How did you know that? I am sure there is not another person of my acquaintance, including that veritable mine of information, Mr. Robarts, who would recognize it."

"I had a good deal of French history as a boy. One of the books my mother gave me when I was quite small contained an illustration of Marie de Guise sitting very stiffly on a chair, or perhaps it was a throne, and in the background was that device. I must still have that book somewhere. I must say

I didn't find it very inspiring apart from the illustrations to which, in obedience to an irrepressible urge, I applied some rather fascinating embellishments."

Fiona laughed. "Of Neill I should have expected that, but I'd hardly have thought that you—" She broke off abruptly, suddenly flustered.

"That I would give in to irrepressible urges?"

Their eyes met and Fiona flushed sharply. Chalmsforth, to his chagrin, felt his own cheeks flush as well.

"What are you discussing so privately?" Gerald's voice broke in on them and, looking up, Chalmsforth found both his brother and Guthrie staring at them. Quickly regaining his composure he replied, "I was admiring Miss Guthrie's work."

He was further annoyed as he caught his brother's soft-spoken innuendo. "I didn't know you for an admirer of *needle-work*, old boy," at which Fiona, seeming to sense antagonism between the brothers, intervened,

"I was explaining to Lord Chalmsforth that Marie de Guise's motto was adopted by Mary Stuart and she had it embroidered on her cloth of state."

Her brother chided, "Oh, don't get started on Mary Stuart, Fiona, or else we'll never be out of here in time for tomorrow's fight," and to Chalmsforth he added, "Fiona just dotes on that woman."

"I wish you wouldn't refer to her as 'that woman,' " his sister replied crossly. "It's hardly a befitting way to describe a queen."

"Just because she once spent the night here, or the week, or whatever it was, I think you feel she is your personal queen," Guthrie teased.

"Well, in a way, she is."

"Did she really stay here?" Chalmsforth intervened in what promised to become a family argument.

"Yes, during her peregrinations of imprisonment. She stayed in the east wing of the abbey—it's still possible to see where she scratched her name on the window."

"Could you show that to me?" he asked, a trifle too eagerly, causing his brother to cast a quizzical look in his direction. Gerald had never seen his brother pay open court to a lady as he seemed to be paying court to Guthrie's sister and, what was even more strange, she seemed to be doing nothing to encourage it. He looked with renewed interest at his host's sister. She was a vastly pretty young woman, he had noticed

32

that on arrival, but he had been full of his infatuation and besides, one could not play fast and loose with the lady of the house, not unless one intended to get tied down. Chalmsforth knew that, and Gerald was sure that Fiona Guthrie was not the sort his brother would pick for a wife. Her family was all right, of course, but Guthrie's financial state was well known—Chalmsforth wouldn't throw away his title and position on a pretty face.

Fiona had gathered up her work and was arousing her aunt.

"I know that you gentlemen have to be off at the crack of dawn, and it is long past our usual hour of retirement. We shall leave you now to indulge in your speculations. I trust that you are all betting on the same man so that your cheers will not be divided."

Chalmsforth rose also. "I, too, must retire. Would you allow me to see you ladies upstairs?"

Under Gerald's puzzled gaze, Chalmsforth took the candle from Fiona's hand and held the door for the ladies to pass through.

Together they mounted the wide stone staircase, Chalmsforth hoping to have at least a moment to speak to Fiona alone, but once at the top she turned to bid him good night.

"I trust you have everything you require. If not, I am sure that your man can procure it for you."

With that she turned immediately to enter her room without allowing him to say a word. To his discomfort and humiliation, he heard the key turn in the lock, leaving him in the cold, dank hallway, lit only by the light of a single candle, to mull over the day's mortifications.

V

"Oh, Fiona, you should have been there. It surpassed everything except that my man didn't win—but what a fight! Everyone was there, even Prinny, and such a mob. I don't know how Chalmsforth did it, but he got us the most magnificent viewpoint and I couldn't see how he could manoeuvre his curricle into such a tiny space, but he did and I swear, though we were among the last to arrive, we had one of the best spots from which to see the combat."

Fiona looked with affectionate amusement at her brother's face, flushed with excitement as he regaled her with details of the morning's prizefight. Neill, together with Chalmsforth and his brother, having just returned from Cagford, were taking a glass of sherry, still attired in their dust-covered clothes.

"But who did win, Neill?"

"Chalmsforth's man, of course. He has the luck of the devil and imagine, he only put up a pony, but if I'd known as much of the man's record as he did I should certainly have had all my blunt on him."

"I hope you didn't go down too much!" Her look of anxiety did not escape Chalmsforth's attention, but then there was very little about her that did.

Her brother flushed lightly. "Oh, don't worry, Fiona, nothing that's going to make such difference in the long run. But what a fight. It was no walkover, I can assure you. Don't you think it was one of the best you've seen?" He addressed this question with great eagerness to Chalmsforth, who replied affirmatively, not wishing to daunt his enthusiasm.

"But I still don't know who won," Fiona complained.

"Well, Chalmsforth's man, as I said."

"But which one was that, Bill Neate or Ned Turner, were those not the names of the combatants?"

"It was Bill Neate who finally took the day, but what a battle it was. Neate was huge, but of course Turner was no midget and he won the toss, so he didn't have to face the sun. He had it all his own way in the beginning, fought just like a tiger and had Neate down, but when he recovered I think Turner was sorry he'd ever taken him on for if Turner was a tiger then Neate was a leopard, jumping at him with an agility the like of which I've never seen. Still, it was touch and go for a while, then Neate opened up a cut over Turner's right eye and the favour of the fight was his. So it went till Turner was battered beyond recognition. Then they sent off the pigeons to Mrs. Neate with news of her husband's victory."

"Oh, Neill, it sounds awful. I'm glad I wasn't there."

"Well, you couldn't have come anyway, for there were no *ladies* watching." Neill winked at Gerald as he spoke.

"Did you enjoy the fight?" Fiona asked Gerald, ignoring her brother's aside.

"Yes, it was colourful, except I got awfully sick of your brother extolling the driving performance of mine all the way there and all the way back. It's a wearisome thing, I can assure you, to have a brother who does everything right."

"Well, Fiona's never likely to find out how that feels," Neill grinned, while Chalmsforth protested his brother's remark by saying enigmatically, at least to two members of his audience,

"I can assure you I do not do everything right. I wish I could say I had done so since my arrival here."

"Come, Peter, don't be modest, it doesn't suit," Gerald snapped. "You know perfectly well people are always coming up to praise something you've done. It gets quite tiresome, believe me. Now you've got Guthrie wild about your driving. I wish all my friends wouldn't give me up as soon as they meet you."

Guthrie began to protest vociferously while Chalmsforth merely added, "I don't believe that is quite true. For instance, you will probably have a long time to wait until you hear praises for me from Miss Guthrie."

"Your brother may have many virtues"—Fiona turned to Gerald—"but I doubt he can sit a horse and jump as well as you. I watched you the other morning when you rode out with Neill and I don't think I've seen anyone take the hedge in the lower field in quite the style you did. Your form was magnificent. I remarked on it to my aunt."

There was no denying the look of pleasure on Gerald's

face. While Chalmsforth found himself admiring Fiona's tact, he was annoyed, despite himself, that her praise was reserved for his brother. Though she had made no mention of his conduct toward her on his arrival and had treated him with the same courtesy she extended to others, he was burdened by it, especially since he had been unable to convey to her his regrets for the deplorable incident. Had she treated him with scorn he might have preferred it to her indifference. It was not even indifference, for she was polite to him, it was simply that she did not single him out at all, treating him just as she did her brother or Gerald, no better, no worse, in fact he was not convinced she did not prefer their company to his. He was so used to deferential treatment that he found it difficult to bear, particularly in an instance when he was at pains to attract her notice. And though he wished to apologize for his abominable conduct, he could not get the memory of the sweetness of her lips from his mind, nor did he wish to, so that while the recollection might be humiliating, it was also a cause of delight. He found himself in the anomolous position of wishing it had never happened, yet not wishing to forget it for the world.

"Perhaps you would like to ride with me tomorrow?" Gerald pressed her, flushed with his triumph.

"I can't tomorrow for I have an engagement in the morning. Perhaps the next day." And so it was agreed.

That night after dinner, when cards were again suggested, Chalmsforth asked Fiona whether she would make up a four for whist.

"Oh, Fiona always wins," her brother complained.

"Well, then, she must partner me," said Gerald, "for I never do."

"Let's see whether we can set them then," she said, and Chalmsforth took up the challenge.

It soon became apparent that the match was between Chalmsforth and Fiona, for Neill was an impulsive player while Gerald played sporadically, either with great abandon or not daringly enough. Chalmsforth watched Fiona as she played. She moved with decision, seeming to know where each card lay, and when defeat was inevitable she took it well. At the end of the long evening, however, it was Neill and Chalmsforth who were down.

"Where on earth did you learn to play like that?"

Chalmsforth asked her with admiration. "I've never seen a woman handle her cards as you do."

"I've spent many hours watching my father. Though he was like Neill, a little too impulsive at times, there was nothing he did not know about the deck, and most of it he passed along to me."

"And a great deal of good it does," her brother grumbled, "for she will not play for money and I'm sure she has it in her power to recoup our fortunes if she wished."

"I enjoy playing cards—for the fun of the game and the pitting of one's acumen against another's. But I detest gambling."

"I tend to agree with you," Chalmsforth replied. "I find little enjoyment in it either."

"Then you must find yourself slightly at odds with the rest of the society in which you move, do you not?"

"At times I may, but I think people know me now and know my likes and dislikes, and accept them."

"I suppose that is the dearest wish of all of us, to be accepted," Fiona said.

"Certainly it is initially," Chalmsforth replied. "Though in certain relationships mere acceptance is hardly enough."

Fiona looked down without reply. It was Gerald who stared quizzically at his brother, a look that turned to one of resentment as Guthrie pressed Chalmsforth to stay on at the abbey for as long as he wished.

"I should like that very much," Chalmsforth responded, then he remembered, with some annoyance, the Orbury's dinner and added, "though I have to be back in town at the end of the week."

He looked over to see whether Fiona showed any reaction to his staying, but her head was bent over her needlework.

Chalmsforth was determined that not another day should pass without his speaking to Fiona. He therefore refused to accompany Gerald and Neill on a shooting expedition the following morning, preferring instead to wait for Fiona to leave the house. Though he knew that she had an engagement, he hoped for at least a few moments alone with her and he was not disappointed.

Midmorning, hearing Fiona in the hallway preparing to leave, Chalmsforth asked her permission to accompany her part of the way. In her usual, friendly fashion, she acquiesced, and together they left the house, walking down the driveway toward the entrance to the park. She talked briskly and inconsequentially of the pleasant season they were having and the prospects of good shooting, until at last Chalmsforth forced himself to intervene.

"Miss Guthrie, since my arrival and the unfortunate mistake I made upon meeting you, I have wanted to convey my deepest and most sincere apologies for my infamous behaviour. My conscience has been even more affected by the fact that you have borne no malice because of it and have, indeed, made no attempt to hold my conduct against me, though you might well have refused to have me as a guest in your house. I cannot too abjectly convey my regrets for what must have been an incomprehensible manner of acting. I can only say that it was caused by a complete misconception of your identity on my part. There is an explanation, but I hardly feel I need go into it."

"Your behaviour was certainly unusual, Lord Chalmsforth. I cannot remember ever having been confronted by a similar circumstance. I would, therefore, be much interested in your explanation if you care to give it."

Chalmsforth did not care to give it at all, however he saw little alternative.

"It had been brought to my attention, quite unjustly it now seems, that my brother had become embroiled with a . . . with a girl of somewhat questionable background, and I was given to understand that he had brought her here to your brother's house, with what intentions I did not know. However, he is a young man often given to wild escapades and this is not the first time my help has been sought to save him from an action for which he would be sorry later. It is an unpleasant duty, one at which he chafes and one I would prefer not to perform, but under the terms of my father's will, which makes me his guardian until he is twenty-five, I have no option. Perhaps my father was unjust in making such restrictions; it certainly does not contribute to a good relationship between us. Anyway, when I saw you, I thought you were the . . . the young woman in question. Looking at you, it was entirely conceivable that you could have swept Gerald off his feet. I sought to attract you instead."

"In order to save him?"

"Yes, I suppose that was it." Chalmsforth realized that in seeking to extricate his brother, he had himself become hopelessly enmeshed. "I had no idea that Guthrie had a sister. I thought you could be no other than the person I sought."

"But I fail to understand. If he finds someone he wants to marry, someone he loves, would you not give your consent?"

Her direct and questioning gaze embarrassed him, but he had no desire to prevaricate in order to please her.

"Surely you must realize, Miss Guthrie, that marriage in our society is not simply based on emotions. There are many factors to be considered before it may be entered into."

"Ah, you mean money."

"Money, to be sure, I cannot deny it, but I speak primarily of background, family lines; those should, in particular, be compatible. You, yourself, must realize the importance of rank."

"I confess I haven't thought a great deal of it. The only marriage I have observed at close hand was that of my parents, and though I suppose they were of equal rank, and I think my mother had a substantial settlement, I cannot believe that either was of importance in their relationship."

"How do you mean, of no importance, you mean it was taken for granted?"

"No, not at all, I mean that it was inconsequential. You see they loved one another and their main consideration was their love and respect for one another as individuals, not as members of a certain rank of society. I suppose you will condemn me as a hopeless romantic, but though my father's tendency to gamble to excess caused my mother some pain, he more than compensated for it by the happiness he brought to the union. I know she was the joy of his life. He was inconsolable at her death and if ever a man died from love, I believe he did. Theirs will always be my ideal of what marriage should be, but I understand matters other than love and respect can decide matches in the world of society. I'm afraid for my part I can never allow it. For that reason, I suspect I shall probably die a spinster."

"But that would be impossible," he protested, "for a lady with your beauty and charm. You must have many suitors."

"Indeed I don't," she laughed. "You see, most gentlemen think as you do, and though I may have rank, my marriage portion has long since been dissipated. I don't want for partners at assemblies, but beyond that little else."

"Will you not come out in London?"

"No, there is no money for that, and indeed, if there were, I don't believe I should wish for it. This is my home. If there is anything to which I am attached, it is the abbey—after my brother, of course."

They walked in silence for a while, then she began again.

"You know, I am almost flattered in being taken for a woman of ill repute." He started to protest, but she interceded. "No, I mean it. I have often wondered how it must be to be born into a different world, one where one must survive by one's wits. I lead a quiet life here and have little chance to observe such things. Do men really pay a fortune to spend a night with a woman?"

The question, asked with such an ingenuous air, disconcerted him. He was at a loss for reply.

"Really, I cannot talk of such things, other than to apologize again that I ever said such a thing to you."

"But I wish you would. What is the difference—a matter of one's birth? We are all women, after all, and must do what has to be done to survive."

"I cannot think you mean that. There is a world of difference between yourself and such a person."

"But where does that difference lie? We obviously do not look different and it would seem——"

"Please, I beg you not to discuss this further. I find it painful to speak of, to compare you with . . . with . . . well, it is odious." He sought to change the line of conversation. "Pray tell me where you are going."

"As a matter of fact, it is because of where I am going I wish you were able to speak of such things to me, but since I see it so obviously embarrasses you to do so, I will not press you further. Anne Robarts, the daughter of our rector, and I have a small school we run for girls of the village and the surrounding farms. I say the girls, though anyone is welcome to attend; however it is mostly the younger girls who come. Probably husbands would object to their women attending, though I don't doubt they would benefit. We teach merely the rudiments of education, reading and writing, a little arithmetic, but more importantly we attempt to teach them to cope with their daily lives, not to accept conduct or conditions from others unquestioningly. You see, had I been a village girl the other morning, you would probably have found it unnecessary to apologize to me for what occurred, but it is just such conduct which I feel they do not have to accept."

Her tone was serious, and he was aware of the truth of her

statement and again was discomfitted by the knowledge. Apparently she was aware of it, for she added hastily,

"Please, I had no intention of censuring you, for after all, I don't entirely blame you for your actions. It is what you have been brought up to expect and it is a manner of conduct that is prevalent. However, I do not find justification in that. I believe that, because of their inferior position in society, women must use all of their wits to develop an awareness of their surroundings and ways in which to survive, in a manner they themselves choose. For instance, it is feasible that a woman might have reason to accept or even seek out such a means of gaining money, but that that is her only means of doing so, is abhorrent."

"These are strange ideas, coming from a lady. Tell me, did they come from your mother?"

"From my mother, from my readings of women's lives in the past, from what I see of women's lives today, from my thoughts, I don't precisely know where. It is one reason that I admire Mary Stuart. She was so truly a lady, a woman with all her strengths and weaknesses, a prey to her emotions, yet always aware of what was being done to her and by whom."

"But surely you should admire her cousin Elizabeth more, a woman who assumed total power, and made a good job of it, from all historical accounts."

"Of course I admire her, but she is never quite real to me. Mary, on the other hand, is entirely real, entirely lovable, entirely human."

They had now reached a small lodge which stood near the main gate and from that direction another young lady approached. She was of about the same age as Fiona, a gentle-looking girl with flaxen hair and fair skin, of small stature and shy demeanour. Fiona introduced her as Anne Robarts. On hearing Chalmsforth's name he noticed that she blushed and was at a loss for the reason. Her first words, however, enlightened him.

"Are you related to Mr. Gerald Chalmsforth?" she asked in a soft voice.

"He is my younger brother. Are you acquainted with him?"

"I had the pleasure of meeting him when staying in London with my aunt."

A look of sudden understanding crossed Chalmsforth's face and he saw Fiona studying him. So, it must be her friend who had captured Gerald's attention and of whom his mother had alerted him. Undoubtedly Fiona was remembering his remarks on the subject of rank, again he felt discomposed. A young woman passed, bound for the schoolroom, and he noticed several ears of corn, tied together with straw, pinned to her dress. Anxious to change their discussion, he asked its meaning. It was Anne who replied.

"The corn, tied with straw in a true lover's knot, has been given to her by her young man who is too timid to propose marriage himself. She has pinned it over her heart with the ears of corn pointing to the right to indicate her acceptance of his proposal. She will wear it throughout their courtship, which will not be long because the marriage must take place before the ears of corn are shelled, and these will be preserved after the wedding as tokens."

"It is an old Cambridgeshire tradition. Men here are often too shy to make their own declaration, they let the corn do it for them—hardly the case in London, I suppose," Fiona added swiftly. "But I fear we bore Lord Chalmsforth with this sentimental custom. We must go. Thank you for accompanying me on my walk."

Chalmsforth bowed. He had, in fact, been charmed by the story and regretted any impression that Fiona might still hold of him as an insensitive, dispassionate blunderer.

VI

Mr. Robarts and his daughter dined at the abbey that evening and Chalmsforth had the opportunity to observe what a proper young lady his mother had feared was attempting to ensnare his brother. Yet in observing his brother's attitude toward her, while he cast many glances in her direction and from his remarks it was obvious that they had met more than once, it seemed to Chalmsforth that Gerald looked as often at Fiona as he did at Anne, and with even more longing, something Chalmsforth found more objectionable than had he pursued the rector's daughter. Miss Robarts was a shy girl, and in her father's presence her timidity increased so that it was impossible to tell her feelings.

Chalmsforth's attention was immediately claimed by Mr. Robarts, anxious to pursue their conversation of that first evening, so that he was unable to join the conversation of the others and was forced to observe Fiona from a distance. Their morning's discussion, while not leaving him in Fiona's confidence, and while he had again blundered in discovering it was the proper Miss Robarts, Fiona's closest friend, from whom he had been asked to protect his brother, had at least allowed him to render his long overdue apology. He was determined to do everything within his power to make her see him favourably, but Mr. Robarts clung to his side preventing him from approaching the beautiful young mistress of the house. She, in turn, continued to treat him with her usual grace and courtesy, nothing more nor less than she had previously accorded him.

Talk turned to Ely Cathedral and he enquired of Mr. Robarts whether it were close enough for a day's outing.

"By all means, and I do think you should visit it before you leave the area. It is well worth it, even for the casual observer, and I know one of your background and interest would find it fascinating and edifying. I cannot urge the visit strongly enough. Were I free tomorrow or the following day I would like to take you there myself, but parish business claims me."

Mr. Robarts sighed at the thought of the upcoming vestry meeting. To a man of God and a scholar, these meetings were tedious indeed, certainly not his favourite tasks, but he knew they were duties that must be undertaken conscientiously, and thus he approached them, conscientiously but without great enthusiasm.

Seeing his opportunity, Chalmsforth turned to Guthrie and asked whether it might not be possible for them all to go there tomorrow.

"But we were to shoot, don't you remember?" Neill replied, not overjoyed at the prospect of a cathedral visit. "And Fiona has promised to ride with Gerald."

"Well, the next day then?" Chalmsforth insisted, determined to have a further opportunity to talk with Fiona before his return to London. Turning to Miss Robarts who, he now thought, would provide excellent companionship for his brother on the outing, and before Guthrie could make further objections, he asked, "Even though your father cannot come, it would give great pleasure if you could accompany us, that is, if he will entrust you to our care."

She smiled and, after glancing at her father and receiving his nodded assent, she readily agreed to join them. Gerald, who passionately disliked religious establishments, had taken up the plan with enthusiasm, and Fiona, though she had visited the cathedral many times, looked forward to seeing it again. It was therefore agreed and it remained only for Guthrie to add his somewhat begrudging assent with outward good humour.

He was compensated for this act by a pleasant morning the next day spent on the fens with Chalmsforth. The marshes abounded in wild birds of all description, since much of the land was undrained and uncultivated. Pheasants, partridges, duck, snipe, bitterns, and ruffs were there for their taking. Flushed out of the coppices by the setters that accompanied the men, they rose like a cloud to darken the pale autumnal sun. Neill, though he considered himself an excellent shot, was amazed at Chalmsforth's skill; such accuracy was rare. With the muzzle-loaded flint-and-steel gun it was necessary to shoot far in front of the prey because of the slow ignition, yet Chalmsforth rarely missed his target. He was extremely skilled in reloading his gun in an amazingly short period of time. Reloading was a difficult and time-consuming business and for Guthrie it was the part he disliked most about shooting, yet Chalmsforth instructed him with patience and precision, so that while he was unable to duplicate his superb timing, during the course of the morning he increased his capability far beyond his wildest dreams. He was elated.

His enthusiasm for Chalmsforth, fanned from the outset, now knew no bounds, and Fiona, listening to him that evening expounding on his new-found friend's accomplishments, his eyes shining with enthusiasm, could not help but think Chalmsforth the best influence to have come into her brother's life, though she hoped Neill would not be tempted entirely to imitate his style. She recognized in Chalmsforth a man to whom money was no object. To the Guthries, however, it was everything. But the attitude of the older man towards the younger was encouraging, for he listened to him and instructed him without the appearance of so doing. He evidenced such understanding of the young man's feelings that Fiona was touched. Chalmsforth had, in fact, enjoyed their morning together and only wished Gerald had half Guthrie's verve and enthusiasm. Meanwhile, Gerald, since his ride with Fiona, had adopted a proprietary attitude toward his fair companion of the morning which Chalmsforth found deplorable.

The journey to Ely the following day was undertaken beneath clear autumnal skies, with only a slight wind from the east and a pale but determined sun. With the size of their party it was decided that two curricles should be taken, and since the ladies did not wish to be separated, it was agreed they should drive with Chalmsforth while the younger men went in Guthrie's conveyance. It was a pleasant, relaxing ride. Anne was quiet and Fiona and Chalmsforth spoke together of the countryside and the cathedral they were to visit.

The cathedral loomed on the horizon long before they reached Ely, dominating the fens like a great solitary ship on a grey sea. Clustered at its base was the little town, where they stopped for luncheon before proceeding on their tour.

Ely Cathedral had originated as an abbey in the seventh century. It had been founded by St. Etheldreda when fleeing from her young Northumbrian husband, and subsequently converted into a Benedictine abbey. Destroyed by the Danes, it was rebuilt and in the eleventh century, close to the time that Culross Abbey originated, it became a cathedral.

The vast interior was dark and rather damp, with an aura of mystery and unworldliness. Fiona led them through the great nave with its twelve Norman bays, showing Chalmsforth, who was the most interested member of the party, the painted roof and the Saxon cross commemorating Etheldreda's steward, Ovinus, and the base of the shrine of the saint herself, which had escaped the Dane's ravage.

"I am always excited when I come here," she confessed. "To see all this majesty and to know it was a woman who began it gives me faith in my own sex."

"But it is ladies who are always behind greatness," he replied.

"Exactly so, *behind* greatness. Etheldreda, however, was the originator of the abbey that in time became this great cathedral. There is a great difference between bolstering greatness in another and actually performing the task oneself. I believe there are now fewer rather than more opportunities for women to act alone than in Etheldreda's day."

"But surely you could not object to a life of providing support for another and in turn being protected and cared for." He had not meant his remark to be so intense as to draw her expression of astonishment, but she replied coolly,

"I feel there is so much to be done in life by my sex, much from which we are precluded by the very protection of which you speak. Our lack of education will always keep us in such a position, I fear. Come now, I want to show you my favourite part of the cathedral, the Lady Chapel."

The chapel was entered by the north transept. Only Chalmsforth showed any interest in seeing it, for Anne Robarts was feeling the cold and as for Gerald, while he was keenly interested in Fiona, that interest could not extend to musty church interiors. Guthrie, who had been anxious to leave ever since their arrival, now suggested that the three of them start on their homeward journey, despite Fiona's protests that it would not take them long.

"With Chalmsforth driving you will soon catch up with us," Neill asserted.

"Well, don't go racing, for that is not the intent of our outing," she cautioned, and turning to Chalmsforth suggested that perhaps they should leave the Lady Chapel until another time. He insisted upon seeing it, particularly when he realized by so doing he would have Fiona to himself for the rest of the day. She acquiesced, though evidencing more haste in showing him the decorated style of the interior, built at the same time as the great octagon of the cathedral. The chapel had been used as a parish church since the middle of the sixteenth century.

Chalmsforth remarked on the hundreds of statuettes it contained, all but one of which had been deprived of their heads, a result, Fiona informed him, of the Reformation. Yet her explanations were hurried, and soon she said, "I really think we should leave now. Perhaps on another visit you may like to take more time to examine this and the rest of the cathedral."

Seeing her anxiety to leave, he accompanied her to the curricle and helped her in, handing her a lap robe, for it had become much cooler with the sun already on the wane. He was determined, however, to drive at a steady pace so as to stay behind the rest of the party, fearing that since his equipage was more spacious and better fitted than Guthrie's, others might join them.

"You must know every inch of the countryside around here," he began as they left Ely behind them.

"I do, for this is my country. Indeed, I should hope that I would, for I know no other place, having lived here all my life."

"You have not then had a London season. I should have remembered you, had it been so. But I collect now, you said you had not."

"That is so." She paused, then continued. "Should I infer, then, that you look over the hopeful crop of newcomers each year."

"I would hardly phrase it that way," he replied, somewhat huffily, for it was indeed what he had been accustomed to do since he knew he must find a wife from their midst. "I do, however, move in London society, and so it is inevitable that I meet those young ladies being presented at some time during their season."

"I find it a most outlandish custom, a sort of marketplace."

"I hadn't thought of it as such, but perhaps you are right."

"And I am sure that it must be a dismal experience for those young ladies who are not a great success, for they have so little within themselves to fall back on. Women are not brought up to think for themselves or to fill their minds as are men. It is a great pity."

They were passing through a village of reed-thatched, half-timbered houses and cottages, many with intricate pargetting, at the end of which was a noble flint-built church. But Chalmsforth found it difficult to pay attention to surroundings that, had it not been for his intriguing companion, would otherwise have interested him.

"Are you happy here?" he asked. "Do you not get lonely with so little companionship?"

"Lonely?" She thought for a moment. "No, I don't think I would describe myself as being lonely, though at times I am restless and feel I should be doing more with my life—not social engagements, but doing something useful."

"Do you not consider that in marriage a lady finds all that is useful?"

"No, that is exactly what is wrong with the way girls are brought up, with marriage as an end in itself. It is not so for men; marriage is an adjunct, albeit a pleasant one it is hoped, to their lives; why should it be otherwise for women?" She looked at him archly. "You are going to say it is because they bear children, I predict, and with that I cannot disagree, yet children grow and should not depend on their mothers all their lives any more than their mothers should depend upon them. Now I shock you, I think."

She smiled at him and he shook his head.

"No, but you consider that life is all good to the male, and I can assure you it is not so." And in answer to her look of enquiry, he went on, "There are many times when I feel my life to be empty and devoid of meaning. I wonder just what I live for. To be sure I have more liberty than you, but that freedom gives me more concern for I feel I am accomplishing little with it. I attend my clubs, discourse a great deal with friends, I am building a library to fill my time—books have become a consuming interest—but I sometimes wonder whether I am on earth for no other reason than to perpetuate the family name. If that is so, I have not yet even accomplished that object."

The bitterness in his voice caught and held her as nothing he had said theretofore had done.

"You surprise me. So many of my brother's friends, even my brother himself I regret to say, lead such frivolous lives yet seem to think nothing of it. The fortunes they win and lose at cards seem their main source of occupation."

"I am cut of their cloth, I suppose," he said thoughtfully, "I cannot assert otherwise. There are times, though, when I feel the only time I enjoyed life was serving with Wellington. Then, at least, I was aware of a purpose in life."

"Life must have a purpose, I agree. I suppose I concentrate my energies in keeping the abbey roof above our heads, at times a daunting task—it certainly keeps me from idleness and frivolity."

"You are far from idle," he asserted. "Though I have been at the abbey only a few days, it has been impossible to find you free to talk as we are doing now. I must admit to have searched for you on many occasions."

"You intrigue me," she said suddenly.

"Do I? I am delighted to know it. May I ask why?"

"I have never met a man with your eye and appreciation for beauty, yet you tell me your happiest days were those on the battlefield. I find that hard to reconcile."

"It may seem strange, yet I meant it. I suppose that in war we see the most sordid side of men, yet somehow we also see their greatest potential. Perfectly ordinary human beings become capable of such heroism—acts worthy of Greek gods. There is a beauty in the comradeship that develops between men in such time, and there is a great sense of purpose. Life, when it is most tenuous, becomes most meaningful, something my life has lacked before and since. I tend to forget those acts of horror I have seen men commit against one another, against women, even against children, in favour of other times I remember, the things said on the night before a battle, the quiet before all hell breaks loose when only an oath or a whispered prayer is heard, that surge of pure energy when the enemy is engaged. Perhaps I should remember the other things, but I don't."

There was silence, and he realized how easily he had confided his innermost thoughts to her, thoughts he would not have spoken of to any other woman, even to his mother to whom he was so close, in fact he seldom spoke so to his most intimate male friends. He wondered what it was about her that drew him to her. Initially it had been her beauty, but he knew it was far more than that. He had known a great many women of incredible beauty, none of whom had ever prompted him to open his heart to them.

She said nothing for a time, and when she did speak it was of the countryside, legends of villages through which they passed, until both became lost in the joy of the red and gold glimmering rays of the sunset across the flat, bleak fens, and an intimate silence ensued which conveyed more than words ever could. Slow though their pace had been, all too soon the gates of the abbey appeared before them and reluctantly Chalmsforth turned in.

"Where on earth have you been?" Neill asked as they entered. "I was sure you would catch up with us, or did you go back and look over the entire cathedral. I swear, imposing pile that it is, these cathedrals and churches have a sameness to them that is wearing."

Fiona began to protest, then laughingly turned to Chalmsforth. "I wish my brother had an iota of your sensitivity. He will never stop to visit a church or admire a landscape no matter how spectacular."

Her affectionate hug was reserved for her brother, yet Chalmsforth felt elated even though she was soon engaged in conversation with Gerald and Anne on the day's outing and in no way singled him out for the rest of the evening. Gerald, in his usual carefree, philandering fashion, had transferred his attentions to Fiona and Chalmsforth observed Anne Robarts sitting aside, downcast, silent. He sensed, for the first time, her rejection, and sympathized with her though realizing that sympathy stemmed, in part at least, from self-interest.

The next day was his last at the abbey, for he remembered, with regret, his promise to dine with Orbury. To Chalmsforth's surprise, when he announced his departure, his brother decided to accompany him back to London, perhaps to save himself from the embarrassment of being thought fickle in having transferred his attentions from one fixation to another, a change Chalmsforth liked as little as Anne Robarts.

Before he set out, Chalmsforth reminded Fiona of her promise to show him the room in which Mary Stuart had stayed during her sojourn at the abbey, and she readily acquiesced, pausing only to get a shawl, for that part of the abbey was shut off and extremely cold.

As they passed through the winding corridors she told him of the Guthrie ancestor who had been given the abbey by James the first after accompanying him from Scotland, and changes which had been made by succeeding generations of the family over the ensuing centuries. As she talked, he found himself watching her lips move across her even, white teeth and remembered the feel of them under his own. A longing to repeat that kiss filled him, but he did not so much as dare to take her hand. He had never before been so completely in awe of a woman and his feelings troubled him.

She opened the door to a room containing a large canopied bed, luxuriously furnished in comparison with the other rooms of the abbey.

"I have not allowed anything to be taken from this room. These are the only objects I have protected since . . . since the reversal of our fortunes. I am afraid I have annoyed my brother by my obstinacy in refusing to part with these pictures and furnishings. I suppose they would be worth something, but the money would go where all the rest has gone." She sighed. "I often come here when I want to think. It is quiet and I have a great sense of the past, wondering how she must have felt as she sat here, how many emotions we share. It is odd that our roof should also have given shelter to some of those who attended her trial and execution at Fotheringay. I cannot feel sorry that those who participated in her imprisonment and gave succour to her enemies were eventually displaced by a Scottish family. You know, I believe that it was her heart that was found by one of the Guthries and buried in the church at Haddenheath beneath the rose stone."

She walked to the window and ran her hand across an etching on the pane.

"How she suffered, yet she etched these words, *'Ne crie point pour moi'*—don't cry for me. Feel them."

He made no move, and she took his fingertips in hers and ran them across the words. He was conscious not so much of the etching on the cold glass as of her cool fingers holding his, and he longed to take her in his arms but did not dare.

"May I come back to see you?" he asked.

"Why, of course," she said, releasing his hand. "I should be delighted, and certainly Neill would; you know, he has taken a great liking to you. I have never seen him respond to anyone else quite so warmly."

He had to be content with her effusions on the part of her brother and said no more, fearing to say too much.

VII

Chalmsforth's return journey to London passed swiftly. He drove at an even more impressive rate than usual, yet scarcely aware of it so deep in thought was he. His brother, also, was unusually quiet. The silence having lasted for the greater part of the morning, Chalmsforth at last broke it by remarking that Miss Robarts seemed to be a very pleasant young lady.

"She is," Gerald agreed without great enthusiasm. "I was quite smitten when I met her in London, however that was before I met Miss Guthrie—I never realized that Neill had such a dashing sister. She rides like a goddess."

Gerald had chosen to depart with his brother rather than stay to pursue his latest infatuation because of the presence of Anne Robarts. He suspected he had aroused more than a passing interest in her breast and, being determined to transfer his attentions to Fiona Guthrie, whom he believed to be the most beautiful, most intelligent, most fascinating woman he had ever met—Gerald dealt always in superlatives—he had sufficient sense to realize that this should not be done overnight. He was, therefore, determined to return at a time when Anne Robarts's ardour would have cooled and he could be free to pursue his new quarry. Not a little of his pleasure was derived from the thought of stealing a march on his brother.

Chalmsforth was provoked. For once, notwithstanding Anne Robarts's lack of rank, he had been prepared to approve his brother's choice; now Gerald wished to press his suit in a direction to which Chalmsforth would never agree. He cast a sharp glance at his brother, wondering whether his own predilection for Fiona had been apparent and whether it was that, rather than Fiona herself, that had caused Gerald's change of heart. His brother's bland expression neither confirmed nor denied his suspicions.

"She has no fortune," was all he allowed himself to say.

"Neither does Miss Robarts," Gerald snorted, "but you don't seem to despise her for that reason. Or have you singled out Miss Guthrie for yourself?"

"No, indeed." Chalmsforth spoke casually, fearing any emotion on his part might provoke his impressionable brother into precipitate action. "She is a charming young lady, and her beauty may be slightly above average, but her want of fortune must always be to her detriment."

Though he spoke to his brother, he spoke also to himself; he found himself dangerously attracted to Fiona, yet he knew she was not a suitable match for him. He knew equally well, however, that he could never allow that intimate relationship to exist which would be forced upon him if she were to become his brother's wife.

The matter was discussed no further and only the merest pleasantries were exchanged for the rest of the journey.

The evening at Orbury's was dismal. They were all there, the beaming Marquess and his equally beaming Marchioness, their classically beautiful daughter, Annabel, who, while he could appreciate her pulchritude, now held no allure for him. There were aunts and uncles, even cousins too numerous to mention, and over it all hovered his mother's friend, the Dowager Marchioness, presiding in pomp and complacency, as though it were she rather than Jason who had found the Golden Fleece and was presenting it to her progeny for posterity. Annabel stayed close to his side before dinner; she must have been instructed to do so, for she spoke little and showed no particular pleasure in being beside him but then, he thought, she showed little pleasure in anything. At dinner, she was placed to his right, while twenty-seven pairs of eyes turned upon him when he requested her to pass the salt. The evening wore on slowly, made no brighter by the fact that after dinner Orbury brought out his finest port and treated Chalmsforth with a familiarity which his own aloofness did nothing to encourage. He pleaded the exigencies of an onerous journey in order to leave as early as he possibly could, his host accepting his explanation with grace, but letting it be understood that he was expected to be a regular member of their circle in future. All the way home Chalmsforth found his thoughts constantly turning to the warmth, the enchantment, the honesty of Fiona, with nary a moment spent on the perfect symmetry of Lady Annabel Telford except to be determined to discourage all overtures from that quarter.

The following morning he called on his mother, anxious to know what exactly had passed between her and the Dowager Marchioness. She was still at the breakfast table.

"Dear Peter," she held up her head as he bent to kiss her cheek. "I have missed you. I saw Gerald yesterday and was glad you got him back safely with no unfortunate encumbrance. It seems he is enamoured of some other young lady now, so it was, as you said, just a passing fancy. Still, I am glad you went, for it set my mind at ease."

"Well, I'm glad I went too, as it happens. Did you know that young Guthrie has a sister? You hadn't mentioned her to me."

"No, I didn't know of it, but now you come to mention it, I believe that is the young lady whom Gerald prefers now, and I'm glad you have had a chance to meet her. I know that there is probably little money there, however, if she is anything like her mother, she would be an entirely satisfactory match for him. He tells me she is devastatingly attractive, though he may be exaggerating. All young men in love do. But from what he says it sounds as though she would be good for him, encouraging him, giving him self-confidence. He needs someone like that. And if she's a beauty into the bargain, as was Ellen, so much the better. And speaking of young men in love, how was your dinner at Orbury's last night?"

Chalmsforth ignored her question to comment with some asperity, "I don't think she is right for him at all. In fact, I don't think they suit."

"Annabel Telford?" His mother looked puzzled.

"No, Fiona Guthrie and Gerald. It simply wouldn't work."

"But why ever not? I am sure if she is Ellen's daughter she is very well brought up and certainly a lady. The Guthries are a very old family, you know. And Gerald will be comfortably off. I think a suitable marriage to a girl of good sense, and a beauty into the bargain, would be good for him. I can't see why you object."

"Well, I do," he replied firmly.

"Why?" she questioned, looking at him directly.

"They . . . their temperaments would not suit at all. Gerald is far too frivolous for her. She needs somebody who is much more . . . much more . . . intelligent, more thoughtful and considerate."

"Yourself, for instance?" she asked quickly.

"No, of course, I didn't mean that. I just meant that a match between Gerald and Miss Guthrie is out of the question."

His mother regarded him quizzically but decided not to press the matter further at that time.

"You haven't mentioned the Orbury dinner."

"It was absolutely ghastly," he responded vehemently. "She simply won't do. I couldn't stand all those relatives of hers and she is so . . . so distant. What on earth did you say to the Dowager Marchioness? They were all standing around me as though I were going to propose on the spot."

"But I thought you were interested. That is what you told me and that is what I told Milly. You said I should. I thought you had decided on her."

"Oh, my God, Mother!" he exclaimed with some exasperation. "No wonder they were so expectant. I didn't say I had decided on her."

"But you said she would do as well as anyone else. I thought that was to be construed as deciding on her."

"Well, she won't do as well as anyone else, I'm afraid," he said, getting up. "They are too pushy by far, and she is as cold and unfeeling as blancmange."

And he departed, leaving his mother to wonder at his enigmatic behaviour. It was so unlike him. She hoped he was feeling quite well and had not caught cold in the damp lowlands.

While Chalmsforth was wondering what was the least decent interval he could allow before his return to Culross Abbey, and what plausible excuse he could give for that return other than a direct proposal of marriage, a course on which he was undecided, Fiona was suffering from difficulties of quite another nature.

Neill had been decidedly out of sorts since their visitors' departure. She put down his depression to the lack of excitement in the country after the prizefight and the quiet of their small family circle. Anne Robarts, too, was quieter than usual. Since Anne had confided her regard for Gerald Chalmsforth to her, Fiona could only suppose his sudden departure without expression of serious intent on his part to be the cause, and her heart went out to Anne. For herself, she had to admit she, too, missed the change caused by their guests and she acknowledged to herself, for the first time, how much she had enjoyed Chalmsforth's company. There had never been anyone who had captured her interest as he had, and with whom she had talked so freely. It had been an interlude, though, nothing more.

A few days after the Chalmsforths' departure, an express arrived for Neill and he shut himself in the library with it without speaking to anyone. When several hours elapsed and he did not come out, Fiona went to him, for it was unusual for him to spend his leisure hours in the library. She saw at once he was unusually pale, and he faced her with a defiant attitude which could only bode trouble. She sat down opposite him, knowing she must be calm and hoping she could handle the matter, whatever it was, as she had others in the past. Surely it could be no worse. But it was.

"All right, Neill, what is it? You might as well tell me, for I am bound to know all in the end. Better that I know everything at the beginning."

"That's just the devil of it, there's no way I can prevent you from finding out about it now. The fact of the matter is that I borrowed money on the abbey to pay off a gambling debt. The note is due next week, and I can't pay it."

"Oh, Neill, you promised you wouldn't do that again . . ." she began, and then realized the futility of that approach. He would become angry and they would fight. Anyway, the thing was done; they must search for a way to repay the debt. "How much is it?" she asked with some trepidation, not, however, in any way expecting his answer.

"Seven thousand pounds."

"Seven thousand!" she gasped.

"Yes, seven thousand." He tossed his head in defiance.

"But you've never been in that deep before. Why . . . how. . . ." Words failed her.

"Well, I suppose I might as well tell you. I was at White's not long ago, playing at a table with the Earl of Newlyn. You don't know him, but he is quite a dandy and he enjoys his cards. Anyway, the others left but he wanted to continue, so we went to his house on Albemarle Street and played piquet."

"But, Neill, you know piquet has never been your game."

"Well, I know I'm not as good at it as you are, but really I play quite well and Newlyn didn't seem that sharp, especially at first, so I thought I was on a winning streak, and when he upped the stakes I agreed. After that the tables turned, I got in heavily, and by the time he suggested quitting I found I was almost seven thousand down. Naturally I had to pay him, so I went to a money lender and got the money. It wasn't easy, though, for no one was keen to advance such a large sum on the abbey alone. No one wants a landless estate, so in the end I'm afraid I . . . well, the man I finally got the money from believed that more of the estate remained with the abbey than is actually the case. I thought I could regain the money before any harm was done, after all, fortunes are won as well as lost. But my luck has been out. The devil of it is that unless the note is paid by next week, I can be thrown into prison not only for debt but also for misrepresentation."

Fiona was cold and shaken, but she sat still, without moving, hearing the words though hardly comprehending them.

"We must find the money," she said at last. "How much exactly is due now?"

"I borrowed something over six, but now it is a full seven thousand with interest. It must all be paid by Thursday, though, he won't let me renew it again." Neill waved the express he had received. "He says here he's been making some enquiries and if I'm not there with the money then he's coming down to find exactly what he can lay claim to."

The thought of raising such a large sum in such a short period of time was appalling, but Fiona's outward appearance remained calm.

"I suppose there are no sources from which the money might be raised?" she asked her brother, without much hope.

"I had hoped to be able to win it in the same way I lost it. You know, if only you had allowed us to play for money when Chalmsforth was here, we probably could have won it back, especially the way you play. And he has it, it would be a drop in the bucket to him. You should see that house of his on Grosvenor Square, not that I've ever been inside it, but they say it is a veritable museum, full of treasures. Just one of his pieces could probably raise the entire sum. Seven thousand may be a fortune to you, but I assure you it is not a great deal in London."

"Neill, that is not the point. Surely you know that you don't play with friends to win money from them."

"But Newlyn won money from me."

"I don't know the Earl of Newlyn, but I thought you liked

Lord Chalmsforth. You sang his praises the whole time. You even annoyed Gerald by doing so."

"Well, you must admit he is a superior sort of man. I don't think he's ever spoken to me before, at White's he's usually so aloof and distant, but here he was quite the reverse. And he seemed to like me."

"All the more reason for not wishing to take his money. Anyway, he's far too astute a card player for either of us to set him if he made up his mind to win."

"I think you could, Fiona, but you won't."

"Anyway, this discussion is beside the point. I am not a gambler and neither is he. I think his pleasures lie elsewhere."

"Oh, you heard about the diamond necklace he gave Grisini, then? It was the talk of London but I didn't think the story had made its way here, or did Gerald say something about it?"

She felt suddenly annoyed.

"No, I didn't know of it. Anyway, that is not the matter under discussion. They are not your diamonds, nor mine, and so they will not help keep you from prison or free you from the talons of this moneylender. But there must be a way."

She got up and paced the floor, and then looked over at her brother, his body slouched on a chair, so young and so dejected. Despite her anger she went over and put her arms around him.

"We'll find a way out, Neill. There's got to be a way out. There has been before and there will be this time. But promise me that when we get out of this scrape you won't let it happen again. The abbey is all we have left and you know how much it meant to father. We mustn't part with it. We won't while I have any say in it."

"Oh, I wouldn't think of selling it either," Neill said hastily, though the thought had often occurred to him that they would be far better off without it. It was a drain upon what little money they did have and hopelessly derelict, but he dared not mention that to his sister. Anyway, in its present condition, it was not worth a great deal.

"I know of only one place I can go," said Fiona at last, "Aunt Clara."

"Oh, Fiona, you can't. You know she won't have anything to do with us. She didn't like father. She said he gambled away mother's money, and I suppose he did. Now tell her we need money because I've been gambling and see how far you'll get."

"I admit it's unlikely that she'll give it, but I can't think of anyone else to turn to. She won't want to see you imprisoned for it would reflect upon her. Anyway I won't say you've been gambling. I'll say we need seven thousand for . . . for. . . ." Her imagination failed her. "Well, I'll think of something."

VIII

At week's end, Fiona posted up to London, taking with her Betsy, her star pupil and daughter of the abbey's housekeeper, Mrs. Pruitt. Fiona could scarcely have travelled unaccompanied, but in any event, she was glad of Betsy's presence for she was an intelligent and willing girl who was thrilled at the thought of seeing the capital city.

Under other circumstances the journey would also have excited Fiona, theretofore she had been little further from Haddenheath than Cambridge, but as it was she was too concerned with their difficulties to give her full attention to the passing scene and the gradual proliferation of towns and villages as the miles passed.

Most of her thoughts were with her aunt and how she might approach her. Lady Clara Benbow was her mother's elder sister. Sir James Benbow, her husband, had a house on Sloane Street where they had brought up their two daughters, Fay, a girl of Fiona's age, and Brenda, three years younger. No close bonds had ever existed between the Guthries and the Benbows, for Lady Benbow had assiduously tried to dissuade her sister from marrying Aaron Guthrie, whom she had regarded as a wastrel and a totally unsuitable match for the beauty of the Berrington family. Time, she felt, had justified her energetic, if unproductive efforts, for Sir Aaron had run through the remainder of his own fortune and that of his wife in an amazingly short time. The most unforgiveable part of all, though, was that in spite of his profligacy, they were so very happy together. It had been unseemly, in Lady Benbow's estimation. Despite Lady Benbow's assertions that Sir Aaron kept her sister immured in the abbey, hidden away on the lonely marshes, unable to enjoy the society of civilized life to which she was accustomed, she knew from her infrequent visits there that it was Ellen, herself, who had no wish to leave Cambridgeshire, that she had grown to love the quiet though bleak beauty of the fens, the great, historic abbey, in fact everything her marriage had brought her. That she did not wish to return to the life on which Lady Benbow thrived was an affront. That she loved her husband despite his detestable gaming habits was inconceivable. Notwithstanding, Lady Benbow had seen fit to announce to the world at large that it had been Sir Aaron's gambling which had killed her sister, forgetting to mention the cold which, despite all care and the attendance of a London doctor at Sir Aaron's insistence, had turned to pneumonia and carried her sister off within a week.

Lady Benbow had sniffed indignantly at the engraving upon her sister's tombstone and muttered loudly about a guilty conscience. Sir Aaron had been too grief-stricken to pay her any heed; it is doubtful that he heard her asides. She had offered to take Fiona back to London with her, but Fiona had refused to leave her father, another unpardonable offence, so Lady Benbow and her husband had returned to Sloane Street in high dudgeon. They met again at Sir Aaron's funeral, four years later, and the offer to take both children had been repeated, though somewhat half-heartedly. Lady Benbow had daughters of her own to bring out and she was not anxious to have a niece on hand who so clearly outshone them. It would not help their chances one bit. It was with some relief, therefore, that she heard Sir Aaron's unmarried sister had offered to live with them. Since that time, apart from annual greetings, they had heard little from one another, a mutually agreeable situation.

Fiona knew the worst thing she could do was to arrive at her aunt's home in this unexpected manner. Lady Benbow liked to plan each event in her life, be it great or small, with the utmost care, making provision for any and every eventuality. Fiona, however, had had no time to apprise her aunt of her visit or to seek an invitation, for circumstances would brook not the least delay if Neill and the abbey were to be saved.

That evening the two young women drew up in front of the neat, well-ordered house on Sloane Street. The sight of her niece in person, as she was shown into the stuffy, plush drawing room where her aunt sat placidly at tea was, therefore, the first intimation that lady had that Fiona was descending upon her. All things considered, while the reception she accorded her young relative was cordial rather than warm, Fiona found none of the frigidity of their last encounter. As a matter of fact, her aunt's thoughts were fastened elsewhere, and after Fiona's preliminary enquiries for her cousins (they were attending an evening party) and her uncle (he was at his club) Lady Benbow found she was glad to have her niece to talk to about a matter that absorbed her. She hoped, she said, to soon have some happy news to impart, and while she was not yet at liberty to give Fiona full details, she could say it concerned her elder daughter, Fay, and a certain young man, Mr. Richard Hardy, whom Fiona would undoubtedly soon meet. While Mr. Hardy had no title, she assured Fiona that he came of a well-settled Kentish family and, since he was the eldest son, stood to inherit a very tidy estate. She and Sir James were very pleased, and the official announcement would be published momentarily. Fiona's arrival was fortuitous, therefore, for it would obviate the necessity of informing her of the news through the vagaries of the post.

The news augured well, for it had clearly put her aunt in a good humour; it was only after Fiona had tended her congratulations on the coming event, and her aunt enquired after the health of Neill and Miss Agatha Guthrie, that the reason for her unannounced descent on Sloane Street was questioned.

Fiona would much have preferred to broach the subject first with her uncle, Sir James. Though she knew he would do nothing without his wife's consent, he was an understanding man. But Lady Benbow would have to be approached eventually, and, since she was obviously in a pleasant frame of mind, perhaps there was no better time.

"I've come to see you, Aunt Clara, on a matter of great concern," she began. "We . . . I need a sum of money, a loan you understand, that will, in due course, be repaid."

In answer to her aunt's raised eyebrows, pursed lips, and unspoken question, she prevaricated. "There are unexpected payments due . . . on the abbey."

"What kind of payments?" Her aunt's frigid tones were not encouraging.

"Repairs to be made, a small mortgage due. . . ." Fiona's voice faltered.

"Well, workmen must be told to wait. If they agree to do work, they must expect to wait for their money. And as for a mortgage, I don't know what mortgage there is. I thought those matters were taken care of when other parts of the estate were sold off. Besides, if there is a note, it can be renewed."

"But it can't be renewed, Aunt, in fact this sum of money must be raised by next week, or else. . . ." Again Fiona found her voice trailing off. She realized she was very tired and it was not, after all, the best time to be discussing such a delicate matter. She needed all her wits about her.

"Or else what?" her aunt demanded sternly.

"Or else we may lose Culross Abbey."

"Lose Culross Abbey for a few measly workmen's wages and a small note? Don't be melodramatic, my child. How much, exactly, is it that you need?" Since she was still in good humour, Lady Benbow mentally decided she might be so kind as to go as high as five hundred, as a loan, of course.

"Seven thousand pounds," Fiona said flatly, expecting an uproar. It came.

"Seven thousand pounds!" For a moment Fiona thought her aunt was going to faint. "Seven thousand pounds . . . did I hear you aright? Is that a small note? My girl, you are just as bad as your father." Her eyes narrowed as they bored into Fiona. "Don't tell me, I know, Neill has been gambling. Just like his father. How many times have I said to James, you mark my words, that boy is going to turn out just like his father, just like his father."

Exhausted though she was, Fiona could no longer endure her aunt's sententiousness.

"Aunt, forgive me but I am very tired and quite hungry. Could we not discuss this in the morning, after I am rested?"

"Why certainly, though what there is to discuss I do not know. It is certain that your uncle will not advance any sum like that, if that is your idea. I shall be glad to call for some cold meats, even though I have already had dinner. Perhaps your visit may not be a failure; we can show you something of London now that you are here. It is, after all, a city worthy of its reputation. You must see Hyde Park, and Bond Street, and the Tower. If the weather is conducive, we may drive along the river toward Ranelagh."

It was obvious Lady Benbow wished to change the subject, and Fiona listened to her plans without relish. Sightseeing was the last thing on her mind, but she nodded her assent and was glad to be released to take an early night.

The next morning, despite a fitful sleep, Fiona felt somewhat recovered and joined her cousins at the breakfast table greeting them warmly, though on the few occasions on which they had met previously she had encountered little kindness from them. She listened, with only half an ear, to their chatter of the party given the previous evening.

"Lor, I thought I couldn't dance another step," Brenda was saying. "John Encross said he had never danced with anyone he enjoyed more. He said I was so light on my feet that it was like dancing with a feather. Wasn't that original."

Feather or feather-brained, Fiona wondered as she smiled her acknowledgement. She thought Brenda the most empty-headed and vain of her cousins. Perhaps it came of being the baby of the family.

"Hardy doesn't care for dancing a great deal, you know," Fay confided, and Fiona replied that some gentlemen didn't care for dancing but that was not to be held against them.

"Of course I don't hold it against him. We sat out and had the best talk." Her mother looked up quickly, hopefully, forcing Fay to add, "I am sure if there had not been so many people around us that he would have spoken more intimately, but there was such a crush. We went into supper together, and he gazed at me most soulfully the whole time." Fiona began to think that he sounded like an awfully dull young man but, desiring to please, she said he sounded most thoughtful.

"Indeed he is. You will meet him this morning, for I am sure he will call. You need not be worried about meeting him, though I know you are not used to London society, but I assure you he is not at all proud and I daresay will treat you just as he would anyone else."

The difficulty was that when Mr. Hardy arrived he did not treat Fiona just as he would anyone else. He could not take his eyes from her.

"I didn't realize you had a cousin, Miss Benbow," he said, bowing on his introduction. "Why did you never mention your cousin to me? What part of Cambridgeshire are you from, Miss Guthrie?"

Much as she would, Fiona could not discourage him from there on from addressing all his remarks to her, to the obvious irritation of her aunt and cousin Fay.

By way of diversion, she drew attention to her cousin's new dress, noting the remarkable shade of yellow, such a bright, cheery colour didn't he think, and how it suited Fay.

"Yes, it is a fine dress, though I suspect it would look better on you because of your dark curls. Brown hair is too nondescript, and there is too little contrast."

Seeing Fay's face fall, and privately condemning the heavy young man for his incivility, Fiona got up and asked her aunt whether she might talk to her uncle, whom she had not yet seen. Lady Benbow, obviously pleased to get Fiona from the room and, at the same time leave the young couple alone together, accompanied Fiona to her husband's study, where Sir James sat reading the newspaper.

"James, look who is here," her aunt called with false gaiety.

"Why, Fiona!" Her uncle got up, folding his newspaper. "What a lovely young lady you've grown into. And how is dear Neill?"

"Well, Uncle, well." Fiona held up her cheek for a dutiful kiss, relieved at his unhesitant warmth. "I'm so glad to see you." She surveyed him at arm's length. "You do look well."

"Oh, I'm not doing so badly, except for a touch of gout now and then, but that happens to the best of us."

Fiona smiled. She was quite fond of her uncle, who was an unassuming man but unfortunately completely dominated by his wife.

She turned to her aunt and asked whether she had told her uncle of their difficulties.

"Indeed, I have, Fiona, but of course he agrees with me that we could not possibly lend you such a sum of money. We are not rich people, you know."

"I realize that," Fiona said, trying to keep her eyes from the diamonds twinkling on her aunt's puffy hands. "It is just that the money must be raised somehow and I didn't know where to turn. Perhaps you could advise me."

"There is only one possibility that I can think of," her aunt said hesitantly.

"What is that?" Fiona could not keep the eagerness from her voice.

"If you were to sell the place."

"Sell the abbey? But that is out of the question."

"Of course, I didn't mean to just anyone, not anyone outside the family."

"Not outside the family? But who could you mean?"

"I mean that we might be willing to let you have the seven thousand pounds if you pass the property over to us. You could continue to live there, at least for the time being. When my own girls are married, I am sure I can find someone for you. Neill can do something, I suppose. Does he have any marriage prospects? It would help if he married into money, though I don't suppose anyone would want to give their daughter to a gentleman with such unfortunate habits. We all know what happened to your dear mother's settlement."

She sighed, but it is doubtful that Fiona had comprehended her last insinuations for she was transfixed in horror at the thought of her aunt and uncle and their stupid daughters and undoubtedly equally stupid husbands installed at Culross Abbey, home of the Guthries for centuries, and of historic significance long before that. To think of it falling prey to the unworthy hands of the Benbows, with their crass, vulgar outlook on life, why, it was preposterous, not even worthy of discussion. And had she come all this way for such a futile solution? She would rather see complete strangers there, even Cits, what did it matter. She would not know what they were like, but these people she knew, and these past few hours had confirmed that they had not changed. They were insupportable.

She became aware of her aunt's voice still droning on.

"Of course, it is in terrible need of repair and we shall probably have to spend a mint on it. You would have trouble selling it to anyone else. But we will take it to help you out since you are obviously in a difficult predicament. It's quite a nice place, and I've always wanted a country estate, though, I confess, I had never thought of anything quite so large."

Her aunt smiled complacently, perhaps at the idea of impressing her few friends and multitude of acquaintances. But her smile froze on her lips as Fiona shouted,

"Quite a nice place! Quite a nice place, indeed! Do you realize you are speaking of one of England's most honoured ancestral sites? Why, the abbey ranks with Ely Cathedral as one of the country's most important structures. Kings of England have stayed there, not to mention queens. It is noted in all the guide books. There is no other staircase in any mansion in England to equal that in the great hall. And you call it quite a nice place! Words fail me!"

Her aunt gradually regained her composure following this outburst.

"Come, come, Fiona. Don't get so worked up. You came to us for help and we are trying to help you. We are your relatives, you are at home among us. If you don't like the suggestion, just say so, though we thought to be generous."

"I don't like the suggestion, ma'am. I don't like it at all. I asked you for a loan, one that, with time, would be repaid to you. I did not ask you to take over the abbey for a mere seven thousand pounds."

"I hesitate to remind you that it is seven thousand of which you are desperately in need. No one is going to let you have an unsecured loan for such an amount. And surely you wouldn't expect it to be given to you?" the buxom lady said in high dudgeon, incensed by Fiona's response.

"No," Fiona admitted, "there is no one who would give such a sum, but perhaps I might get a loan using the abbey as security. It belongs equally to myself and my brother."

"Then I hope he informed you before he got in this mess," her aunt said shrewdly, Fiona's answering flush confirming her suspicion that she had only just discovered the entanglement.

"Come, come, Clara." Sir James, who had been silent during the exchange, though its content did not surprise him, now intervened. "Fiona does not seem to like the idea of parting with the abbey. It is understandable. Perhaps we could lend her the amount for a period until she can arrange matters."

"Seven thousand pounds! And me with a wedding on my hands any day now. There will be clothes to buy, and don't forget Fay's portion. No, indeed, it is a most inopportune moment. We could not spare such a sum just now, nor any time for that matter. Besides, how could they ever repay such a loan?"

"Well, perhaps you are right," he conceded, looking rather shamefaced.

"Of course I am right."

"Then I obviously should not have troubled you, and I will no longer. I thank you for your kindness, but I think I must return to Cambridgeshire without delay."

"Not now," her aunt intervened. "At least wait until tomorrow."

"Very well." Fiona turned to Sir James. "Perhaps you would be so kind as to arrange for a post chaise for me."

"But you must use my carriage, I insist upon it." Sir James was anxious to make some amends.

"I have no wish to trouble you," she replied with dignity.

"Indeed, it is no trouble," her aunt put in, "as long as you send it back directly. We shall undoubtedly be needing it rather frequently now, what with shopping and calls and a million things which will have to be done."

Fiona agreed reluctantly. It was not worth a fuss, and it would save some money, though it counted little given the vast debt that hung over them. She spent the remainder of the day ruminating on plans of action, taken up and discarded, all either absolutely impractical or totally impossible. Had she been less pragmatic, she would have hoped for a miracle to happen, but she believed nothing could be accomplished without effort. Something must be done, but what?

IX

Lady Benbow was in a positively black humour that evening, for Mr. Hardy, despite being left alone with Fay for an inordinate length of time, had not only not proposed during his visit but, as Fay sobbed to her mother later, had asked repeatedly when her cousin would return. Thus, Lady Benbow thought better of resuming her idea of pressing Fiona to stay and see the sights, considering the sooner her disturbing influence were out of sight the better.

Fiona, only too willing to comply, was ready by eight the following morning, but, at the last moment, Lady Benbow decided she must take the carriage to return a bonnet she had ordered but which had not been constructed to her liking. Thus, Fiona's departure was delayed until almost noon. Adieus on both sides were cool, though Fay looked unusually satisfied when the carriage at last pulled away carrying with it her distracting cousin.

Fiona stared abstractly at the passing London scene, the sumptuous houses, the well-clad people, thinking dully how easily some of them might raise the sum needed, large though it was. But even if she knew any of them and they were willing to advance the money, what could she offer in return? Only the abbey itself, and she had already refused to do that. There was nothing else in her possession that could be worth that much. It was hopeless. She was defeated.

As the carriage entered Park Lane on its route to the Edgeware Road, an obstacle barred their way. A cart loaded with fresh provisions from the country, bound, no doubt, for the kitchens of one of the fashionable houses in the vicinity, had been overturned by a cabbie. Fresh fruit and vegetables littered the street and a fight was in progress between the two burly drivers as to who was at fault. Sir James's coachman would much have preferred to stay and cheer for the cabbie, a cockney like himself, but he could see that it would clearly be a lengthy business and they already had a late start. With reluctance, he turned down a side street to pursue another route. Fiona, realizing the coachman had changed direction, called out to ask where they were.

"Grosvenor Square, ma'am," was the reply.

Grosvenor Square. It sounded familiar, but why? Then she remembered Neill's speaking of Chalmsforth's townhouse there, and a sudden, desperate thought occurred to her.

"And which is Lord Chalmsforth's house?" she demanded.

The coachman indicated a stately mansion on the opposite side of the square. With sudden decision, Fiona ordered him to stop there and go and enquire whether his lordship was within.

The coachman, though surprised and somewhat annoyed at yet another delay, did as he was bid and returned shortly to announce that his lordship was at home and would Miss Guthrie kindly step in.

Fiona, closely followed by Betsy, entered the house with a determined yet reluctant stride, as though part of her insisted on her going while another part would much have preferred to remain in the carriage. Inside, she had never encountered anything to equal the luxury and splendour of the decor and furnishings. The dark blue carpets were thick and soft underfoot. Marble busts of figures of English history and literature graced niches in the panelled walls and a gracious, curved, marble double staircase led to the rooms above.

The footman informed her that his lordship would be down immediately and that he would show her to the saloon where his secretary, Mr. Nicholson, awaited her. Instructing Betsy to wait in the hall, Fiona followed the footman, her mind now determined on the course she must take.

In the great saloon a rather nervous, bespectacled young man introduced himself as Lord Chalmsforth's secretary.

"His lordship will be down directly. He had not expected you."

"No. I was passing through the square and thought to call on him," Fiona replied distantly, unwilling to converse.

Though Nicholson showed no surprise, he was, in fact, quite shocked. That a young lady, at least she gave every evidence of being a lady, should call on his lordship accompanied only by her maid was hardly proper. Perhaps she was a relative or friend of some long standing, for his employer had been so obviously pleased by the news of her arrival, elated

70

might better describe it; it was not a state in which he had previously seen him. That the visitor was quite, quite beautiful went without question, despite her lack of style; that her beauty obviously must add to Lord Chalmsforth's pleasure in seeing her was also apparent when Chalmsforth made his appearance some moments later, apologizing profusely for keeping her waiting. He was elegantly attired in white breeches, knee boots, and blue velvet coat. Never had he tied his cravat in such haste, though it showed no sign of being anything less than immaculate.

"Miss Guthrie! You have no idea the happiness this gives me. I heard no inkling that you were in town. Did you come up with your brother?" He held her hand slightly longer than necessary in greeting her and looked into her eyes with such genuine pleasure that though she felt little inclined, she gave him a full smile in return.

"No, Neill is in Cambridgeshire, at least he was when I left a few days ago. My coming to London was . . . unexpected."

"I hope there is no difficulty."

She paused before answering and he, realizing Nicholson was still in the room, turned to dismiss him.

Fiona found her courage to follow her determined course dissipating following her host's warm greeting, and she was unable to broach the subject of her visit directly, saying instead,

"I have been visiting my uncle and aunt, Sir James and Lady Benbow. They live on Sloane Street. I don't know whether you are acquainted with them?"

"I believe I have met Sir James Benbow on occasion, though I was not aware that he was your uncle."

"It is rather that his wife is, or was, my mother's sister."

Her voice grew cold at the thought of that lady, and her heart grew cold at the thought of the things she meant to say, and a silence ensued. He, for his part, wondered what lucky star had guided her to his doorstep and saved him from the dilemma of finding an excuse to visit her.

"Oh, but excuse me, would you not like some refreshment?" And he pulled the cord for the footman before she could refuse his offer.

She sat, still silent, holding the glass of sherry which had been offered to her, and wondering whether, in fact, she could bring herself to the subject of her visit. It was Chalmsforth who opened the way for her.

"But did you not say that you had been visiting your uncle and aunt? Am I to gather that your visit is at an end, that you are now leaving London?"

"Yes, that is so. As a matter of fact, I am on my way home to the abbey at this moment, but as I found our course had led through Grosvenor Square, and I recalled that that was where you lived, I decided to stop to see you, to talk with you, before my return." She felt she could not go on; his smile of infinite pleasure made her task more difficult.

"And I am delighted that you did so, though I find myself provoked that you only come to me as you leave London. Surely it is possible that you can stay longer."

"My visit was not a social one. It was, rather, one of business and it did not serve to stay longer on Sloane Street."

"But this I cannot allow. London is awake now, there are all manner of amusements here. You really should stay, at least for another week. Could it not be arranged?"

"I cannot return to my uncle's house."

The note of finality as she spoke made him pause to consider.

"I am, indeed, flattered that you thought to call on me. I have thought of you . . . and your brother, of course, often since my visit to Culross Abbey."

He saw her eyes fixed upon him with a certain determination and asked slowly,

"Are you sure that *I* cannot be of assistance to you?"

She took a deep breath and her lips trembled slightly as she quickly replied,

"As a matter of fact you can. I need seven thousand pounds."

In the deep silence that followed, after her words had reverberated through the great saloon, bouncing off the delicate-eggshell-blue walls, resounding from the sparkling chandeliers, echoing from the frescoed ceiling, she heard nothing but her own quickened heartbeat. She continued to look at his face, which showed no sign of surprise or annoyance, in fact it showed nothing, nothing at all. At last he said quietly, as though he spoke of the weather,

"Seven thousand pounds. Why certainly, I am sure that can be arranged without difficulty. You may have a draft on my bank. To whom shall I draw it?"

His calm acceptance left Fiona at a loss. She had expected questions, demands for explanations, shock at her coming to him in such a matter, anything but his phlegmatic reply as though she had asked for a glass of water. That he would give such a sum to her freely, without hesitation, was beyond belief. It was, also, quite impossible to accept on that basis from a virtual stranger.

"You misunderstand me, I fear. I cannot accept this as a gift, nor can I ask it as a loan for that matter, for I am not sure that I can repay it at any time soon. In fact, the money is needed by Thursday in order to repay a note which is due then, otherwise. . . ." Her voice broke off and she looked down at her gloved hands, afraid she might burst into tears now, when she most needed her self-possession.

"Otherwise?" he prompted gently.

"Otherwise there is the possibility that my brother may be in some legal difficulties." She squared her shoulders believing she had the fortitude to continue.

"Well, in that case, I must write the draft without delay. I would not want Guthrie to meet with any dire consequences, whatever the reason."

He turned to go, but she stopped him.

"Please, the matter is not settled between us. I have told you I cannot accept this sum as a gift, nor could I allow you to loan such an amount without adequate hope of recovery. I have discovered how difficult it is to raise money when one has little of tangible value to offer. I came to you with another proposal."

Something in her voice and her eyes puzzled him and he turned back and sat down opposite her.

"What is it that you propose?" he asked curiously.

She looked down for a moment, unable to meet his frank gaze, but gaining courage at last she raised her head to look at him directly and when she spoke her voice was flat, without emotion.

"When you first met me in the library at my home, you made me a certain proposition. You said I could ask my price for spending a night with you." She raised her chin slightly and continued with a coolness without which was not reflected within. "I am now asking for seven thousand pounds for that night."

He did not move but kept staring at her, only his hands on the arms of the Chippendale chair tightened their grip so that the knuckles stood out white against the taut skin. While outwardly his expression did not change, inwardly he felt as he had when he had found a soldier looting a house in Lisbon, pulling an irreplaceable Velazquez from the wall, tearing at the canvas to loosen it yet with no idea of its worth, ruining a priceless work of art. Such a senseless waste of beauty. How could there be beauty without nobility, beauty without honour? He looked at Fiona now as she sat opposite him without moving. He had thought she was everything that he wanted in a woman, vivacious, brave, loyal, honest, and beautiful beyond belief. Now, in the space of a moment, she had shattered that dream. To even consider selling herself, it was incredible. He would have given her anything and asked nothing, he would have considered it a privilege to do so. He rose from his chair and put his hand to his brow, fearing she might recognize the disgust he felt at her proposal.

"I assure you, it is quite unnecessary," he said dryly. "I thought I had explained my gauche error and that you understood——"

She interrupted him.

"You did explain, and I did understand that explanation though I may not have agreed with your reasoning. But you see, I am in dire need of this money and it must be raised without delay. I have applied to my aunt and uncle, but they are unwilling, or unable, to help. Now, I cannot accept such a sum as a gift, particularly from a virtual stranger, of no blood relationship. My aunt has pointed out to me the impossibility of raising such a sum without collateral, or the sale of something of equivalent value. I could not possibly remain in anyone's debt. It had not been my intention to come to you, but when we were passing through the square I remembered that you lived here, and I remembered your offer."

"But that offer was not made to Miss Guthrie of Culross Abbey. I thought you were a woman . . . a woman of light moral character."

"I realize your misunderstanding, but does it make a difference?"

He grew impatient in answering. "Of course it makes a difference. A lady cannot . . . cannot . . . a lady cannot sell herself."

"Does my rank make me less desirable then?" she asked in that straightforward manner he had grown to know so well and that always had the power to disconcert him.

"It is not a matter of desirability," he said harshly, "it is a matter of propriety. There are certain things a lady cannot do, and what you suggest is one of them. Do you not realize that should you embark on such a course no respectable man would ever marry you?"

"I do not particularly care to marry, so that hardly perturbs me. If marriage were usually contracted for love, it might be different, but so few are based upon that as far as I can see. Anyway, I believe if any man truly wished to marry me, my past would matter little."

"How little you know of men! But perhaps a suitable husband could be found for you now who would have money and could take care of such debts. You are an exceedingly beautiful woman."

"I find that quite repugnant! To be married in such haste and to immediately extract a large sum of money from some prospective husband prior to the ceremony. Worse yet, to have to live with him after for the rest of my life! No, I'm afraid that will not answer. I find it disgusting. Besides, I see little difference between such a marriage and selling myself, as you put it, in the manner I suggested. Though you did not realize who I was that day at the abbey, yet it was to me you made the offer. I did not accept it then, but now I do." When he made no reply, she added, "I had understood then that you . . . that I . . . attracted you."

"I was not impervious to your charms." There was a strained edge to his voice. A silence, broken only by the sound of a tall corner-case clock, continued as Chalmsforth walked over to the window and stood with his back to the room. Then, at last, he turned.

"To whom do you wish the draft to be drawn? If it is to a moneylender, I think you should not deliver it. I shall entrust the mission to Nicholson. You may rely on his discretion."

He had neither accepted nor denied her suggestion. She was unable to read his expression. He looked suddenly weary and his eyes were blank. She gave him the name and direction of the moneylender, then added softly but with a certain dignity, "You know, I cannot take this as a gift."

"You have made yourself quite clear on that point, Miss Guthrie. Now where are your things?"

"They are in my uncle's carriage. I . . . I should not wish him to know."

"I rather imagine you would not," his tone was harsh. "But

do you suppose you can make such proposals and no one will ever know?"

"I suppose not. Eventually, I suppose all would be known, but not now."

"Very well."

"And Betsy is with me, my maid," she explained.

"At least I suppose I should be grateful that you did not come on such a journey on your own. And I suppose you would not wish her to know either?" The harsh quality of his voice did not abate and served to remind Fiona of the enormity of her plan of action. But it was done, there was no going back now, and Neill would be safe.

"I said nothing of that, my lord, I was merely informing you that she was with me," she answered coldly, determined to maintain her dignity come what may.

"Very well." He turned and quit the room, leaving her alone. She put her head in her hands and at last gave in to the palpitations she had felt since the interview began. It was not so much that she feared the act itself, though she had no great knowledge of what was to come; she had no married ladies among her intimate acquaintances, and there had only been intimations gleaned from books or remarks her brother had made. It was, however, a natural act and therefore could not be totally frightening. She had no great value for innocence for itself alone, the prize set on that commodity in young women seemed beyond proportion to its worth. It was, however, the intimacy she feared. She acknowledged that she liked Chalmsforth. Now, if the deed were to be done in such a cold manner, she would have preferred it to be with someone to whom she was indifferent or even disliked. And though Chalmsforth had originally shown preference for her, she had reason to believe that now he despised her.

It was some time before he returned and by then she had regained her composure. She was surprised to find him wearing a top coat and carrying a tall beaver hat.

"Are we going out?" she asked, rising immediately.

"You can hardly expect me to immediately conduct you to my chamber above, before the servants and your own maid. I thought you wished for discretion in the matter."

She did not reply, but held her head high as he opened the door for her and led her to his waiting curricle. She noted that her uncle's coach had been dismissed and wondered what had become of her box. Nor was there any sign of Betsy. She was acutely aware that she was alone in a city where she had no acquaintance except for her aunt and uncle, from whom she had parted on none too amicable terms, alone with a man of whom she knew little and with whom she had just proposed to have the utmost intimacy. She dared not think of her home or Aunt Agatha. Neill must never know, she affirmed to herself.

She kept her eyes ahead of her, oblivious to the bustle of the London streets as Chalmsforth guided his horses through the maze of pedestrians and carriages with a sure hand. She wanted to ask him where they were going, but one glance at his profile had shown a countenance so forbidding that she found it hard to recognize in it the debonair gentleman who had talked so freely and so emotionally on that journey to Ely.

As though reading her thoughts, Chalmsforth turned to her.

"Are you not curious as to our destination?"

"I was sure if I waited long enough you would tell me or, if you did not, then I should find out when we arrive. Perhaps it is better that I do not know."

"Perhaps not," was his laconic reply.

At that moment they turned into Brook Street and drew up at a smart house on the corner. Chalmsforth threw the reins to his groom and alighted, holding up his hand to assist her down. She gazed up at the windows of the house, unable to hide her apprehension. As dismal as she felt, it somehow did not seem nearly as forbidding as had her aunt's dwelling. The windowpanes sparkled and the striped damask hangings were drawn back to allow the light and what little sun there was to penetrate into what were obviously spacious, comfortable rooms.

She did not know what to expect as the footman admitted them. Obviously Chalmsforth was not unknown there, in fact the footman acted as though he were master of that establishment as well as of the one on Grosvenor Square. She waited for some clue, but when it came it was the last thing she anticipated.

"Is my mother at home?"

She could not restrain herself from turning to him and crying in astonished, even shocked, tones,

"Your *mother!*"

One look silenced her until they were shown into the

morning room to await that lady. Then she turned on him in fury.

"And what, sir, has your mother to do with this?"

"I felt it best that you stay with her for a time." His glance swept over her faded travelling dress. "I prefer women of fashion, after all. My mother will direct you to the right dressmakers and introduce you into society."

"But that was not part of the bargain."

"Bargain?" He raised his eyebrows in aloof comment.

"The arrangement . . . I mean . . . you said . . . you know very well what I mean. . . ." But before she could extricate herself from this jumbled sentence, Lady Chalmsforth entered the room and greeted her son warmly and then turned amicably but questioningly to Fiona.

"Mother, I would like to present to you Miss Fiona Guthrie. She is Ellen Berrington's daughter and Neill Guthrie's sister. I believe I mentioned to you that I met her in Cambridgeshire a short while ago. Miss Guthrie, my mother, Lady Chalmsforth."

"Indeed you did, Peter. And are you to stay in London? I do hope so. I was so fond of your mother. We came out together, you know. I was Florence Pryor then."

Fiona warmed to Lady Chalmsforth instantly.

"Then she has spoken of you often. I did not realize that you were Lady Chalmsforth. She liked you a great deal, you know, though like is not strong enough; she loved and respected you."

"And I, her. Peter, what a delightful surprise. I was feeling quite blue today and now I am to have the pleasure of this young lady's company. You are so like your mother, my dear, it takes me back more years than I care to remember. And Ellen is gone now, along with my own dear husband. But I must not get mournful. Where are you staying, Miss Guthrie?"

"Please call me Fiona," she said, but knew not what to reply. How could Chalmsforth bring her here and embarrass her so. She turned to him, unable to keep the fury from her eyes.

"Miss Guthrie has been staying with Sir James and Lady Benbow on Sloane Street, and was about to quit London for Cambridgeshire, but I prevailed upon her to prolong her stay a while longer and remain with you."

"Oh, I am pleased. Gerald will be also." She smiled, but her son ignored this last remark.

"I have notified the Benbows of Miss Guthrie's intention. Her maid and her luggage will arrive shortly, but I think it would be wise to take Miss Guthrie to your dressmaker, since I know one of her reasons for coming to town was to refurbish her wardrobe. Have them direct the accounts to me. I promised Miss Guthrie's brother that I would take care of these matters for him," he concluded by way of explanation, but Lady Chalmsforth took all these instructions with perfect equanimity, as though she were daily used to young ladies being dropped upon her doorstep and then being ordered to feed and clothe them and send the accounts to her son.

She took Fiona's hand. "We're going to have such fun, my dear, and you will look absolutely perfect in almost anything. Why I saw some rose-pink satin only yesterday that I was dying to buy, but it simply wouldn't do for me. It will be adorable for you. And I can't wait until Mlle. Estelle sees your face, such structure and colouring, I know it will arouse all her creative millinery endeavours. Dear, dear Peter, what a simply capital surprise. Thank you for bringing Fiona to me. But then, you always do the nicest things."

Fiona looked from mother to son, seeing the likeness between them and the affection they so obviously held for one another. She suddenly felt very low and was embarrassed to feel tears come to her eyes. She looked away, but Chalmsforth must have noticed for he said quickly,

"Miss Guthrie has had quite an exhausting day, being quite prepared for the return to Cambridgeshire until I persuaded her otherwise. I don't doubt that she rose with the lark for the journey and has been busy ever since. It would be best that she rest until dinner. There will be time enough to talk and shop tomorrow."

Fiona could not help but feel grateful to him, and she was able to withhold her sobs until she was alone in a pretty daffodil-yellow bedroom upstairs.

X

Everyone—milliners, mantuamakers, shoemakers, haberdash-ers—was in raptures over the outfitting of Fiona, everyone, that is, except Fiona herself, who took little part in it all except to express a preference for plainness over adornment and a horror at the extravagance and cost of it all. Lady Chalmsforth would have none of it, however, and the business of acquiring the wardrobe was left in her capable hands. She had unerring taste and was delighted to be able to order clothes which appealed to her but were much too youthful for her own choosing. Her first act was to purchase the rose satin she had so admired. It was a happy choice, for it was perfect with Fiona's dark hair and fair skin, though her cheeks were still pale. Lady Chalmsforth hoped she would regain her bloom in time for Lady Sefton's ball the following evening, at which time she planned Fiona's first formal introduction to the *grand monde*. She knew she would take London by storm as her mother had done before her.

Lady Chalmsforth arranged that the dress chosen for that ball, a bell-skirted creation made of the rose-pink satin, ribbon-trimmed in a darker rose with a low, scooped neckline designed to set off Fiona's fine neck and shoulders, would be finished by the following afternoon. As they left the dress-maker's establishment, Fiona protested, for she was sure that such a requirement would entail some poor seamstress's staying up all night in order to finish it, but Lady Chalmsforth assured her that any inconvenience suffered would undoubt-edly be added to the bill, which again occasioned Fiona to protest the vast amounts of money being spent on her account. Lady Chalmsforth would not hear of it, for if her son had promised he would settle all the accounts, he would un-doubtedly do so and whatever arrangement he had with her brother need not concern Fiona, it was between the two men and not a cause for Fiona's worry. But worry she did, though seeing that her concern caused discomfort to Lady Chalmsforth, for whom she already felt a growing regard, she hid her feelings as much as she could. There was little to be done. If it was a woman of fashion Chalmsforth wanted, she must accept that role though she felt it little became her. She had entered into an agreement with him and had been handsomely rewarded at a time when she most needed it. If he wished to fritter away more money on his whims, it was not for her to argue. She only hoped that matters would soon be settled between them and she could return to her beloved abbey.

Nor was Fiona oblivious to the fact of how much enjoyment Lady Chalmsforth was deriving from outfitting her in the last word of fashion. Never in her life had she been so indulged nor had so much attention paid to her. Dressmakers and milliners raved over her beauty to a degree she found embarrassing, yet since they seemed genuinely happy to lend their talents to a task which would show their work to best advantage, she obliged them by turning this way and that and then listening to their torrents of delight when a certain something had been achieved. In the end it became something of a game, a game in which she found herself taking part though she could never manage to bring herself to their same pitch of excitement. Try as she would, when she looked in the mirror she still saw Fiona Guthrie of Culross Abbey under all the finery, a young woman caught in a distressing dilemma.

Lady Chalmsforth was delighted with everything in which she saw Fiona. She was determined to make her the hit of the season which, given her looks, her pleasant manner and ready wit, notwithstanding her lack of fortune, she felt was a foregone conclusion.

Thus it was that Lord Chalmsforth, passing Brook Street on his way to White's that evening, came upon the two ladies in high spirits sitting over their evening tea and discussing the events of the day. Lady Chalmsforth had just been relating to Fiona a story of her own coming out. It seemed she had mistaken a certain gouty admiral by the name of Fenwich for a dashing Mr. Fenton, who had been spoken of as a possible match for her; on being introduced to the venerable naval hero she had run from the room in a torrent of tears to the great consternation and mystification of both the old gentleman and her parents. Admiral Fenwich had never understood her mistake; he thought he terrified her and ever after he had assiduously avoided her, thus causing her even greater discomfort. The retelling of this anecdote resulted in gales of laughter especially occasioned by Lady Chalmsforth's imitation of the old admiral. This laughter only slightly abated on Chalmsforth's entrance, for Fiona found it impossible to completely quell her good humour though she found his presence daunting. Lady Chalmsforth gave her son a minute account of the day's activities, not omitting Fiona's concern for the seamstress who might be forced to sit up to finish her rose satin for Lady Sefton's ball.

"I shall see to it that she is personally recompensed," Chalmsforth promised with a grave look at Fiona.

"Thank you," she smiled. "I am sure she will be able to use the money, whoever she is. I am well aware that the owners of these establishments do not lack for ample emolument judging from the sums I heard mentioned today, but I wonder how much of it filters down to the hands that actually ply the needle."

"Your social concerns are commendable," Chalmsforth replied. She looked at him sharply but nothing on his face indicated sarcasm, so the matter was dropped. "Then I gather you have had a satisfactory day."

Fiona and Lady Chalmsforth both started to talk at once, then laughed, both stopping and starting to talk at the same time once more. It was obvious that they had formed a fast friendship and Chalmsforth, looking from one to the other, felt somehow gratified.

"We have had a simply marvellous time," his mother said at last, "and I can't thank you enough for bringing Fiona to me. Now, are you going to accompany us to Fanny Sefton's tomorrow night? We shall be leaving about eight."

Chalmsforth said he would be unable to be there that early, but he would see them later in the evening, causing his mother to observe that if he were going to be late it was doubtful whether Fiona would have any dances left. That, as it happened, was the case.

Chalmsforth arrived at Lady Sefton's just before eleven and joined his mother, who with Amanda Markham was watching Fiona going through the intricate steps of a quadrille with Sir Brian Fennister, a gangly young man who obviously took great pains with his appearance but to no great avail. His elation at the grace of his partner made his own clumsy efforts appear even more ludicrous.

"Peter, you should have been here earlier. Fiona has caused a sensation. I knew she would. She is simply charming everyone, including some of the crustiest dowagers, and she has been overwhelmed with partners."

"Lady Fennister doesn't look all that charmed," Chalmsforth observed wryly.

"Well, this is the second time her son has stood up with Fiona, and you know how possessive she is. Besides, he is so obviously absolutely besotted with her."

"I can see that, and it does not improve his appearance one bit. I'm surprised Miss Guthrie can stand it, he is stepping all over her."

"Don't be unkind to him, dear, he tries so hard. And she has simply accepted whoever asked her to dance without question, being even more kind, I think, to the shy and less desirable young men. She declined a dance with Lord Elton, and he is not used to being refused, as I'm sure you know, just to dance again with Sir Brian. I think she knew how important he considered it to dance with her. She is a most amiable girl."

"I can imagine that surprised Elton, but I hope all these attendant swains are aware that Miss Guthrie is totally lacking in fortune. It would be awful to disappoint them after they have fallen in love, far better it be known before."

"Peter, you are so cynical. It is simply because she is so very lovely and so very kind also, I might add, that she has caused a sensation. It does not mean that all her partners look upon her as a future wife, but they are undoubtedly captivated by her and are vying to dance with her. Anyway, despite her lack of fortune there are plenty here who have large enough fortunes in their own right that they do not have to marry money. I must say I would not be averse to her as a daughter in the least." She looked pensively at the ivory fan he had given her as she spoke, examining the lotus design. "Gerald came by earlier today and was quite upset that he had refused Fanny's invitation. He had no idea that Fiona was to visit us and would be here."

"I don't imagine he did."

"Well, you might have told him. You know he likes her."

"Since I, myself, had no forewarning of it, I could scarcely have told him. Besides, he has hardly been near me since we returned from Cambridgeshire."

The dance ended and Fiona joined them, accompanied by Sir Brian whom she thanked handsomely for dancing with her. Sir Brian was obviously unused to being complimented and he scrutinized Fiona to make sure she was not having fun at his expense, but being assured of her sincerity, he flushed with pleasure as he reluctantly withdrew. Lady Fennister came over to join Lady Chalmsforth, apparently anxious to get full particulars of the young lady who was claiming so much of her son's attention, leaving Fiona and Chalmsforth momentarily alone.

"You look very lovely," Chalmsforth approved. "Mother was certainly right in her choice of that colour, yet there are not many women who could wear it. She tells me you have been deluged with partners."

"I've enjoyed the dancing and I'm glad you approve of the dress," she replied frankly, and then paused before asking him abruptly, "Perhaps I am now woman of fashion enough for your taking."

Though his first remark had been amiable in tone, now she saw again a look of cold fury in his eyes. The half smile faded from his lips and his eyes narrowed.

"Let me be the judge of that," he replied tersely, turning on his heel. As he did so his arm was seized by a broad-shouldered, dark-haired man in the dashing uniform of the Tenth Hussars.

"Farendon!" Chalmsforth's whole attitude changed to one of complete joy. "I had no idea you were expected home."

"I might know I would find you with the prettiest girl in the room. Well, don't just stand there, won't you introduce me?"

"Miss Guthrie, may I present Colonel Farendon. We served together in Spain. This is Miss Guthrie, sister of Sir Neill Guthrie of Culross Abbey in Cambridgeshire."

"I know that part of the country well. My uncle lived in Fordham for some time. Marvellous shooting down there and even though it is flat, that is some of the loveliest country I've ever known."

Fiona warmed to the newcomer immediately.

"You couldn't have said anything to please me more. I miss my fen country and everyone I talk to seems to think it the least interesting place in the world. But it takes a trained eye such as yours to appreciate its beauty. It is indeed a lovely part of England. Is it long since you have visited Fordham?"

Farendon very definitely had a trained eye for beauty, though at that moment it was not the beauty of the fens that captivated him, but before he had a chance to press his advantage, Fiona's hand was claimed by her partner for the next dance, the Earl of Newlyn.

From the look Chalmsforth gave him as he said, "My turn at last, dear lady," with a flourish, it was obvious he held him in little admiration. Newlyn's attitude was equally distant.

"Evening, Chalmsforth. Didn't know you were here. Are you just home, Farendon?" But without waiting for an answer from either, he took Fiona's arm possessively and led her to the floor, though not before she had observed the look of animosity which passed between the two gentlemen.

"What an absolute beauty," Farendon murmured. "If I'd known someone like that would be here, I would have arrived ages ago. Have you known her long?"

"No, not really. She is a guest of my mother's."

"Lucky chap. I wish my mother knew girls like that. The ones she introduces to me always have buck teeth and squint."

"And probably large fortunes. Miss Guthrie, I regret to inform you, is singularly lacking in that quarter."

His friend observed him closely. "Not warning me off, are you old chap?"

"No, but your mother is right, you know. It would be helpful for you to cast your attention where there is money."

"Chalmsforth, you are always so practical. And I suppose buck teeth and squints can replace alluring blue eyes and soft pink lips for a mere few thousand."

"Not all girls with money have buck teeth. But I don't care. Make a fool of yourself if you wish. For the moment I want to hear how things are going with the Tenth. And how's Wellington doing? Has it been hot over there? You look as though you've been out in the sun quite a bit. Have you seen any action recently? How about Bucky Wynne, did the wound in his leg heal all right?" And, tucking his arm through that of his friend, he drew him off to an anteroom but, since they were so often disturbed there he insisted they leave and go over to White's and get them to rustle up some of their superior port while they talked in peace.

Thus Fiona saw no more of Chalmsforth or his military friend that evening, but if she noticed his departure, she made no comment upon it. Lady Chalmsforth was too busy enjoying Fiona's success, so it was some time before she noticed her son was no longer there. The Marchioness of Orbury, however, noted his departure and whispered to her husband, who was plainly disconcerted by Lady Chalmsforth's newly-arrived guest and determined that Chalmsforth must be brought to book with all haste.

Despite all, Fiona found that she had enjoyed Lady Sefton's ball. She was unused to being a centre of attraction, and she could not quite grasp the devastating effect she seemed to exert over some of the gentlemen there. Sir Brian Fennister's attentions had become so pronounced that his mother was forced to leave early and to command her son to see her home, this following a consultation with Lady Chalmsforth in which it had transpired that though Miss Guthrie possessed a very pretty face, that, in itself, was her fortune. Her son, however, seemed undaunted by his mother's lack of enthusiasm for that young lady, for the following morning found him at Brook Street paying his respects to Miss Guthrie to discover that even in the brightest light of day and after a late evening filled with dancing, her beauty was undiminished one whit, in fact, he found it quite enhanced. Being a rather gangly youth, without great wit, he was unused to women, particularly beautiful women, treating him as kindly as did Miss Guthrie. She seemed to regard him with as much favour as she did Lord Elton and the Earl of Newlyn, who also arrived to pay their respects. Lady Chalmsforth, not in the habit of having a morning room filled with gentlemen following a ball, was entertaining Amanda Markham and taking in the scene with enthusiasm. She was delighted with the way in which her protégée had conquered at her first ball and took not one particle of credit upon herself, but felt that for once society had chosen to honour someone truly worthy of its attention.

It was upon this scene that Lord Chalmsforth arrived, accompanied by Colonel Farendon, who had been most insistent that they pay a morning visit, ostensibly because he had been unable to pay his respects to Lady Chalmsforth the night before. Actually, he had been sorry to leave the ball without getting to know Fiona better and he hoped to make reparation that morning.

Chalmsforth did not appear altogether pleased to see Newlyn reclining in a slim Hepplewhite chair beside Fiona, discussing his latest purchase of matched Percherons that he was most anxious that she should examine. Did she ride in the park, or would she do him the honour of accompanying him for a drive that afternoon, he was enquiring, but before Fiona could reply, Chalmsforth interrupted with,

"Miss Guthrie is engaged to drive with me this afternoon. I don't believe she would care for your Percherons, especially if you got them from Slade-Waring. Speedy, perhaps, but not at all smooth paced. I trust you looked them over carefully before you purchased them."

Newlyn flushed. He had indeed bought the greys from Slade-Waring and thought he had struck a hard bargain.

"I'm not addle-brained," he replied testily. "You probably wanted them yourself. You know they're a fine pair. I'm well satisfied, and I believe Miss Guthrie will be also when she sees them."

"Then that must wait for another day, since she is engaged to ride with me today."

"Then another day perhaps?" Newlyn questioned Fiona eagerly.

She was in a quandary. It was Newlyn who had been the cause of her brother's indebtedness, not that she blamed him entirely, though he was certainly a great deal older than Neill. She did not particularly care about driving with him, but she was irked by Chalmsforth's imperious attitude toward her. She knew she was bound to him, though he had not until now made any move to assert that authority. Remembering his set-down of the previous evening and piqued by Chalmsforth's evident dislike of Newlyn, she turned a ravishing smile upon the earl and promised that at any other time she would be delighted. She gave Chalmsforth a defiant glance but his only response was to say he would call for her at three.

Farendon, having chatted with Lady Chalmsforth and having watched Fiona from across the room, now eagerly joined them, bowing his tall scarlet-and-gold-sashed figure to Fiona.

"With all this talk of excursions in the park, Miss Guthrie, perhaps I can prevail upon you to ride with me."

"I often ride at home, but I regret to say that here I have no mount."

"Allow me, ma'am, to send you over one of my horses that

is particularly well suited to ladies," Newlyn interposed. "You may keep her as long as you wish. I assure you it will give me the greatest pleasure to know that you are riding her."

"That is quite unnecessary since Miss Guthrie's horse has just been sent up from Cambridgeshire." Lord Chalmsforth turned to Fiona, who received this news with some astonishment. "Your brother informed me that he was sending Sappho to town for your use while you are here. The horse was received in my stables yesterday. As a matter of fact, I called this morning to inform you of its arrival."

"Sappho?"

"Yes, but perhaps this was not the horse you wished sent. If you would rather have had another, I'm sure it can be arranged," Chalmsforth informed her, ignoring her obvious confusion.

"No, no. Sappho will serve very well. I'm glad Neill thought of sending her," Fiona recovered, though feeling that her ties of entanglement were increasing.

"In that event, perhaps we can ride tomorrow morning." Farendon beamed.

"I should be delighted, Colonel. It seems I shall get my fill of fresh air with all of these planned outings; that is quite splendid, for I am a country girl and though London is exciting, I feel most myself when out of doors."

A playful discussion ensued between the gentlemen, in which Chalmsforth took no part, at which it was decided that no matter what the setting all believed Miss Guthrie would reign with equal merit.

"You flatter me, gentlemen, with all this banter," Fiona laughed good-humouredly, taking none of it to heart though in truth she did not find their overdrawn compliments and Chalmsforth's grave silence greatly to her liking. She looked to Lady Chalmsforth to relieve her from the situation, and that lady took her cue.

"I'm afraid I must ask you to leave now, for Miss Guthrie and I are engaged to go to the library this morning and if we are to return in time for her to change for her drive, we should soon be leaving."

The gentlemen obediently rose at her remark and began their leavetaking, as did Lady Markham who, despite Lady Chalmsforth's desire that she accompany them to Hookham's, said she was in no mood for reading since the last novel she had had from there had put her to sleep each time she picked it up. It did not escape Fiona's attention that Chalmsforth made no attempt to leave with the others but she overheard Newlyn turn back to enquire of him when his engagement to Lady Annabel Telford might be expected.

"My engagement to Lady Annabel?" Chalmsforth's eyebrows shot up in surprise and indignation.

"I heard you were to offer for Orbury's daughter. Such an equal match of temperament, I thought."

"I do not know your sources, Newlyn, but I suggest you reexamine them for you seem to hear a great deal more than those involved."

"But it was Orbury himself who spoke of it only yesterday at White's." Newlyn smiled triumphantly as he again bowed his departure.

Chalmsforth swore silently to himself. How dare Orbury loose a rumour like that. He had no right to do so. He would certainly do nothing to encourage him in future. He saw Fiona's eyes fixed questioningly upon him and was even more annoyed by the exchange, though he made no comment upon it.

"I'm on my way to examine Lord Roedean's library," he announced. "Young Roedean tells me he plans to sell everything and gave me the first opportunity to look it over before it goes on the auctioneer's block. Would you like to come there instead of going to Hookham's?"

"Oh yes," said Lady Chalmsforth with enthusiasm. "We can go to Hookham's another time. What a shame, though, that young Lord Roedean should sell everything when it took his father so long to gather the collection."

Lord Roedean had recently inherited his father's title and property. He was a younger son, something of a profligate, and not expected to be heir, but his older brother had died unexpectedly and he had found himself with a title and house which he enjoyed but with a collection of books and antiquities for which he had no earthly use. He was anxious to turn this memorabilia into ready guineas as soon as possible, and since it had been pointed out to him that Chalmsforth had an ample supply of that commodity plus his father's odd habit of collecting dry volumes which only attracted dust, his own personal preference being for collecting something quite warmer and more cuddlesome, Roedean had sought Chalmsforth out.

On arrival, they were shown into a room filled with bookshelves from floor to ceiling. It was obviously not a library where reading had been encouraged, for behind locked glass doors row upon row of shelves were lined with books of uniform binding placed so tightly together that only an unusually determined reader could have wrenched one free. In the midst of the room were more glass cases, also locked, containing vases and ornaments of various epochs, each carefully labelled.

It was a neat but somehow forbidding room and Fiona could not help but ask,

"Is this like your library, Lord Chalmsforth?"

"Mine is not nearly as tidy, or as austere I might add. I suspect you would consider it quite a jumble after seeing this, for I am forever pulling down volumes that interest me and leaving them opened at some place here or there. In that respect, I am the bane of Nicholson's life, I fear, for he's always picking up after me. Sometimes I wish that he wouldn't. Books are meant to be read, not just looked at."

"I can't help but wonder whether these books have ever been touched, let alone read," Fiona mused, pointing out the locks on the cases.

Chalmsforth picked up a volume from the table to show her its pages uncut. "I suspect not. Uncut pages are, of course, desirable to a collector; nevertheless, I could never leave my own books so."

As Chalmsforth proceeded to examine bindings and titles and note those in which he was interested, Fiona and Lady Chalmsforth found greater interest in the artifacts. It was a casual interest though, until Fiona noticed a small broach fashioned of heavy gold in a fine but outdated style, designed in the form of a wreath of thistles intertwined with fleur de lys. Unlike the other items in the case, this one was unmarked.

"Oh, Lady Chalmsforth, do look. No, not the vase but the broach close by, the one with the thistles. I believe that may have once been owned by Mary of Scotland. We had a painting of her at Culross Abbey in which she wore a broach very much like that at the neck of her dress. I am sure that is the one because do you notice the small fleur de lys where the thistles are entwined? It is most unusual to see them together. I have looked at that painting so many times as a child that I can remember every detail of it."

Lord Roedean, a young man of the highest fashion in every detail, had been talking to Chalmsforth, but now he joined them.

"It is a nice broach, but quite plain don't you think? Do you not prefer jewelry encrusted with gems? I regret that most of the ladies of my acquaintance do, as, I hear, do those of Chalms——" Here he broke off abruptly, directing an embarrassed glance at Lady Chalmsforth, who appeared quite unperturbed at his rather obvious reverence to Chalmsforth's gift to his opera diva.

"This is not just a piece of jewelry though," Fiona insisted, "can you not see that? It is admirable because of its history, not simply because of its metal or encrustation."

Chalmsforth, coming near then, smiled at her enthusiasm.

"I expect you would buy anything if the seller assured you it had passed through the hands of Mary at some time."

"No, indeed," was her spirited rejoinder, "I'm not such a gull. But this piece I recognize and I doubt there could be two like it."

Chalmsforth examined the broach carefully before returning to his book selection. He offered to purchase any books the ladies desired. Though Fiona had in her hand a slim red-leather-bound volume of Burns' poetry that she did, indeed, desire, and though it was, she knew, an infinitely small matter to Chalmsforth, she replaced it, saying nothing, perhaps because her wish for it was personal. For matters of her own pleasure she refused to be indebted to him.

Lady Chalmsforth, for her part, complained that it was a dry collection, but then what could one expect of such a dour man. While Chalmsforth was making his final arrangements with Lord Roedean, Fiona again went over to the glass case to look longingly at the broach. She wondered what had been its path between leaving its original owner's hands and ending up in that cold, sterile case. Who would be the next to possess it? She knew it was without purpose to enquire its price, for she had nothing with which to buy it. Ironically, of all the luxuries which had been bestowed upon her since her arrival at Lady Chalmsforth's, this was the only one she really wanted, yet she would not, she could not ask for it.

Fiona was ready and waiting for Chalmsforth at three when he drew up at Brook Street in his low-slung phaeton drawn by his magnificent Cleveland bays. He looked at her pearl-grey dress and straw bonnet trimmed with a large cerise bow with obvious approval as he handed her up and they set off smartly, weaving their way through the crowded London streets towards Hyde Park.

Despite their pleasant morning in Roedean's library, Fiona had been much offended by Chalmsforth's earlier high-handedness and she found herself forced to speak.

"Though I said nothing of it before, Lord Chalmsforth, and though I am very happy to be out on this beautiful afternoon, I would wish you to have asked me this morning rather than simply announcing that I was to drive with you. In my brief acquaintance with you it has been quite clear to me that you are used to having your own way and satisfying whatever may be your desires, and I realize that my position here is . . . shall we say an unusual one, but I see no need to set aside all proprieties. We may have struck a bargain, but you do not own me."

For the first time she saw Chalmsforth embarrassed as his haughty face flushed at her words.

"I do owe you an apology; I was brusque. It was my intention to ask you first, but you must know that I intensely dislike that blackguard, Newlyn. Of all people, I did not wish you to ride with him."

"Why is he so distasteful to you?" she asked curiously. "Has he at some time come between you and the lady of your choice?"

He looked at her sharply and waited a moment before replying, "Miss Guthrie, there are many types of men with whom I am acquainted; thank God they are not all like me, for as you point out I have my faults. Of those types, there are many with whom I disagree, many of whom I dislike, but Newlyn is so despicable in character that I wish to have as little interchange with him as possible. Since we move in the same circles, of necessity I see him often, but I make no attempt to encourage him in any way and neither should you. His conduct, especially towards members of your sex, is particularly reprehensible. This, in itself, since you have already enlightened me with your views, should not recommend him to you."

"Yet I have seen nothing amiss in his conduct."

"At a ball, no, nor on a morning visit. But I assure you that he is not the sort of person with whom you should become better acquainted. I would prefer that you did not, though I realize my preferences carry little weight in your eyes, and therefore I merely warn you of him."

"You did not seem to mind the attentions paid to me by Sir Brian Fennister or your friend Colonel Farendon."

"Sir Brian is a young fool, nice, but a fool nevertheless. And, as you pointed out, Colonel Farendon is my friend. I could not object to your friendship with either, though in the case of Sir Brian I might wonder at your choice. He is a harmless youngster, terribly henpecked by that formidable harridan of a mama of his."

Fiona laughed at his description of Lady Fennister and he smiled back at her and they entered the park in good spirits. It was unusually crowded, perhaps because of the exceptionally fine afternoon. Though a newcomer, Fiona encountered many acquaintances from Lady Sefton's ball and Chalmsforth, finding it impossible to ignore the admiring glances thrown her way, wondered how long it would be before she haughtily discarded the ineffectual youngsters of the ilk of Sir Brian Fennister and adopted the attitude of aloof indifference commonly found in society's most beautiful women.

She was in the midst of returning the salute of one of her partners of the previous evening when she suddenly remembered something and she turned to Chalmsforth as soon as the gentleman had passed, asking accusingly,

"And who, may I ask, or what is Sappho?"

"I thought you needed a horse to ride while you were here and since my mother has no riding horses now, and none in my stable are suitable for your weight, I found a nice little mare yesterday that should suit you well. I thought you might appreciate the name Sappho, but perhaps you don't approve. You could change it as you wish."

"It is not a matter of the name. I simply cannot accept a horse from you, that is all. These clothes I have—the bills are simply staggering I have no doubt. I realize you are rich and perhaps it may not signify to you, but from my point of view you are spending a small fortune on me, not to mention the enormous sum which——"

But he cut her off abruptly.

"We will not mention that, or any of it. You are not accepting anything from me. The horse is for your use. If you do not wish to use it, you do not have to. It was amazingly underpriced, so I assure you that if you truly do not want it, I can sell it without difficulty, probably at a handsome profit."

"And the clothes? When I go will you find someone who will fit them also?"

His voice filled with arrogance and disdain as he drawled,

"Miss Guthrie, I really do not care what happens to them. If you do not like them or do not wish to keep them, it matters little, though I was not aware you were already thinking of leaving."

It was her first opportunity to speak of her London stay and the reason for it, but before she could do so a curricle drew alongside drawn by the offending Percheron greys of Newlyn, who was tooling them with an experienced hand.

"I think you'd be much better off over here, Miss Guthrie," he called over after greeting them. "I've never had a better team than this. I'll match them any time against yours, Chalmsforth."

Chalmsforth looked them over condescendingly.

"The hindquarters of the one on the right are slightly higher than those of the other. You must find that terribly inconvenient."

"You know they're well matched and fine goers into the bargain. What say we race our teams to Brighton? Wouldn't you like to see a race, Miss Guthrie? Winner gets the loser's team."

"I wouldn't allow a horse in my stable after you had handled it, Newlyn," Chalmsforth retorted.

Newlyn flushed. "One day you'll go too far in your insolence," he warned.

"I wonder how far I have to go to make you keep your distance."

Fiona, realizing that there was no longer any amusement in the eyes of either man, quickly intervened.

"Lord Chalmsforth, your mother is expecting me back by five. We are engaged for cards tonight at Lady Markham's and I know she will not want to be late. It was so pleasant to see you again, Lord Newlyn." She smiled at Newlyn. "Your greys are really admirable and you drive them exceedingly well."

When they pulled out of earshot, Chalmsforth turned to her.

"Are you deliberately trying to encourage him to spite me?"

His bitter tones took her by surprise.

"No. I merely wanted to avoid an open quarrel that would

94

hurt all involved. You were very rude to him, you know. I actually have no reason to particularly like him, for Newlyn was the cause of Neill's indebtedness. My brother played with him for higher stakes than were within his means."

"I might have known Newlyn would stoop to robbing young gulls like that."

"He may not be blameless, but I am not convinced he was entirely at fault. My brother should have known better. Nor can I believe he is such a reprobate as you would have it, for your mother receives him and I don't believe she would if he were such a bad character."

"My mother does not see him in men's company as I do, listening to his boasts and threats. He uses his name and position in ways in which they were never intended to be used. A name such as his should stand for something other than the debauchery and license with which it has become associated."

"And Chalmsforth, what does that stand for?"

He caught the ire in her tones.

"I am aware that you do not think highly of me, Miss Guthrie. I admit I am not entirely blameless, but I believe that in any association I have had I have acted with honour. That is what my name stands for. If I do not uphold that honour, I should not feel entitled to my inheritance."

As he spoke, a high-perch phaeton approached from the opposite direction bearing a young lady with golden tresses peaking from under a bonnet of white ribbed silk, the pale pink of her pelisse matching the pink lining of the interior of the phaeton, as did the pink ostrich feather which decorated her bonnet. The lady smiled sweetly at Chalmsforth, who bowed his acknowledgement of her greeting but made no attempt to slow his horses or to introduce her to Fiona. She noticed no crest on the phaeton to identify its occupant and turned to Chalmsforth to enquire,

"Who is the beautiful young lady?"

"A singer at the opera," was his terse reply.

"That wouldn't by chance be the famous Grisini, would it?"

"Yes, it would," he answered, no more communicatively.

"She of the famous diamond necklace."

"And how has that tale reached your ears? Not from my mother, surely?"

"No, it was my brother who mentioned it."

"I might have guessed."

"I should like to meet her."

"I regret that that opportunity must be denied to you. It is impossible for you to have social acquaintance with such a young woman."

"But not for you?"

He flushed, but did not reply.

"I see very little difference between her position and mine."

"Fiona!" It was the first time he had used her christian name and it was that which drew her attention rather than the fury in his voice. His face was stern as he said, "I never wish you to refer to your . . . your proposition again."

As they bowled through the streets she was left to ponder how she could ever be freed from her obligation if she were not allowed even to refer to it.

XI

In the ensuing days, Chalmsforth's name and all that it stood for was often spoken of, for though the owner of that name rarely appeared, his friend Colonel Farendon was a constant visitor. There could be no doubt of the affection and esteem with which Farendon held Chalmsforth. He told her of his bravery on the field of battle and the high regard in which his men had held him because of his unfailing fairness, his willingness to first perform any act of danger which he demanded of them, and his uncanny ability to remember their names and some particulars of their lives. So oft repeated were his praises that Fiona would have thought Chalmsforth had commissioned his friend to speak on his behalf and influence her in his favour had she not known that he would foreswear any such action. Indeed, he had no reason to try to impress her for already she was his, in body if not in spirit, of that they were both aware.

There could be little doubt that London society had indeed taken Fiona to its bosom and she, unknowingly, became a style-setter and was greatly sought after, particularly by those hostesses who wished to attract the most elegant and desirable gentlemen to their routs and assemblies. Yet she appeared not to notice her popularity or, if she did, she paid it little heed. She treated gangly youths such as Sir Brian Fennister with the same deference as London's most eligible gentlemen, like Lord Elton. She made no attempt to attract any man; possibly that was the reason she did not fail to attract even those who had formed the habit of eying each crop of aspiring debutantes with a jaundiced eye and pronouncing England's most beautiful girls as merely passing, for without attempting to please, by speaking her mind on any issue under discussion, by being totally herself, she swept all before her in the beam of her smile and the aura of her amity.

All, that is, except Peter Chalmsforth, who watched it all

from afar, showing her every civility but not attempting to single her out in any manner. His mother had become very fond of Fiona in the weeks they had spent together and she was at a loss to understand why her eldest son visited Brook Street less now that Fiona was there than he had previously. Not that their house lacked for visitors, far from it. Gerald was always underfoot, as was Lord Elton, a widower with a large Lincolnshire estate, who was content only when he was part of Fiona's inner circle, at her side, within earshot of all she said. Chalmsforth's friend Colonel Farendon came, sometimes riding with Fiona in the park or accompanying the ladies on their shopping excursions. The Earl of Newlyn also was a frequent visitor, though Lady Chalmsforth noticed that Fiona steadfastly refused to drive with him and accepted only those engagements with him to which she, herself, was also invited.

Kitty, George Chalmsforth's widow, had come to look over the beauty ensconced in her mother-in-law's home, but she failed to see what all the fuss was about and usually confined her visits to those times when she knew that Newlyn would be there. She sought always to divert his attention to herself, they were friends of some duration, but often her efforts were in vain for he was plainly attracted to Fiona. Kitty did not hesitate to mention to him, on more than one occasion, the penniless condition of London's reigning belle, a fact of which he was painfully aware, for had she had fortune he might have sought her as a lawful partner. He knew he must marry eventually, though in the past he had avoided that binding state, but in exchange for his name and title he needed more than limpid lilac eyes and soft lips. As it was, however, despite her powerful connections he did not rule out some sport, in fact her association with Chalmsforth made her even more desirable.

Perhaps, though, of all the visitors to Brook Street, it was Kitty's daughter, Susan, who was most taken with Fiona. It had been an immediate and firm attachment on the part of the young girl, equally reciprocated by the person she most desired to emulate. She came often, usually accompanied only by a woman of inferior education and, worse yet, inferior sentiments, who was her governess. Fiona had quickly discerned Susan's quick mind and her desire to learn and soon was assigning her readings which they discussed over their needlework on those afternoons when she stayed at

Brook Street. Often their talk ranged far from the subject of the book and, for the first time, Susan found herself able to talk freely to an adult about those things that troubled her or those she held most dear.

So the days passed in a round of visits, shopping, balls and routs, all quite delightful in their way, yet Fiona often wondered how this prolonged stay could ever be concluded to allow her return to the abbey where she belonged. She knew there was no one to prevent that return except herself; she, it was, who would never leave until accounts were settled. Chalmsforth, cold and distant, made any discussion of that matter impossible.

Fiona had seen nothing of her aunt and uncle since leaving Sloane Street. They did not move in the same circles as the Chalmsforths and she made no attempt to draw them into it. She was surprised, therefore, one morning to hear the names of her aunt and cousins announced; that they should call with no previous acquaintance of Lady Chalmsforth was hardly proper. Lady Benbow hastened to explain that since she had so often caught sight of her niece's name in the *Gazette*, and since Lady Chalmsforth was going to so much trouble on her behalf, she had called to ascertain whether Fiona might not be proving a burden; it might, she said, be preferable for her to return to Sloane Street. Had she realized previously that her niece wished to remain in London, she would have pressed her to stay with *her own family* as long as she wished. Lady Benbow emphasized the words with a reproachful glance at Fiona that took in her handsome lavender China silk morning dress. Fiona was sure that she knew to the penny how much it had cost and was astonished to find her so magnificently attired.

Fiona presented her cousins to Lady Chalmsforth, who privately noted that they had inherited none of the Berrington looks, nor did she find a great likeness in either looks or manner in Lady Benbow to her former friend, Ellen Berrington. She was, however, perfectly cordial in her manner toward the visitors.

Since Fiona had noticed no announcement of her cousin's engagement, she decided against mentioning Mr. Hardy's name, and confined her conversation, polite but without enthusiasm, to their welfare.

"And how is dear Neill?" her aunt responded.

"He has written to say he will be in town next week." Neill

had not graced London with a visit since his debacle with Newlyn, and Fiona had been secretly glad, for she had not yet had to explain to him where the money had come from to repay his debt. Now her aunt raised that very subject.

"And how did he fare on that little matter you came to me about?" Lady Benbow asked in penetrating tones, showing both by her voice and expression her displeasure.

Fiona noticed Lady Chalmsforth's glance of questioning from one to the other of the speakers, but she replied calmly enough,

"Well, Aunt, well. It is all taken care of."

"I am glad for that, I must say. I should hate to see you lose the abbey because of Neill's impropriety. I know it has been in Guthrie hands for a great while and means much to you. Your uncle and I would certainly have helped you if we could. However, you seem to have been well taken care of."

"Of course, Aunt." The subject was painful to Fiona, but to silently implore her aunt to desist from this line of questioning would avail nothing, so she took a line which was bound to provoke displeasure but was equally bound to lead the conversation elsewhere or, she hoped, stop it altogether.

"And how is dear Mr. Hardy? Are we still to expect an announcement soon?"

She smiled sweetly as her aunt gave her a vicious glare, as did Fay, though Brenda was far too busy conversing with Gerald, who had been ushered in just prior to their arrival, to notice anything.

"Mr. Hardy?" Her aunt looked as though she could not quite remember the gentleman. "Ah, yes, Mr. Hardy. No, no, he would never do. Your uncle and I talked it over and decided that it was not at all a connexion we desired."

"Indeed, I hope no hearts were touched by that decision."

"No, Fay took it very well."

Lady Chalmsforth silently applauded Fiona. Though Fiona had scarcely spoken of her London relations, she was aware that little love was lost there. It was the first time she had heard Fiona utter anything less than amiable, but everything about this visitor indicated her to be an ill-natured woman. She had no desire to encourage her.

"And how long do you plan to remain in London?" her aunt continued coldly.

"My plans are uncertain."

"I wish she would never leave," Lady Chalmsforth put in.

"I have never enjoyed myself more. I have half of London in my house daily, at least the most dashing half. I would never have so many gentlemen of elegance and charm gracing my drawing room if Fiona were not here. And we have such great fun together."

"Then I take it you do not wish to come back with us?" Her aunt's enquiry was cold, though in truth now that Fiona was so popular she would not be at all miffed to have her drawing her powerful friends to Sloane Street.

"No, Aunt, I have no wish to leave Lady Chalmsforth," Fiona replied, as the door opened to admit that lady's eldest son. As Lord Chalmsforth was introduced to Lady Benbow, who became utterly fawning on taking in his appearance and his imperious manner, Fiona rather feared one of his famous set-downs from which she might feel forced to come to the defence of her relative, but after greeting the visitors and his brother, he merely announced he had come to see whether the ladies would care to accompany him that morning if they had nothing else to do.

Lady Benbow reluctantly withdrew with her daughters. Since all the effusion had been on her side and neither Lady Chalmsforth nor Fiona had said anything that could be construed as wishing to further their acquaintance in a more intimate manner, she was left to rail at her daughters all the way back to Sloane Street on the stuck-up attitude of her niece now that she had managed to worm her way into the graces of one of England's finest families.

Lady Chalmsforth was delighted to see Peter and delighted he should ask them out with him. She had pondered his absence from Brook Street, wondering whether he so often stayed away because Gerald was always there. She was now inclined to agree with Peter that a match between Fiona and her youngest son was not altogether suitable. It was obvious that while Fiona regarded Gerald with affection, it was the affection of a sister rather than a prospective wife. Though Lady Chalmsforth thought that Fiona had been and would continue to be a good influence upon him, she doubted that Gerald would ever be able to control such a forthright and beautiful woman. Fiona would always have the upper hand. With her eldest son, however, it would be a different story, though who would gain ascendancy she would not venture to say. While Peter had stayed away from Brook Street, she knew from the Dowager Marchioness of Orbury that he had also kept well clear of that family, much to their concern. Lady Orbury had asked her to intervene with him with regard to the match but she had steadfastly refused to do so, saying that her son made his own decisions.

"And where are we off to?" said Lady Chalmsforth, settling back into her son's carriage.

"To Westminster Abbey," he replied.

"Westminster Abbey! What on earth for?"

"I thought Miss Guthrie would like to see the tomb of her favourite queen."

"I would, indeed." Fiona was enthusiastic.

"And who is that?" Lady Chalmsforth asked.

"Mary Stuart. Don't tell me she has never mentioned to you her admiration for that lady in all the time she has been with you?"

"No, she has not. But looking at monuments is hardly my idea of great fun, Peter."

"Come, Mother, a little history won't hurt you. Goodness knows, you made me read enough of it when I was small. I am only returning the compliment and in a much pleasanter manner. After the abbey I want to show Miss Guthrie another statue of her queen that I just ran across on Fleet Street, and then I plan to treat both of you to luncheon at Grosvenor Square."

"Well, that is an honour. I rarely get asked to your mansion, Peter, it must be a special occasion."

"It is," he replied.

"But what is it?" Lady Chalmsforth was puzzled.

"Today is Miss Guthrie's birthday. Didn't she mention that to you either?"

Fiona blushed, wondering how he could possibly have known. She had said nothing of it to anyone. Lady Chalmsforth turned to her accusingly.

"Oh, Fiona, I am disappointed. I could have planned such a lovely party and now you have let Peter steal the thunder from me."

"But I did not tell him," she protested. "I have said nothing on the matter, indeed it is of no import." Yet she could not refrain from demanding of Chalmsforth, "How did you find out?"

He smiled and she realized how rarely she had seen him smile since she had been in London, though that had not been the case when he had been in Cambridgeshire.

"I saw it in your family Bible in the library at the abbey."

Their eyes met for a moment before Lady Chalmsforth broke in to say she wished that at least her son had been kind enough to inform her.

"I know this is the evening of the Westphalls' rout, but we should be doing something quite special."

"But, Lady Chalmsforth, we are doing something quite special," Fiona insisted.

And it was special. Fiona lingered long, though not as long as she would have wished, before the white marble monument Mary Stuart's son had erected, some years after he had ascended the English throne, when he had removed his mother's remains from Peterborough where they had rested for twenty-five years to the abbey. A Guthrie had been among those who had escorted the body to London. The epitaph, placed by the Earl of Northumberland, was in Latin. As she had before, Fiona regretted she had never studied that language and was forced to ask Chalmsforth to translate it for her; the inscription extolled Mary's virtues and deplored her misfortunes and her wrongful imprisonment in England. Fiona quietly thanked him, and stood examining the queen's figure lying full-length beneath the great canopy, her hands clasped in prayer. The face, taken from a death mask, was of such silent repose that, though it was not youthful, it shone with that even greater beauty that can only come from within.

Lost in thought, she almost forgot she was not alone until Chalmsforth touched her elbow.

"We can come back another day, if you wish."

"I should very much like that," Fiona replied almost shyly.

"Now I want to show you the discovery I made just the other day. I can assure you, Mother, it won't take long and then we'll be in the warmth and comfort of Grosvenor Square."

They drove down Fleet Street, past the taverns and coffee houses, past the Temple Bar, built by Wren, past Childs' Bank, which still used the sign of the Marigold because it was built on the site of the old Marigold Tavern, past the church of St. Dunstan-in-the-West, which stood opposite Hoare's Bank which, in turn, had adopted the inn sign of the Golden Bottle, until they came to number 143 where, in the doorway, stood a life-size statue of Mary Stuart. Fiona gasped with pleasure.

"How strange, to place it here!"

Only she and Chalmsforth dismounted from the carriage to examine the statue, Lady Chalmsforth preferring to remain inside. On the right-hand wall of the doorway was a poem dedicated to Mary by the French poet Beranger, translated into English on the opposite wall, *"Adieux de Marie Stuart à la France."*

"But how on earth did you find it? And who placed it here?"

"I was in this vicinity not long ago, quite by chance, and of course it caught my eye. I made enquiries and it appears that the statue and poem belonged to a Scottish laird, Sir John Tollemache Sinclair, a former owner of this property."

"The Sinclairs are another Scottish family that migrated south with James, as did the Guthries. What a splendid thing to do, and right in the midst of the city of London. How bold!"

She smiled up at him and he caught the pleasure in that smile and returned it, but all he said was,

"I thought of you when I saw it and thought you would like it."

"I do." She hesitated and then added, almost shyly, "Thank you for a lovely day."

"But it isn't over yet," he said, helping her back into the carriage.

At lunch they lingered long over the magnum of champagne, long after the *terrine de foie gras*, the *homard à la portos* and *haricots verts*, and the last vestiges of the *charlotte russe* had disappeared, then only then did Chalmsforth lay two small packages before Fiona.

"Are these for me?" she asked in surprise.

"Of course they're for you; it is your birthday we are celebrating, is it not?"

Inside the first package she opened was the red-leather-bound volume of Burns' poems, the one from Lord Roedean's library.

"How did you know I wanted it?" she asked.

"I saw you with it and when you put it back I saw it was Burns—so, you see, it was not hard to deduce."

"Peter is quite admirable in selecting gifts," his mother put it, "so do open the other box, Fiona, for I can't wait to see what is in it."

It was the gold broach, the wreath of thistles with fleur de lys, the broach that had once belonged to Mary Stuart. Now it was hers! She had an urge to hug Chalmsforth; her smile of gratitude did, in fact, do so by its warmth.

"Oh!" she exclaimed in delight, holding the broach up in her hands and letting the pale rays of the sun shine through the window onto the burnished gold. Then, "Oh! There's nothing that could have pleased me more. How did you know?"

"By the look on your face when you first saw it, of course."

"I didn't realize it was that obvious. May I wear it now?"

"It is yours to do with as you wish."

Fiona pinned it at the neck of her nile-green challis morning dress, and throughout the afternoon Chalmsforth could not help but notice how often her fingertips ran back and forth across the thistle design. From that time on she was never without it.

"Now we have you cornered in your lair, Peter," Lady Chalmsforth intervened, "and you are in such a good mood, I want to ask you whether you would consider having Fiona's ball at Grosvenor Square instead of Brook Street."

"I didn't know I was to have a ball," Fiona protested. "You have done so much already, I really don't think it necessary."

"But of course, every young lady of distinction who comes out must have her own ball. I did, your mother did. And I shall certainly hold one at Brook Street, but Peter's is so much larger and so much better equipped to handle entertaining on that scale that it would be preferable to have it here. I have picked out a date and have ascertained there are no conflicting engagements at that time, but before I send the cards I want to settle on the location."

Though Chalmsforth was loathe to allow even the cream of the *ton* entrance *en masse* to his house, one look at Fiona decided him that if a ball were to be held for her it should be held in no other place than under his roof, so that to his mother's surprise he agreed with only a token protest at the disarray it would cause.

"Don't worry, Peter," his mother assured him. "Fiona and I will arrange everything. All you have to do is to be here."

That was not quite the case, however, for though Lady Chalmsforth provided the guest list, it was Nicholson who arranged for the invitations to be written and despatched and

Chalmsforth's major domo who took control of the kitchen, ordering supplies and provisions, and the myriad other tasks necessitated by such an occasion, and Chalmsforth himself who decided on the arrangement and decor.

The ball was the cause of great excitement long before the date, for since Chalmsforth usually entertained only his most intimate friends there, few people had been inside his house and invitations were most highly sought after. Lady Chalmsforth found herself accosted by people she could hardly remember, who invited her to functions she had no wish to attend in the hope of being repaid by an invitation to Grosvenor Square. It promised to be the event of the season.

Even Neill Guthrie seemed excited about it when he called at Brook Street the following week, so much so that he accepted without argument his sister's quite vague explanation that she had borrowed the money to repay his debt with another unspecified loan. Possibly he was glad to be rid of a troublesome matter and preferred not to enquire further into it. With Chalmsforth's renewed friendship toward her, Fiona was finding herself in a more difficult position, for though she had been forbidden to speak of the debt she owed him, she, herself, could not overlook it, nor could she see how it was to be repaid. She knew, however, she could never leave London until the matter was somehow resolved.

Lady Chalmsforth loved Fiona, and Peter's renewed attentions to her young friend delighted her. She did all she could, within the bounds of discretion, to encourage them. Neither Peter nor Fiona, she knew, would endure intervention, even from herself, but she could not resist helping along a match desired by herself and also, she believed, though neither would acknowledge it, by the parties themselves.

The day before the ball Lady Chalmsforth arranged a day's outing to Richmond for the three of them, with luncheon at the Star and Garter on Richmond Hill. When Peter called for them early that morning, however, she complained of a headache and begged them to go without her for she had no wish to be unwell the following evening. She would not hear of the outing's being cancelled, pointing out that Fiona had long looked forward to seeing the Thames at Richmond, and to her delight her son, with only the slightest demur, accepted the palpable lie of her indisposition.

It was a clear, cool December day as the two set forth, but

Fiona found it exhilarating to feel the wind brushing her cheeks as they sped on their way.

"My mother has romantic notions," Chalmsforth said laughing, "but I wish she would plan them at more conducive times of the year. Outings such as this should be saved for the spring."

"It is a little brisk," she agreed, "but it is lovely to get away from town even if only for a short while. You have no idea how daunting it can be for someone like me, brought up in the quiet of the fens, to be surrounded always by such hustle and bustle."

"Yet you seem to have survived well."

"Only because of the congenial company with which I have been surrounded, I can assure you."

"You and my mother do seem to get along very well."

"She is a wonderful woman. I am extremely fond of her," she said thoughtfully. "And she has been most kind to me."

She wanted to tell him of the mixed feelings she had had when he had first taken her to his mother's house that morning—it was little over a month ago yet it seemed forever—she could not, though, for to do so meant raising the reason behind her presence in London at all and she had no desire to break the spell of the happy day.

They passed through Walham Green and Fulham, where Chalmsforth pointed out to her the Palace of the Bishop of London, then on to East Sheen, past Marsh Gate, and the hour had passed noon before they pulled up on Richmond Hill before the Star and Garter, lately taken over by Christopher Crean who had been cook to the Duke of York and whose gastronomic feats were drawing the gentry and nobility from miles around. But though the meal was sumptuous in appearance, aroma, and taste, it was the view of the river and the surrounding countryside from their table by the window that took Fiona's breath away, that and the clear, pure air, and the presence of a man who, no matter how many times she might try to deny it, intrigued her beyond any other.

"May we walk by the river?" she asked when they had finished their luncheon—splendid fillets of partridge with Saint Pierre caper sauce followed by slices of Stilton cheese marinated in port. Somehow she longed to prolong the day away from the flurry, the turbulence, the superficiality of London.

So they strolled down the long sweep of the lawn, through the avenue of limes at the bottom of the garden until they came upon the tow path where they paused to admire the swans on the river, the royal birds belonging to the crown, and Chalmsforth explained to her the custom of "swan-upping," where each year the year-old cygnets were identified and marked for the crown.

They followed the tow path, keeping their pace in time with the slow flow of the meandering river, feeling contented in one another's company, completely at ease.

"You never cease to amaze me," Chalmsforth said suddenly.

"Why?" she asked with curiosity. "I can think of nothing I have done which is amazing."

"But here you have half of London swooning at your feet and you pay it not the least heed. It is very rare to find a woman, indeed anyone, whose head would not be turned by so much attention and admiration. I swear that wherever I go I hear someone talk of your beauty or charm."

"I'm glad you hear only the good things. I have overheard remarks which, I can assure you, have been distinctly less than flattering."

"But that is hardly to be wondered at. You can't expect others, particularly other women, not to be envious of your taking the town by storm. Yet I see no difference in you today to the young lady who accompanied me to Ely Cathedral."

"That is because there is no difference," she began, and then paused to correct herself. "No, that is not entirely true, there is a difference, but it is not caused by any sudden popularity. This has been my first chance to observe society, much vaunted society, at first hand, and though I have greatly enjoyed myself and I have certainly had every advantage, I know that I could not live such a life forever. I suppose I have become more critical of others, especially of other women. I find a terrible shallowness in them, a lack of interest in anything of substance. It does not make me despise my own sex, rather it makes me feel sorry that we are not earlier given the chance to broaden our minds so that we do not have to rely on frivolities to fill our lives."

"You may be right. I have never given the education of women much thought, for in truth our own education wants for much. I should hate to think that Susan, who has always been such a serious child, would grow to become as frivolous as her mother."

"She is given little encouragement for her natural bent of

108

learning, and that is a great shame. I sometimes wonder whether Kitty is afraid to acknowledge her child's intelligence, afraid it is somehow unfeminine and to be avoided, that nothing is to be encouraged except the cultivation of beauty."

"But you have both, and no woman could more perfectly represent her sex than you." The fervour of his voice made her falter in her step. She glanced up at him and as she did so, a ribbon from her bonnet caught on a low-lying bare branch of a birch that overhung their path.

He reached up to detach the silken strip from the tree, but in so doing the bonnet fell back from her head. He was about to retrieve it, but suddenly stopped, looking down at her with an expression so changed, so filled with longing and ardour that she scarcely knew what to expect. Then she was in his arms and he was kissing her as he had on that first occasion in the abbey, the first time he had seen her. All the longing he had since endured to feel her soft lips once again beneath his own was contained in that kiss. All the feelings those lips had evoked that first time returned to him once he had possession of them again. He held her to him, repeating her name softly in the dark silk of her hair, acknowledging his desire and, as he did so, that same passion rose also within her so that her arms clasped tightly around him and when he again turned to kiss her upturned mouth, his kisses were returned with a warmth he had not expected nor dreamed possible.

At last he drew back, releasing her yet holding her at arm's length to look more fully into her face.

"Oh, Fiona, forgive me. I had not the right, I know."

Her eyes were soft, yet she had a puzzled, troubled air.

"But of course you had the right," she replied slowly. "You know you have the right."

His look was uncomprehending at first, then the ardour in his grey eyes turned swiftly to anger as he understood the meaning of her words. He removed his hands from her arms and stooped swiftly to retrieve her bonnet.

"Was that the reason for the warmth of your embrace?" he asked, almost savagely.

"I don't know," she replied truthfully.

"Come, it is time we left here, more than time."

Though he guided her arm on their return journey along the path, there was no intimacy in his touch, nor did he speak any but the merest civilities on the homeward journey. He left her at Brook Street, declining to wait to see his mother, and returned to Grosvenor Square feeling an emptiness and disgust inside which he could ill abide. That evening he consumed more than his usual amount of wine, so that when Farendon arrived to accompany him to a gathering of Hussars at Peek's Tavern, he found his friend stretched out in an armchair staring unseeingly into a smouldering fire, his chin on his chest, decidedly bosky.

"Well, well, Chalmsforth, you have got an early start on all of us."

"Go along without me, old fellow, I just don't feel up to it tonight." Chalmsforth's voice was unusually thick.

"Why on earth not? You've been in excellent spirits these last few days. What's happened to put you in such a brown study?"

"Nothing. I just don't feel particularly sociable tonight, that's all."

"Well, if you don't go, I won't either." His friend sat down opposite him, after filling a glass from the bottle of port on the table beside Chalmsforth. "I've rarely seen you like this. What is it? Some woman?"

"There's no woman worth the trouble," Chalmsforth muttered half to himself.

"Then it is a woman, and if it is, it can only be the charming Miss Guthrie. I wondered why you hadn't fallen for her along with the rest of us. Come on now, what happened? Did she refuse you?"

"Hardly," Chalmsforth replied, then not wishing to discuss the matter and seeing Farendon would not let it alone if he stayed, he got up somewhat unsteadily from his chair.

"Very well, let's go to Peek's and see what the Hussars are up to."

XII

On the night of the ball, Chalmsforth determined that he would pay no more attention to Fiona Guthrie than custom demanded. He had been bitterly mistaken in allowing his affections to be won over by a woman for the first time in his life, that woman so completely wanting in delicacy and propriety as to offer to sell herself to him, no matter the cause. From her first coming to London he had tried to quench the passion he had experienced when first he had met her, but instead that passion had grown to become a consuming fire, one that threatened to engulf him as he came to know her better, particularly since her birthday. He had put aside the imprudence of her proposition until the previous day at the river when she had again insisted on reminding him of it. To think that at that moment he had been on the point of proposing marriage to such a person! It was unthinkable. The Chalmsforths had always contracted alliances, they had never worried about love matches, and their marriages had survived. Well, now, he would set aside his emotions and form an alliance with Orbury's daughter. It was certain that Lady Annabel would no more think of proposing such a travesty than she would think of abandoning her stately and fashionable life to run away with the gypsies. At least he would always know where he stood with her; he would never have known with Fiona, disturbing, wanton creature that she was.

But try though he might to draw comfort from this commonsensical notion, the moment he saw Fiona arrive with his mother that evening, it was all but forgotten. He had always known that she was lovely, yet never had he seen her quite as lovely, quite as radiant as that night, and the smile she turned upon him on her arrival nearly made him forget his earlier resolutions.

Clad in a gown of soft white velvet with an Etruscan bor-

der of gold, her gown was a dressmaker's triumph, for it was
not so much that she wore it as that it clung to her as though
it were part of her skin, soft and white, moving around her as
she moved and creating an aura when she twirled before him
to show its effect. It hung loosely from her shoulders at the
back, and in front was caught at the waistline by the ever-
present gold thistle broach he had given her. In her dark hair
was a diadem of pearls, but that and the broach were her
only adornments. In response, all he laconically remarked
was, "You will do very nicely."

Fiona was disappointed. Ever since the previous afternoon
she had tried to examine her feelings toward him, for they
could no longer be ignored. Since her birthday she had un-
dergone a change of emotions which had culminated in that
scene by the river. She felt a greater closeness to him than to
anyone; he seemed to understand her feelings more than she
had ever thought it possible for one person to know another,
divining what she was thinking and where her sensitivities
lay. And because she found her thoughts so often turning to
him, she realized the quandary in which they placed her. If
he seemed to forget the debt she owed him, she could not.
She had wondered what she would do in the unlikely event
that he offered her marriage. It would, of course, absolve any
indebtedness to him, but she could not allow herself to think
of it. Ever since her arrival in London she had heard
rumours of his impending alliance with Annabel Telford, the
Marquess of Orbury's daughter. Though, to her knowledge,
he saw little of that cool, imperious lady, nonetheless it was
clear that the Chalmsforths married in a direction where fortune favoured them, and certainly nothing was to be gained
by an alliance with a Guthrie. Yet when, by the river, he had
kissed her, she had been unable to contain the emotions that
were awakened with that kiss. She had exulted in his kisses,
even though she was unsure of their meaning, nor could she
wholly understand her own reaction. That night she had lain
awake long remembering that moment, forgetting his silence
on the way back, thinking only of his arms around her and
how she felt herself belonging within that encirclement, as
she had never thought to belong to any man. She acknowledged to herself that she loved him, that she wanted to
be with him always. It was for that reason she had dressed
with especial care for the ball at his home, it was that feeling
which accounted for the especial radiance of her smile. Yet

his distant attitude and the lack of warmth in his regard could not escape her. She felt suddenly lowered in spirits, noticeably, so that Lady Chalmsforth was forced to exclaim,

"Peter, to say that Fiona will merely do is an insult, worse than saying nothing. You are like a bear with a sore head today. And speaking of sore heads, I was disappointed you didn't have a minute to see how mine was after you had been gallivanting all day in Richmond. How was your day, by the way?"

Lady Chalmsforth had remarked when he had not come in with Fiona on her return. She had noticed also that Fiona was unusually quiet and preoccupied that evening, which made her feel that something had occurred between them. But her son's brief acknowledgement that the day had passed well coupled with Fiona's silence made it seem that the day she had so carefully schemed to put them together had passed in vain or, if anything had happened, neither of them was about to enlighten her. In any event, it appeared there would be no announcement that evening with which to startle their guests. It was a shame, for she loved Fiona dearly. She had come to regard her as her own Sarah, so beautiful yet so unpretentious, so sought after yet so thoughtful of others in her every action. Fiona was all she would have wished Sarah to be.

But Lady Chalmsforth had to put aside these thoughts for the guests were beginning to arrive and she stood between her son and Fiona to receive them.

Everyone was there, everyone who was anyone and many who thought they were someone. Sir James and Lady Benbow and their daughters had been invited as a courtesy and were among the first. Fiona saw them hasten to Neill, undoubtedly to get all the details of the settlement of the debt. She was glad she had told him so little, for he would not be forced to lie, something at which she was glad to say he was completely unaccomplished. Whatever might be said of the Guthries, she thought, they acted with probity despite their tendency to impulsion.

Kitty Chalmsforth came, sumptuously arrayed in orange chiffon with a richly spangled border, to plant a perfunctory kiss on her mother-in-law's cheek. She was quite miffed at all the fuss they were making over a girl who was nothing to the family. Well, when her Susan came of age she would see she received not one jot less. She had wondered whether

Chalmsforth had any intentions toward Fiona. She was a beauty, perhaps, but there was no money there. Chalmsforth would never marry without money, no matter that he had so much he didn't know what to do with it, investing it in dusty old books, what a waste. She thought her brother-in-law a cold fish, though she would never tell him so to his face, rather fearing him for his rages which were cold and polite, so unlike the fierce, hot battles she had waged with her husband. She could not abide cold men.

Newlyn arrived shortly after Kitty. There was nothing cold about him, she thought, watching him with some satisfaction. She wished he would settle for marriage, but he had such a wandering eye she wasn't sure that she would ever pin him down. Nevertheless, he had done much for which she was grateful to console the solitude of her widowhood. She noticed the appraising look he gave Fiona as he greeted her, kissing her hand, that look did not escape Chalmsforth's attention either. He was spending far too much time at Brook Street, silly man. She was sure he had no serious intentions toward Fiona and surely even he, attractive as he was, would not expect to get anything from her without marriage. In all the gossip which floated through the *grand monde* about her, there had been none that could imply Fiona had acted with any impropriety since her arrival in London, and before that she appeared to have lived the life of a total recluse in that abbey of theirs. Well, she smiled at Newlyn as he came toward her; *she* knew how to warm the cockles of his heart.

It had been arranged that Fiona would open the ball with Chalmsforth, but she was startled when she moved to take her place in the set with him to hear him say tersely, almost against his will (in truth prompted because he had heard Newlyn speak of them),

"You will also dance the two waltzes this evening with me."

Her surprise was caused as much by his terse, impolite manner of commanding rather than asking as by the fact that to dance more than two dances in the same evening with one partner was bound to cause comment, even in London. But the dance floor was no place in which to settle the issue, especially since the quadrille gave them little opportunity for private discussion.

It was rather daring that there was to be waltzing at all, for the waltz had only just made its way to England from the

114

Continent and was regarded in some circles as quite scandalous. It was Chalmsforth who had taught Fiona how to waltz, for when they had discussed the ball he had thought it would be a novel idea to introduce it, having learned it when he had been serving in Europe. Lady Chalmsforth had protested that it would not do when the person in whose honour the ball was being held did not know how to dance it and he had offered to teach her, impulsively pressing upon his mother to play the piano and ordering the servants to clear the floor of furniture and rugs. She could feel his arm around her waist now and his voice insisting, "You must listen to the music and let your body flow with it. Relax and let my hand guide you. No, no, you really must let me lead you." And she had relaxed and allowed the melody to engulf her and had given in to the sensuousness of the music and his arms around her. She thought of the way he had looked down at her as he held her, nothing like tonight when his expression had been little short of forbidding. No matter what her situation, she resented his imperious tone. If she were free she would dance with whomsoever she pleased, but she was not free. She felt some satisfaction, however, in having Newlyn claim her as soon as the first set finished. She knew Chalmsforth hated him and for that reason she gave Newlyn one of her more ravishing smiles and laughed perhaps a trifle more than necessary even when, as they saw Chalmsforth move through the dance with Annabel Telford, Newlyn remarked, "Well, there's a match created in heaven if I ever saw one, two icebergs about to create an avalanche."

Gerald was, of course, dogging her footsteps as usual, but also paying attention to Lady Markham's youngest daughter who had just come out, oblivious of the fact that Brenda Benbow had been casting cow eyes at him ever since she arrived. Fiona thought of Anne Robarts as she watched Gerald dancing with young Miss Markham. It was a pity, for she knew that Anne had been truly fond of him in her quiet, intense way, but Gerald was far too young to settle down. He still had a lot of growing up to do. Since being in London she had become better acquainted with him and could now understand Chalmsforth's concern over his unpredictable actions. Like Neill, he was too easily led by his impulses, but like Neill he was young and would undoubtedly outgrow these tendencies. She hoped, however, that he would not break any more sensitive hearts as he did so.

Fiona danced with Lord Elton who, as usual, said little, unless one could count the expression in his eyes which could be said to say everything. She had grown used to people staring at her since she had been in London, but somehow she found the soulfulness of Lord Elton's gaze difficult to bear. She liked him, he was a kind, gentle man, but quite uncommunicative. She had no wish that he should form a passion for her, eligible though he was. It was not the fact that he was older than she that deterred her, nor because he was a widower with three growing daughters, but simply that there was no answering spark of passion ignited by his smouldering gaze.

As the dance finished, she was almost glad to have her attention again claimed by Newlyn.

"Come," he said quietly, taking her by the elbow, "there is somebody in the conservatory who wishes to speak with you."

"Who is it?" she asked curiously, then looking around her she realized that Neill was nowhere in sight. Surely he had not been gambling with Newlyn again. She felt her anger mounting. If he had, she would leave him to suffer the consequences on his own this time; she was still embroiled in rescuing him from the last episode.

She followed Newlyn into the dimly lit conservatory, filled with ferns and exotic blooms unseasonably gay against what little could be seen through the glass panes of the drear night. It was a place of Chalmsforth's own design and she remembered how he had shown her round one day, naming each plant and explaining its peculiarities to her. But she paid little attention to the blooms or the warm, damp air, looking only for her brother, ready to rebuke him if this mission should prove to be another imbroglio. The conservatory, however, was empty, and turning back she realized that Newlyn had closed the door.

"There is no one here," she said coldly.

"Am I not here?" he asked playfully.

"Well, of course you are here, but you did not say it was you who wished to see me, but rather that there was someone else here. I thought, perhaps, it was my brother."

She wanted to mention his last encounter with her brother but decided against it for there was something unidentifiable in his expression, something which made her wary.

"Your brother, I trust, is still talking with our host—at least he was a moment ago. It was I who wanted to ask you why you gave away both the waltzes to Chalmsforth after I most particularly mentioned them to you. That was not a civil thing to do, Miss Guthrie. Tell me, is there something between you—some understanding? Is it you he likes rather than the Iceberg?"

"No, it is not," she retorted.

"And you, do you like him?"

"No, though I fail to see——"

"Then why give the waltzes to him and not me?" He came over and looked down into her eyes. "I do like you and you do owe me a waltz."

"Another time, Lord Newlyn." Fiona tried to preserve her poise, though she felt some alarm.

"Why not tell Chalmsforth you've changed your mind? The waltz is next, you know."

"No, I can't."

He studied her face. "Then I claim my waltz now."

He put his arm around her waist and pulled her to him.

"We cannot waltz, Lord Newlyn," Fiona cajoled, determined to make light of his behaviour. "There is no music."

"I have a very vivid imagination and you've been inflaming it all evening."

"I'm sorry, but I must go back."

Fiona tried to pull free from him but he held her fast.

"One kiss and I shall forgive you for giving away my waltz."

Though frightened, Fiona was determined not to show that fear, and she said lightly, "Only after you have slain a dragon."

"Before I risk my life I must know whether the prize is worthy of such a sacrifice."

As his hold upon her tightened, Fiona fought, bracing herself against him, using all her strength, but he had her pinioned so that she could barely draw breath and she was powerless to prevent him savagely fastening his lips upon hers. His mouth was warm and wet, thoroughly revolting to her, and the more she struggled against him, the more he savoured his victory. At last, in fear that he would tear her dress and cause a scene impossible to conceal, she stopped struggling and let him have his way.

Suddenly, his iron grip was wrenched free and Fiona was pushed aside, just as Newlyn was sent reeling across the conservatory, colliding with a range of orchids and ferns in his path and narrowly missing the glass door which led to the garden.

Chalmsforth, his face white with rage, standing where he had struck the blow which had sent Newlyn on his spinning course, waited until Newlyn struck the ground before avowing,

"If you wish to play such games, I suggest you not do so under my roof. Confine them to your own, or to the hell halls you frequent." Turning to Fiona, he said tersely, giving her his arm, "I believe this is my waltz, Miss Guthrie."

He said nothing as he led her onto the floor; his eyes were expressionless though she knew he was angry by the tension of his fingers as they encircled her waist. At last he spoke.

"I don't know whether you have been purposely encouraging that man, but I have warned you about him before. Now, I hope you have learned your lesson."

She knew he was right and had, until he spoke, had every intention of thanking him for rescuing her from Newlyn's clutches, yet she was infuriated by the imperious manner which he had adopted toward her all evening. Newlyn had kissed her, it was true, yet Chalmsforth himself had done so only the day before. He seemed to overlook his own conduct in condemning another's. That Newlyn had been totally repulsive to her, while she had wanted Chalmsforth's embrace, she forgot in the moment of her anger.

"Then I hope you have also warned Kitty against him," she replied coldly, glancing across the ballroom to where Newlyn was now waltzing with Kitty, his demeanour again composed though keeping the greatest distance between himself and Chalmsforth.

"Kitty does as she pleases. She is her own mistress."

The bluntness of his reply caused her to turn on him angrily.

"And are you implying that I am not?"

She felt the pressure of his fingers on her back as he reversed the step and saw only the inscrutability of his expression as he drawled,

"You, my dear, as you were so careful to remind me only yesterday, are mine. You are the one who will not let me forget that I have paid for that privilege of calling you my mistress."

His cool reply infuriated her. She longed to push him aside, to walk off the floor leaving him to the embarrassment of being abandoned by his partner before all his guests, yet she knew there was reason in what he said, detestable though it was. He had paid for that privilege, though not till now had he spoken of it; he had even forbidden that it be mentioned. It was unjust of him, though, to bring it up in the middle of the ball, her ball. It was wrong of him too, to believe that she had encouraged Newlyn. She could have explained exactly what had happened, why she had followed him to the conservatory; but Chalmsforth probably would not deign to believe her; despite his anger, she doubted whether he really cared. This ball, which was to have been the happiest since her arrival, had become the most insupportable. She felt the tears rise to her eyes, but she would never, never allow him to make her cry. Swallowing her distress she finished the dance without another word.

As he escorted her to a seat he tersely reminded her, "Remember that the remaining waltz is mine."

She tossed her head without reply, afraid of what she might say to him in front of his guests. She could not forget Lady Chalmsforth was there and all she owed to that dear person.

She watched Chalmsforth cross the room to talk to Annabel Telford who eyed him coolly though not without interest. Newlyn had been right there at least; they were a perfect match. She saw the Marquess of Orbury approach Chalmsforth, obviously glad he was again showing an interest in his daughter. Nothing could be more calculated to put Chalmsforth off, she thought, but turned, determined not to concern herself with the affairs of a man she now found insupportable and, seeing Lord Elton standing alone, she went up and spoke to him with such vivacity and earnest desire to please that he quickly took the opportunity of asking her to go down to supper with him, a privilege he had not counted upon and therefore was all the more elated, in his quiet, sedate way, by her acceptance.

Fiona was determined that she would have nothing more to do with Chalmsforth that evening and when the next waltz was struck up and he approached her, she frigidly refused, feigning a twisted ankle. Those nearby were startled to hear the impeccably polite Chalmsforth reply coolly, "Waltzing can be the very best cure for that," as he grasped her hand in a relentless grip. Fiona might have protested his forcefulness had she not seen Lady Chalmsforth smile at her from the other side of the room. She could not make a scene, so she acquiesced with a grace she was far from feeling. She was determined to ignore him and assiduously kept her face turned from him throughout the course of the dance though once her eyes caught his and she saw something there that puzzled her. Anger was in those grey, forbidding eyes, yes, but did she not also see injury? Yet that was ridiculous, she was the one who was hurt.

"You waltz well now," he said, breaking the silence, but when she made no attempt to answer him, he added, "though occasionally you tend to be a trifle too rigid."

She did not deign to reply; in fact she said not a word during the entire dance. If her silence perturbed him, he gave no sign of it, adding insult to injury by saying when the waltz finished,

"I am glad you gave your full attention to the step. There can be no doubt that your performance profited by it."

She ignored that remark also, and was determined not to speak to him for the remainder of the evening. By dancing with her more than twice he had placed her in the anomalous position of making everyone in the room believe that he must have serious intentions toward her, and there were expectant whispers wondering whether an announcement might be made before the night was out. Yet she confused this rumour by being exceedingly pleasant to every gentleman in the room except Chalmsforth, while he, on the other hand, confined his attentions to Annabel Telford; such unpredictable behaviour caused tongues to wag even more. Orbury did not know what to make of it and whispered to his wife that Chalmsforth had better come to the point or leave Annabel alone. He was not going to have his daughter played fast and loose with and he was thoroughly fed up with this young woman Lady Chalmsforth had brought under her roof, a pretty face and nothing else to recommend her. They were obviously searching for a husband for her, else why go to the trouble of the ball in her honour. If Chalmsforth had ideas of taking her for himself, he would most certainly cut him in future.

Fiona could not clearly remember how the rest of the evening passed, concerned as she was with that hidden interior conflict of tumultuous anger and hurt, though outwardly she gave no sign of it. She had to take Lady Chalmsforth's word that it had been the party of the season.

In the early hours of the morning, when Fiona finally returned to Brook Street, she vowed that she would free herself by one means or another of her indebtedness to Chalmsforth. She did not know how she would do it but only that it would be done. Never again would she allow herself to be indebted to him for any reason.

XIII

Chalmsforth desperately wanted to get away from London and the day following the ball he decided to leave for Perrynchase. He had hated the previous evening. He was infuriated with Newlyn for attempting to take advantage of Fiona and aware that his own behaviour had been far from commendable. He had allowed his emotions to run away with him again. He found Fiona had the ability to make him feel first and think later; that had not happened to him before. He had prided himself on his clearheadedness—his behaviour had even been called calculating by some—yet Fiona made him speak and act without preconceptions. He knew that he had been horribly rude to her and that he should apologize, but he could not bring himself to see her while his own feelings were in confusion. He wished she had never come into his life, but a few days away from her disturbing presence might set things aright within himself.

He was giving instructions to Nicholson when his mother arrived. He had not expected to see her so soon, in fact he had been on the point of writing her a note, something her visit obviated. She so clearly had something she wished to discuss with him that he immediately dismissed Nicholson, and pouring her a cup of coffee, he invited her to join him at the table.

"Such a fine evening last night, Peter; everything was beautifully arranged. I really believe you know how to entertain your guests better than I ever did. The vol-au-vents were superb, and I heard so much talk of the fine music, in fact nothing but compliments all round. Amanda Markham says you must be the best host in London for you forgot nothing."

"I appreciate your pleasantries, Mother, though I doubt you would make a special morning visit just to convey them. There must be something more—I'd appreciate it if you would get to the point for I'm on my way to Perrynchase for a few days and there are a number of matters to deal with before I go."

"Oh, dear, that is a nuisance. I didn't know you were planning to go to Hampshire just now. You didn't mention it before."

"I didn't mention it because I only just decided on it."

"Oh." Lady Chalmsforth looked relieved. "Then it can be nothing important. You can surely put it off for a few days, can't you?"

"For heaven's sake why? Don't tell me Gerald's in trouble again?"

"Oh, no, dear, nothing like that. As far as I know Gerald is doing quite nicely. He seems to have taken a liking to Lady Markham's youngest—I forget her name now—but you know there can be nothing wrong there."

"Well, that's a relief. Then what is it?"

"Well, I had a visit from Lord Elton this morning. He asked last night if he could call on me, but I didn't think it was a matter of any particular consequence. However, when he called this morning he asked to see me alone. The upshot of the conversation was that he has made an offer for Fiona."

There was silence. Chalmsforth looked away from his mother down at the invitation card he had been holding in his hand, not reading it, merely lost in contemplation. Then he looked up.

"And what did she say?" he asked at last.

"She didn't say anything. You see, I haven't mentioned it to her yet."

"Well, then, I suggest you do so without delay. It is a matter for her to decide and nothing to do with me."

"Well, dear, I was hoping you would speak to her about it. You know Elton much better than I do, and I thought you could advise her."

"Advise her! Really, Mother, this isn't something in which I should be involved. You know there is nothing wrong with Elton. Perhaps he is a little old for her, and I'm not sure he has the right temperament—but that is for her to decide. He is certainly financially sound, and though he has daughters, he undoubtedly wishes to beget an heir." He found this biblical expression used in connexion with those involved strangely unappealing and without thinking he crushed the card in his hand. "I'm really unable to understand why you came to me with this."

"I can explain that. You see, I had an urgent letter this morning from Charlotte Mytton. She is decidedly under the weather and asked me if I could come immediately to be with her for a few days. You know, she is among my oldest friends and I know she wouldn't write such a letter unless she really needed me. She hasn't yet recovered from the death of her husband. I've tried to persuade her to come to London to live, but she won't leave their home in Surrey. I think it a great mistake and mean to ask her to come back with me; indeed I shall insist upon it. I leave to see her today."

"But why can't you discuss this matter with Miss Guthrie before you leave?"

"Susan is with her today; I can't talk in front of the child. Besides, I somehow feel it would be better for you to discuss it with her."

"Well, I don't," he said flatly. "Let it wait for your return."

"Dear Peter, you are being difficult this morning. You know Elton is going to want an answer one way or another. Fiona will see him anyway tomorrow night at the Drayforths' rout, and he will expect her to at least know of his offer. It would be most awkward if she were not apprised of it."

He was about to refuse when his mother leaned over and took his hand. "I would appreciate it, Peter. You know how I rely on your judgement in these things."

"Very well," he replied reluctantly. "I won't leave for Perrynchase until tomorrow then, and I'll stop at Brook Street in the morning before I go."

"Could you make your departure the following day, I wonder? You see, since I shall be absent I was hoping you could escort Fiona to the Drayforths'," Lady Chalmsforth cajoled.

"Really, Mother, I might as well not go at all," he expostulated. "Oh, very well. I suppose it makes little difference to wait another day. Now I hope there is nothing else in your bonnet which will confine me to London for the rest of the season, for I am heartily sick of these balls and routs."

"Spoken by the man who has just given the ball which will be a landmark for many a season to come, how can you!"

"I am even more heartily sick of that one than all the rest combined."

"I think you are overtired. You're like a bull among the bumble bees this morning. Perhaps I should leave you."

She got up and he rose hastily and took her hand. "Forgive me, Mother. You're right, I'm not in the best of humours today. Enjoy your drive and give my kindest regards to Lady Mytton."

"I shall, dear." She patted him gently on the cheek. "And perhaps I shall be back before you leave. I do so hope Charlotte will not take a great deal of persuading for I know your busy schedule. Especially with Fiona here, London would do her the world of good."

The following morning Fiona was engaged in writing a letter to Aunt Agatha when Chalmsforth called.

He bowed stiffly to her and she greeted him with an equal coolness of manner. He decided to come directly to the point of his visit, a point he would have preferred in Hades, but he had been charged with the matter.

"My mother has asked that I speak to you."

From the writing desk, she looked over at him saying nothing. Her quiet, composed manner as she sat with her hands folded, clad in a pale blue morning dress, made him forget the manner in which he had planned to disclose Elton's offer and he walked over to the window, the better to think, and stood with his back to her.

"My visit concerns Lord Elton."

Since he went no further, she at last prompted him in cool tones,

"And what does Lord Elton want?"

"He has"—he paused before continuing—"he has made an offer for your hand. Mother asked that I speak to you about it."

"Oh." Her tone was noncommittal. Again there was silence, broken at last when he turned to her.

"I know nothing of your feelings for him, but apparently he holds you in high regard." He hated to plead Elton's suit, yet he felt it incumbent to say more. "He is a steady man, possibly a little old for you, but he is financially secure."

"You advise my acceptance, then?"

"I advise nothing," he replied coolly. "I am merely conveying the offer to you. You must make your own decision."

She stood up and paced the floor slowly, for the first time appearing disconcerted as though she were troubled. Then she seemed to make up her mind and she turned to him.

"I thank you for coming in this regard. But surely you must realize I can consider no offers of marriage, nor make any other plans for my future life until the matter between us is settled. We are both aware that I am in your debt. It cannot continue. I came to you when I needed help and asked for a sum of money, not as a gift but . . . in return for certain favours. Those favours have never been given. Yet I feel myself as bound by that agreement as any man would feel himself bound by a debt of honour. Had I the money with which to repay you, or the means of raising that money from some source, it would solve the matter. But I have not. The debt must, therefore, be settled between us as agreed in order to close the matter."

His mouth twisted slightly as he retorted, "Are you, then, in such haste to get into my bed?"

His words, in their bald contempt, took her off guard and her face turned scarlet with embarrassment and anger.

"That, sir, is distasteful in the extreme."

"Madam, your entire proposal has been distasteful in the extreme to me from its very inception."

"I was unaware that you found me so distasteful," she replied hotly. "I had thought otherwise, else I should not have conceived the notion of making such an extreme suggestion in the first place."

"I did not say that you were distasteful to me, but that your proposal is, has been, and always will be distasteful to me. How can you propose to repay a debt of honour, as you call it, by losing your honour?"

"Because that was the agreement made between us," she replied quietly.

"It may have been your agreement, ma'am. It was not mine, I can assure you. At no time did I intend to carry it out. That you could believe I would act in so base a manner toward a lady of your birth, that you could believe me so little a gentleman that I would even consider such a scheme, to ruin the character of a person of genteel upbringing, the daughter of my mother's friend, that is what has hurt me and wounded my self-esteem since the day you first walked into my house."

"Yet it was your own conduct on our first meeting at the abbey that led me to believe otherwise. I should never have thought to so settle a debt had that not occurred. Indeed, until then I did not realize that such offers were made. As you indicated, I had led a sheltered life."

"You know very well that I did not then realize who you were, nor that your mother was a person held in friendship and esteem by my own."

"Yet after, you brought me here and put me in an intolerable position by having your mother, as you say my mother's friend, introduce me to society, all the time knowing of the arrangement that had been made."

"How many times do I have to apologize to you for the mistake I made at the abbey?" He was infuriated. "I can assure you that when I knew who you were I never, at any time, had any intention whatsoever of taking advantage of you in the way you suggested, or any other for that matter."

"No," she retorted. "Far better to leave me forever in your debt, I suppose, to live my whole life in that knowledge. I suppose I should say that I am obliged to you, but I cannot. I cannot force you to take me, yet I wish I could to end the matter."

"As far as I am concerned, the matter is at an end. You owe me nothing. You have more than repaid me by the pleasure you have given my mother."

"Yet I have derived equal, if not more pleasure from her company. No, sir, the agreement was not to give me seven thousand pounds to become a companion to your mother. I cannot delude myself with that. The agreement when you gave me the money was that I should spend a night with you. That has not been done, but in order to absolve myself from all indebtedness or the necessity of gratitude to you, I wish it to be finished and over. Then I may return to my former life."

"And could you," he asked slowly, "enter into such intimacy with me so coldly, so unfeelingly, in so mercenary a manner?"

Under the scrutiny of his gaze, she flushed and was forced to lower her eyes, but her voice was firm when she answered,

"Under the circumstances, sir, I believe I could."

"Then, I assure you, I could not," he flung at her angrily, "nor ever shall. It was a hard and sordid bargain, totally wanting in delicacy or sensitivity, which you proposed. There could be no satisfaction in it for anyone."

"Yet you, yourself, originally proposed it. When you did so, you made it clear that I have only one negotiable asset, and that is myself." When he began to protest, she went on swiftly, holding up her hand to silence him. "I do not say this in retribution. Indeed, you did me a favour, for in an instant you opened my eyes to something it might have taken me a lifetime to believe possible."

127

"If I did make you so believe, I did it only on the presumption that you were a person who performed such services—professionally."

"Ah, yes, a professional person. I have often wondered why it was favoured with the term 'profession,' the oldest profession is it not called, but now it is obvious, a woman's person is all she has with which to make any sizeable income in life, in the event she is born with none of her own, and since few women stand in line to inherit, that is usually the case. Woebetide that she is ill-looking or plain, for she must rely on her looks and charms to make her way."

"If a lady uses her person in such a manner, it can only be done in marriage."

"And what, sir, is the difference between a wife and a mistress in such an event, except that it seems to me the former has a worse lot, for she is forever tied to the person to whom she has sold herself in just such a mercenary manner as the latter, except that in her case it is done with society's full approval, I believe she is even said to be fortunate to make such a match."

"And what of the issue from either arrangement, ma'am? You seem to overlook the fact that one woman bears lawful offspring, so regarded by the world, while the other bears children of doubtful patrimony by a varying series of lovers, unless she is so fortunate as to discover the means of preventing such occurrences."

Fiona's eyes widened in interest.

"There are such means by which childbirth can be prevented despite——"

But he cut her off abruptly, in exasperation.

"Fiona! Why is it that you make me discuss things that can never be discussed in front of a lady, let alone with a lady?"

"But surely this is a matter that should be known to women above all."

"Certainly not. I cannot agree with you."

"You mean it would free them and you cannot have that."

"I mean no such thing. You twist my words. I mean . . . I mean . . . What I came here to discuss was Lord Elton's offer for your hand."

"Lord Elton is a good man as far as I know him, and kind, but I have no love for him. I might be able to develop an affection, but that would be all. It would be an entirely unscrupulous proposition on my part if I were to agree to the match, one with which I would have to deal for the rest of my life. Even to rid myself of my indebtedness to you, I could not abide such a lifetime. Far better a few hours of unlawful . . ." she paused, unsure of herself.

"The word for which you search, ma'am, since you insist on frankness, is copulation—unlawful copulation. You can think of it in no other way for that is the sum and total of it, whereas between man and wife it is a bond that goes much further to entwine their hearts, their lives, as well as their bodies."

"Is this how you feel about marriage to Annabel Telford?" Fiona asked curiously, aware of a pang of fear that it might prove to be so. It was his turn to flush under her scrutiny.

"I have not proposed marriage to Lady Annabel," he replied abruptly.

"Yet," she prompted.

"It is not that proposal which is at hand, but Lord Elton's. Am I to take it that you refuse his offer?"

"I cannot even discuss it until the matter between us is decided. I asked something of you under certain conditions. Those conditions have not been met. Had you a gaming debt and you were told you need not pay it, would you consider the matter settled?"

"But that is a completely different matter."

"I fail to see the difference, nor do I regard this obligation any less seriously."

"But it is altogether a different thing for a gentleman not to pay his gaming debts."

"Why, because a gentleman's honour is worth more than that of a lady?" she demanded.

He flushed. "I didn't mean that."

"Then what did you mean?"

"I meant that you are under no obligation to me whatsoever. I assure you of my sincerity. Can you not understand that if you ever engaged in such conduct no gentleman would ever consider marrying you? If it were to be known, I am sure Elton would withdraw his offer."

"I don't give a fig if he does. I did not ask him to offer for me, nor did I want him to offer for me, and I have no intention of accepting him under any circumstances. I have already expressed my views on that. And despite all you say, I

129

believe that if someone truly loved me it would not make one whit of difference what I had done in the past."

"How little you know of men."

"Perhaps. I hardly count myself an authority."

"Then you wish me to tell Elton you decline his offer."

"You may tell him whatever you wish." She turned her back on him, afraid that the tears she had been holding back might begin to fall, for she would never allow him to see her in tears.

"If it is because you regard yourself as being under obligation to me that you feel unable to return to Cambridgeshire, I assure you it is not so. I will send my carriage to take you home whenever you wish."

"Then early tomorrow would be as good a time as any other."

"My mother will miss you, of course," he said, in softer tones, but she made no reply.

"I understand you are invited to the Drayforths' this evening. At what time shall I call for you?" He wished she would turn back to him and felt an urgent desire to go to her but did not dare to do so, apprehensive of her feelings but more afraid of his own.

"I have no intention of going to the Drayforths'. You need not trouble yourself on my behalf. In fact, I shall count it a great blessing never to lay eyes on you again."

"Very well, Miss Guthrie. You couldn't be more precise in your sentiments." He walked to the door, but turned before he left. "I am quite of the same mind."

The door slammed behind him with a reverberating crash. Fiona sank into a chair, her head in her hands, and allowed hot tears of pride, anger, mortification, and frustration to fall.

XIV

Fiona was in her room getting together the few things she had brought with her in preparation for her return to Cambridgeshire—not a lengthy business for she planned to take none of the clothes Chalmsforth had paid for—when a servant announced that Lord Newlyn was below and wished to see her. She was about to refuse but abruptly changed her mind. It would be a small revenge upon Chalmsforth for him to learn that the last visitor she saw in London was the one whom he most detested, so she examined her eyes in the mirror to see whether their swelling had sufficiently subsided and tidied her hair before descending.

"My dear lady," Newlyn began, "I feared you might not see me after that little contretemps last night. I am sorry I allowed your beauty to carry me away in that manner, though I found Chalmsforth's reaction unnecessarily harsh. I trust I have your forgiveness."

"Of course you do." She smiled at him.

"I really came in the hopes I could atone for my conduct by driving you in the park this afternoon."

Fiona hesitated. She had always before refused such invitations, but a drive with Newlyn in Hyde Park at the fashionable afternoon hour would inevitably reach Chalmsforth's ears. That was enough to make her decide in favour of the proposal.

"I'd be delighted. Allow me time to get my bonnet and change my dress."

If her reply was unexpected, Newlyn gave no sign of it.

"You may take all the time you wish, Miss Guthrie. For you, no wait is too long."

The park was crowded as they entered. She half hoped that Chalmsforth would be there, but saw no sign of him. However, it was a pleasant afternoon, and she was glad to have come on this, her last outing in London. Newlyn talked a great deal of his team, elucidating their finer points, as they nodded to their acquaintances. Before nightfall it would be common knowledge that she had driven with Newlyn; she thought with some satisfaction of Chalmsforth's chagrin.

"I can't tell you what pleasure you give me by accompanying me today," Newlyn smiled at her. "I so seldom get a moment alone with you and this is a privilege I have long wished, to have you beside me here. Do you not find my greys far more to your liking than those ramshackle nags of Chalmsforth's?"

"Yes, indeed," she replied without thinking, for hearing Chalmsforth's name reminded of how much she hated to leave without having repaid the sum she owed. Life was ironic, she mused, had it not been for her companion that afternoon she would not have been indebted to Chalmsforth, and how different their friendship might have been—and all because of that foolish game of piquet Neill had played. He should never have done so, he should have known piquet was not his game . . . Fiona's stream of thought stopped abruptly —but it was *hers*.

She could play piquet, her father had taught her all the intricacies of that game until she could beat him handily, but she had never played for money. She detested gambling and all the sorrow and sacrifice it had caused. Yet . . . a plan began to form in her mind—it might be her only chance.

"I noticed you at the card table at Lady Markham's the other evening, Lord Newlyn," she began. "You handle your cards with great skill. I do admire that, and you were playing piquet au cent, it is the game I most adore."

"Then why did you not join the table?" he asked.

"The stakes, alas, were far too rich for my pocket."

"I should gladly have staked you."

"The stake must be one's own, and it must be high, to demand from a player his full potential," she contended.

"My dear lady, how I do agree with you; a woman after my own persuasions if I may make so bold," he eyed her speculatively as he spoke.

Fiona was silent for a moment before broaching, "Still, I am sorry I shall be leaving London without ever having had the opportunity of testing my skill against yours. You would be a worthy opponent."

"Need it be so?" he demanded.

"I leave tomorrow."

"But tonight remains."

"I am promised to go to the Drayforths', though I should much rather. . . ." she stopped.

"Rather play?"

"No, no. It is impossible. I am without funds and to play without a wager is no sport."

"But perhaps, perhaps we could contrive somehow to make it interesting."

"How?"

"Miss Guthrie, you may be without a monetary stake, but nevertheless you have other assets of even greater value."

Fiona flinched and was forced to lower her eyes as his own ran assessingly over her. There was no misconstruing his meaning, and he was heartened by her offering no disclaimer.

"Well, well, Miss Guthrie, so you are not the simple country girl you would have made me believe last night, but I suppose that was because you were then under Chalmsforth's aegis." He laughed suddenly. "Cold fish that he is, I doubt he suspects the most amenable and tractable nature of his fair guest."

"I don't care to discuss Lord Chalmsforth," she maintained coldly.

"Nor do I—I should much rather discuss the matter at hand, and I take it you are willing."

"Such an arrangement would allow me to play," Fiona mused, half to herself, astonished at her own coolness. "Very well," she decided abruptly, "but I must warn you, I do not undervalue myself."

"Nor should you, madam," he concurred. "It is for you to say."

"Then five hundred points at ten pounds a point, with an extra four hundred for each rubber."

Newlyn whistled softly between his teeth. "High stakes, indeed, but no more than is justified."

In his face was the same fervour that had been there before; she recoiled, remembering his lips, hot and clinging, the way he had pinioned her in his hold so that she could scarcely breathe—dare she take such a risk? Yet there was no alternative, not if she wanted to free herself from her obligation. And she did, most heartily she did.

Yet still she wavered, looking into Newlyn's avid and assessing eyes, recalling suddenly Chalmsforth's warning, "His conduct, especially toward members of your sex, is particularly reprehensible." Well, she vowed to herself, in that event she must not allow herself to lose. Purposefully, she squared her shoulders.

"This evening, then, I shall come to your place. Albemarle Street, is it not?"

He smiled, and for one awful moment Fiona felt she had walked into a trap, but if it was, it was a trap she herself had made.

"Shall we say eight?"

"That would be perfect," he smiled. "May I send my carriage for you?"

"No!" she replied quickly, a trifle too quickly, for he smiled even more knowingly. "No, that won't be necessary, I shall find my way."

"I shall do everything within my power to make this evening a fitting climax to your visit. I think I can safely promise you memories never to be forgotten."

"Memories I can carry away in both hands. You should know, Lord Newlyn, that I require bank notes rather than a draft."

"I shall arrange it."

"You should also know that I am quite determined to win."

"No less am I, but all will depend on the fall of the cards. Whatever the outcome, neither of us should have cause for regret."

When Fiona returned to Brook Street she stopped only to write two letters, one of which she put on the mantel in her chamber and the other in her reticule. Then she summoned Betsy and asked her to finish the packing and go to the Belle Sauvage at Ludgate Hill and take a room there for the night and to purchase two tickets on the morning stage for Cambridge.

She changed into a gown of tussaud silk, plain though not too severe, and took only a light meal before summoning her courage to leave. Then she had Lady Chalmsforth's coachman drop her at the Drayforths' but dismissed him for the evening saying that she would return with Lord Chalmsforth. When he was safely out of sight, she found a hired carriage and gave the driver Newlyn's address. It was evidently not unknown to him and she thought she caught a slight wink as she gave him instructions on arrival to return without fail at midnight and wait there for her. She paid him sufficiently, promising to double the amount later, and gave him a look to discourage any conversation which might cause her to lose heart.

Newlyn awaited her in his drawing room, a room of large proportions with the Chinese decor that had become so much the rage. Despite the room's size, it was surprisingly stuffy. An enormous fire burned in the hearth and beside it was set a small table with a wine decanter and glasses.

"How delighted I am to see you. I was beginning to be afraid you might have changed your mind."

"No, indeed, I did not forget we have a wager to settle."

"Do have some wine before we start."

Fiona noticed that he had evidently already partaken quite freely of it before her arrival. Well, so much the better, she thought, but for her part she was determined to keep a clear head. She took only two sips of the claret before suggesting they should start for it would take some time to reach five hundred.

"I have set my wager here." He opened a small box to reveal a stack of bank notes.

"Then let us begin at once," she said briskly.

She won the cut and chose to let Newlyn deal, thereby gaining an immediate advantage which allowed her to win with ease the first ten points. She leaned back and began to relax. If her luck held, she could easily have the wager by midnight.

But her luck did not hold. By ten she was down one hundred and eighty points and her losing streak continued. She could get no long suit of any consequence and was unable to employ her usual strategy of discarding those cards unsupported by aces, for she saw precious few aces. Nor could she get carte blanche, a hand without a single honour which would have awarded her an immediate ten points for, as luck would have it, there was always a jack or a queen to deprive her of it. Never had she had such bad hands. Newlyn said little as he played. He paused only to drink. She tried not to notice the way in which his eyes dwelled on her mouth and breasts as he played his cards casually, almost carelessly, but always so winningly.

The room was hot and stuffy and Fiona began to feel worried and uncomfortable. She had never thought to lose in this manner, not at piquet, it was her game. Why, she had even been able to beat her father, an excellent player who had taught her all he knew. Yet never had she had such miserable cards which, no matter how skillfully she used them, robbed her of any victory. As the night wore on she saw little opportunity of regaining her momentum.

She watched Newlyn closely as he dealt but could discover no improper handling of the cards, nor did her scrutiny reveal that he made any attempt to palm or change them in any manner. Yet always, whatever suit she decided on, he seemed to know exactly what she held and have a counter to it. She would have thought he was cheating, she even checked to make sure that there was no mirror behind her to reveal the contents of her hand.

"Lady Luck seems with me tonight," he slurred his words, leaning across the table and caressing her hand.

She snatched it away. "You have won nothing yet, my lord."

"No, not yet. I can wait."

He smiled and she realized how much he repulsed her. She reflected that never at any time had the idea of giving herself to Chalmsforth aroused the feelings of disgust which she now felt in looking at Newlyn. She wondered how she had ever allowed herself to be so entrapped, but remembered that it was she herself who had suggested the stakes. She was now badly shaken and took another sip of her wine before remembering that that could only make matters worse. She still had a chance if only the cards would favour her. She looked down at the design on the back of the cards as they fell slowly from Newlyn's hand as he dealt. It was an intricate pattern of entwined snakes, blue outlined in gold.

"Be good to me, please," she thought, watching one card fall on top of another. Then something caught her eye. The gold outline on the snakes was not of equal width on all the cards. There was a slight variation, not very much and impossible to notice casually unless under scrutiny. As Newlyn went to deal the last card to himself she noticed the wider band on the middle snake and reached across to grasp his wrist before he dropped it.

"That card, sir, I believe, is an honour, most likely an ace."

She twisted his wrist sharply to reveal the ace of hearts. Then she turned over the rest of his hand, two other aces, three kings.

"These cards are marked," she said tersely. "You have had this game set against me all along, allowing me to win those first hands to lull my suspicions. Rarely have I heard of such a despicable cheat. Is this how you played with my brother when he lost so heavily to you? You are monstrous, sir. I suggest you renounce the game by default."

"I admit to nothing," he said huffily. "And I have no intention of giving in while I'm ahead. If you wish for fresh cards, you may have them. I'll get rid of these if they're not to your liking."

With that he gathered up the cards and threw them on the fire, ringing for a servant to bring an unused pack and commanding that refreshments be laid for them.

"I swear I am prodigious hungry." He ignored her malevolent stare. "You are a good player, I must admit it. I am enjoying myself tremendously."

She did not deign to reply.

It was almost midnight before play resumed, for though she had no appetite she had had to join him at supper. Now she needed to regain the lost points before she could build her own lead, but she had carefully examined the new piquet pack and could find no irregularities in the cards. It remained only for her to be on her guard against other treacheries on his part. But with the new pack, her luck changed and two hours later she was almost four hundred points ahead. She breathed more easily, though she did not relax her scrutiny of her partner. Thus, when she found him attempting to *sauter la coupe*, to insure the turn up of an ace on his deal, she quietly told him to redeal the hand.

"Quite the little card sharp, aren't we," he said, not altogether pleasantly. "And where did you learn all this? Not from your brother, I know."

"How like you to take advantage of unsuspecting innocents," she said before she realized she was speaking Chalmsforth's words, and she suddenly wished desperately that he was there, for though she now knew that she would win, she also realized that she was completely alone with Newlyn; she had not counted on the difficulties she might have in leaving. Newlyn seemed to have resigned to losing for, despite his last attempt at trickery, his efforts were only half-hearted at best. Neither did he seem to care particularly which, in itself, emphasized to Fiona her precarious position. No one knew she was there and he must be aware that she would have told no one she was coming, certainly not Chalmsforth. She concentrated on her last hand, determined he would not rob her of her victory.

"And that, my lord, is pic, repic, and capot," she said, laying down her last cards. "And I believe that takes me over the five hundred points we agreed upon."

"You may be right," he smiled at her lazily, without moving.

She got up and stretched.

"I see it is after four. How late the game lasted," she said, determined not to show the fear caused by his slow smile and heavy-lidded gaze. "I really must go."

She hoped the hired driver would be outside, but her thoughts were quickly drawn away from the possible difficulty of being alone on London streets at night by Newlyn's rising.

"But there is no rush, is there? As you point out, it is early morning and no one can be awaiting you. An hour or so more can make little difference."

Almost involuntarily she stepped back as he came toward her. Reaching out, he grasped her arms, holding her fast in his grip.

"You didn't really think I would let you leave without some little reward for myself, did you?"

Fiona twisted to free herself from him, but that only caused him to tighten his hold.

"It was I who won my bet, not you," Fiona contended. "No gentleman would behave in such a manner. I'm sure you will regret it if you force me to do anything against my will."

"Who said I was a gentleman? You knew I was not, otherwise you wouldn't have suggested this little caper—do I have to remind you that it was you who put yourself up for the taking, not I. Hardly the action of a lady, so we're a pair and, I think, a well-matched one."

Roughly he pulled her to him, just as with an equal force, she pulled away and, catching him off guard for a moment, she broke free and ran for the door. Despite his inebriated condition, he was quicker than she expected; she felt his hands seize her by the waist and, pulling her against him, he began to fondle her breasts at will. She struggled to free herself but she was hopelessly, helplessly trapped and he, enjoying the game, enjoying his domination, revelled in his victory. Forcing her against the table which held the remains of the

138

supper he had consumed, he fastened his lips on hers, sighing with satisfaction. Fiona braced herself, to prevent herself from being pulled to the floor. Reaching back she found the fruit dish and with it the sharp paring knife. Instinctively her fingers closed around its handle and swiftly raising it, she plunged it into the back of her persecutor.

The blade entered Newlyn's body at the shoulder, not to a great depth, for Fiona pulled it out as swiftly as she had struck him. Nevertheless, he screamed with pain and dropped his hold upon her. She faced him, knife in hand, his blood gleaming red and ominous on its blade. She was sickened by the sight of it, yet she knew it was her only protection.

"You bloody witch," he roared. "How dare you turn on me in my own home. You're nothing better than a street trollop. You. . . ."

Still holding the knife, she rang the bell for the footman.

"Do you wish to give orders for my pelisse, or shall I?" she asked with a coolness she was far from feeling.

Newlyn was gently feeling for the wound on his shoulder and moaning as he did so.

"You needn't think you can get away with this," he shrilled. "I'll be sure all of London knows the kind of viper they have taken to their bosom."

"I suggest you try nothing more. My next blow would be much lower and preclude any activities of the type you planned for tonight forever."

"You hussy!" he spat at her through clenched teeth.

A footman came, glancing nervously from Newlyn to Fiona. She ordered him to get her pelisse and to see her to the door. He didn't move, however, until Newlyn nodded slightly, giving his approval. Fiona picked up the box containing the banknotes, laying down in its place the paring knife, and followed the footman into the hallway.

Outside she breathed a sigh of relief. The carriage was there. Once safely inside she instructed the driver to take her to Grosvenor Square and, taking the bank notes from the box, she put them in with the letter she had written earlier. Before closing it, she reached up and reluctantly removed the gold broach from her dress and tucked it in with the bank notes and then sealed the bulky envelope.

At Grosvenor Square, she instructed the driver to deliver the letter, which was taken without comment by a bleary-eyed footman. Then it was on to the Belle Sauvage at Ludgate Hill.

It was not until Fiona was seated beside Betsy in the stage bound for Cambridge that she leaned her weary head back against the seat and compared the Fiona Guthrie now returning to Culross Abbey to the young woman who had left. Chalmsforth had said she had not changed. It was not so; she was changed beyond all recognition. She could never again be that guileless creature who had entered the fashionable world of London believing she knew exactly what she was doing. Life played tricks upon people, it was impossible to know what was in store. Newlyn had sickened her, yet he was not entirely to blame. She had laid herself open to such conduct, she had known the cast of which he was made. Had he played with a man it might have been different, as it was he probably felt quite justified in treating her less than honourably—there was no honour in gambling with a woman, he would take whatever he could get whether it were freely given or not.

It was not Newlyn who unnerved her as she thought back on the night, but herself. To find she had the ability to strike out at another human, whatever the reason, even the ability to kill. Had the knife entered his body nearer the spine, who could say what might have happened; she shuddered at the thought. He was a rake and a lecher, but the realization that she might have murdered him was horrifying. Oh, to find peace again at the abbey! She closed her eyes and dropped into a troubled sleep, her head falling onto Betsy's shoulder, nodding in time with the rhythm of the coach wheels on the rough road.

XV

Chalmsforth awoke late the next day feeling decidedly under the weather. For the second time that week he had consumed far too much wine, he had, in fact, become quite inebriated. It was not his habit, and therefore he found his sore head all the more painful. He had been out most of the night, he was not entirely sure where, and his manservant had put him to bed, he was not entirely sure when. By the look of the light creeping through the crack in the heavy window coverings it must now be past noon. He groaned. His head was heavy, his eyes rasped, and his mouth was unpleasantly dry. He tried to remember the previous evening and couldn't. All he could remember was the earlier encounter with Fiona which had led him to cast caution to the wind. How foolish he had been, all over a woman, and a woman who was completely unworthy. His head told him he was paying for his folly.

Gently he put his feet to the floor. He found the impact with solidity jarring and sat a few moments before ringing for coffee. At least by this time Fiona would be out of his life. He would leave for Perrynchase immediately. There was no reason to await his mother's return, a note to her would suffice. He presumed Fiona would have left some word of explanation for her return to Cambridge, she was always punctilious about such things. But he really didn't want to think about her.

He reached for the morning paper and glanced at it as he sipped his coffee. The King's Own had embarked from Ramsgate, he wished he could have been with them. There had been a fire at the premises of a Mr. Gilet, a bookseller. There was no change in the King's condition. He scanned the marriages and deaths, nothing of significance.

By the time he had bathed and dressed it was almost two before he descended the stairs, and Nicholson awaited him, peering nervously over his glasses. The fellow must think I'm an ogre, thought Chalmsforth, and I probably look like one today.

"And what have you for me," he said, as cheerfully as his aching head would allow. He really must try to be more pleasant to Nicholson, he must be frightening the fellow somehow.

Nicholson handed him a bunch of invitations which Chalmsforth flipped through rapidly, without interest. Then he handed him the bulky letter which had been delivered early that morning. Chalmsforth tore it open as he walked toward the library but stopped short when he saw the stack of bank notes inside. He knitted his brows and turned the envelope over to look at the hand, then he hastened to pull out the accompanying letter. With it, out fell the gold thistle broach.

Sir, I thank you for the loan of the seven thousand pounds which you gave me at a time when I most needed it. Your action was kind and I appreciate it now as I did then. But it was a loan, to be repaid. I believe that it may be within my power to obtain this sum before I leave London. If it is possible, I shall have it delivered to you, along with this note.

Your servant,
Fiona Guthrie

Chalmsforth looked in disbelief at the money, and then turned sharply to Nicholson.

"When was this letter delivered, and by whom?" he asked tersely.

"It came very early this morning, my lord. I was told it was delivered by the driver of a hired vehicle, someone not known to Wilkins, who took it in. I think he said that he thought there might have been someone inside the vehicle, but he wasn't sure. It was not then light."

"Send him to me," Chalmsforth said abruptly. "What time did my coach leave to pick up Miss Guthrie at Brook Street this morning?"

"It left before eight but returned within the hour. She wasn't there."

"Wasn't there?" he shouted. "Then where the devil was she?"

Nicholson became more flustered than ever. "I'm afraid I don't know."

"You don't know! And yet you let me go on sleeping without waking me!" Chalmsforth thundered.

"I'm sorry, my lord. I did put my head around the door but you were sleeping so soundly I thought you would be angry if I awoke you. You see, I thought the arrangements had been changed."

"You thought!" Chalmsforth snorted. "Have my coach brought around immediately."

"Yes, my lord. By the way, I did accept an invitation from the Marquess of Orbury for dinner next week." Nicholson put in in an attempt to redeem himself. He pondered for the rest of the day on the angry scowl Chalmsforth gave him as he strode through the hall.

Chalmsforth gained little information from Brook Street. His mother had not yet returned from her visit to Lady Mytton. The housekeeper told him that Miss Guthrie had left for the Drayforths' the previous evening. The coachman had dropped her there and she had said she would return with his lordship. Her absence had gone unnoticed until the morning when his coach called for her. Then it was discovered that her maid had also gone and that some of her things, those she had brought with her when she arrived, had been packed.

"But why wasn't I informed?" he snapped.

"But I thought you would know of it as soon as your coachman returned this morning," said the housekeeper defensively.

Chalmsforth paced the floor. She could have taken the stage, it would be easy to ascertain that, but where could she have been all night? If she had been at the Drayforths' she would have been seen, but she could not have stayed there throughout the night, and she had certainly not planned to return with him, as she had indicated she would, not after all that had passed between them. He hated to go around London asking after her whereabouts, especially if it could be something better left unknown. And where on earth could she have obtained seven thousand pounds? Not at the Drayforths' rout, that was certain, and none of the ideas which poured into his head appealed to him.

"Did she write to anyone, other than the note to my mother, or did anyone call?" he questioned.

"Well, of course, you were here in the morning."

"I know that," he rasped irritably, "but anyone else?"

"And then Miss Guthrie went driving in the park with the Earl of Newlyn for about an hour in the afternoon, and then she came back and changed and left for the——"

"Newlyn," he shouted. "Why on earth didn't you tell me that when I got here?"

Taking up his hat, he ran down the steps and climbed into his carriage, giving Newlyn's Albemarle Street address.

Newlyn had passed an uncomfortable night. His shoulder throbbed and he kept clenching and unclenching his right hand, terrified it might be affected by the wound. God, what he would have given to have had that girl there. To think he had let the little snip outwit him. It infuriated him so that he had had very little sleep until morning. He had, therefore, only just arisen and was still in his bedchamber when Chalmsforth arrived.

Chalmsforth walked in without waiting to be announced. One look at his face made Newlyn think that perhaps last night hadn't been a complete loss after all, not if he had managed to discompose Chalmsforth.

"Do come in, old boy," he motioned to a chair. "This is a delightful surprise. You'll pardon my informal attire, but I had rather a hectic night last night, if you know what I mean." He gave Chalmsforth a conspiratorial smirk.

Chalmsforth stood, his hands gripping the back of the chair so tensely that his knuckles showed white while he raked Newlyn with a flinty stare.

"No, I don't know what you mean. Perhaps you would care to explain," he said evenly.

"Oh, yes you do, old boy. I don't kiss and tell. It wouldn't be fair, particularly in this instance."

Chalmsforth restrained himself with difficulty from dashing the chair over Newlyn's head.

"Out with it. You might as well, for if you don't I'll beat it out of you. Was Miss Guthrie with you yesterday?"

"But surely you must know she was, otherwise you wouldn't be here."

"I know that you drove in the park, but what happened after that?"

"I wish you wouldn't press me into telling you something I'm sure she would not wish you to know."

In reply Chalmsforth threw aside the chair, crossed the room, caught his adversary by the lapels of his ample dressing gown, and shook him until Newlyn, fearing for his shoulder, yelled to be set free.

"Just what is it you want to know, Chalmsforth? Are you going to force me into ruining a lady's name?"

"I want to know what happened last night."

"Then sit down and have a glass of port and act in a civilized manner and I will tell you, at least all that can be told."

"No wine, just get on with it," Chalmsforth said tersely, returning to the chair and sitting down stiffly.

"Miss Guthrie rode with me in the park and then it was arranged that she should come back here and spend the evening with me, which she did. We had a very pleasant time together."

"You blackguard! I know she wouldn't come just like that. You must have forced her to."

"I assure you I did not. In fact it was her suggestion. She came here herself. She said she preferred it to going to the Drayforths'. I agreed with her. Don't you find them dull? Anyway, we had a much more amusing evening."

Newlyn was now rather enjoying himself, especially as Chalmsforth's face had turned white. He'd really touched him where it hurt, something he'd been longing to do and had never thought to find the opportunity.

"We had a delightful evening," he gloated. "She's a charming and I might say a very affectionate young lady, most perfectly constructed. I can't remember when I've had greater satisfac——"

But he didn't finish. Chalmsforth had risen from his chair and, seizing Newlyn, he pulled him up from the lounge on which he was reclining and hit him solidly on the jaw, sending him to the floor on top of his wounded shoulder.

"Don't, don't!" he screamed as Chalmsforth bent over him, intent on hitting him again. "Stop it, for God's sake, stop it."

"I'll stop when you reconstruct that story you just told me. Do you think I'm going to leave here and allow you to run blowing your horn all over town besmirching a lady, a friend of myself and my family? I want you to retract everything you have said and promise never to repeat the lady's name again in any context."

Newlyn was pinned to the floor by Chalmsforth's gleaming boot. His shoulder throbbed painfully and Chalmsforth's expression was daunting.

"Very well, just get off me and let me go."

Chalmsforth removed his foot and Newlyn rose, straightening his dressing gown.

"I have a mind to call you out for your remarks, except knowing your lack of prowess with a weapon it would be nothing short of murder."

"It would amount to murder at the moment for I've hurt my right shoulder. It wouldn't be an even match."

"It wouldn't be an even match at the best of times. But it would be one way to silence your busy tongue."

"You couldn't stay in England if you did kill me, Chalmsforth, I trust you realize that."

"I can assure you that there is life outside England."

"But what about your precious family name?"

"It might suffer, perhaps, though I suspect society would feel I had done it a favour in ridding it of you."

The two men glared at one another with outright hatred, both members of the same class, both brought up with the advantages of wealth, education and name, yet Chalmsforth knew he had far more in common with his manservant than with the man opposite him.

"Well, then, I'll give you my word not to mention what happened here last night," Newlyn said at last.

"Your word is worth nothing and you know it," Chalmsforth retorted. "I need greater assurance than your word. Perhaps, after all, the only assurance I can get is by calling you out."

"Now, don't be hasty, old fellow. If it was known you fought a fellow who was already wounded in the shoulder, it wouldn't look at all well for you."

Chalmsforth's eyes narrowed. "How did your shoulder get wounded, anyway?"

Newlyn looked away to hide the half smirk on his lips. He couldn't resist.

"I'm afraid the lady bit me in her ecstasy."

This time he didn't see the blow coming, but he felt its impact far more than the last. He tasted blood in his mouth and knew his mouth must be cut. Gingerly he felt to see if his teeth were still in place.

"I assure you," he said through rapidly swelling lips, "that I will never mention her name again."

"If you do, I shall have you blackballed at White's. I think I can gather enough evidence of your unsavoury practices to ensure you will no longer be welcomed there. I know of several men who have been fleeced by you and I suspect I would not have to look too hard to find some strange coincidences. I don't doubt some very interesting evidence would come to light. I can also promise you that the first time a murmur reaches my ears that you have said anything, anything at all, about the lady in question, I shall call you out no matter what condition you are in, and I will shoot to kill, that I can promise. I suggest you take a few weeks away from London on your estate to recover your equilibrium. The rest will do you good. It may also help you to forget anything which it may be to your advantage to forget."

Chalmsforth left as Newlyn's manservant arrived to change the dressing on his shoulder. Seeing the state of his master's face, the man hurried away for more warm water and cotton bandages.

XVI

The fool, the damned little fool! To ruin herself with a rake-hell like Newlyn to repay that wretched sum of money for which he had no earthly need. Chalmsforth thought of her expression as she had spoken of it as a debt of honour. It was ridiculous to so regard it. Women never had debts of honour—then he remembered, that was just what she had objected to. Well, none of the women he knew would have so regarded it, but, of course, she wasn't quite like the women he knew. He couldn't imagine any woman, any lady that is, making the arrangement she had made to repay her brother's debt. It had shocked him. Now, for the first time, he realized the courage that it must have taken to make such a suggestion. He remembered the quiet dignity with which she had uttered the words which had crushed him, remembering too the reason she had sought the money, to save her brother from debtor's prison. It had taken courage and determination to take such a step, qualities he had always admired and which he had never denied belonged to her as to no other woman of his acquaintance. This latest event proved that, but why Newlyn of all men? How could she have allowed him to touch her?

Perhaps she actually liked him, he thought savagely, feeling disgust. After all, had she not gone to the conservatory with him and allowed him to kiss her? At the time he had thought she was glad he had rescued her, but now he realized she had never said as much. And then, a mere two days later, she had gone to his home. How could she do such a thing? And then to take money from him. It made her no better than a common—he stopped, finding, despite his disgust, he could not bear to think of her in such terms. Of one thing he was glad, she had left London. He had checked at the Belle Sauvage and ascertained that she had been on the stage that morning with her maid. He had no reason ever to see her again. It was done. He would put her from his mind and from his life forever.

This resolution, however, was easier said than done. Fiona's sudden departure from London following, as it did, on the heels of the ball in her honour, caused a stir of speculation among the society in which she had moved and he was often asked about her. Terse though his answers were, it was noted that the question seemed to cause him pain and discomfort which, in turn, caused further speculation that there had been more in the relationship between the elegant Miss Guthrie and the arrogant Lord Chalmsforth than had been known. People remembered having seen them together here and there, words which had passed between them, looks which had been exchanged; as time went on, people even remembered words which had never been spoken and intimacies which had never taken place. So rumour had it that Miss Guthrie had left town after a lover's quarrel. It was presumed that Chalmsforth had trifled with her affections and then not wished to marry her, for it was inconceivable that a girl with nothing to recommend her but her name and face could have refused him, he was far too eligible a *parti* for that. So it was that Chalmsforth's name was firmly linked with Fiona Guthrie's while Newlyn's was never mentioned in that connexion.

Lady Chalmsforth was greatly disappointed to find that Fiona had returned to Cambridgeshire in her absence. Luckily, she had persuaded Charlotte Mytton to return to London with her so she didn't feel too solitary, though Charlotte could in no way replace Fiona.

Lady Chalmsforth, too, joined in with those who questioned her son about Fiona's sudden departure.

"But she left you a note, did she not?" was his less than helpful response to her worried enquiry.

"Yes, but it said little except that she had been away too long and that she was needed at home, something about her aunt being unable to manage any longer without her. I think she could have at least managed until the season was over. There are so many upcoming events that Fiona would have enjoyed, the Armbrusters' masquerade party and that new Italian singer at Covent Garden."

"I'm not at all sure she was all that keen on life in town. She told me she preferred the country."

"What else did she tell you?" Lady Chalmsforth eyed him curiously.

"What do you mean, what else did she tell me? You were the one who was in her confidence, more than I," he replied irritably.

"Now, don't get huffy, Peter. It was just a shock to me to get back and find her gone. I'd told Charlotte so much about her and she was dying to meet her."

"In that case, I'm sorry she didn't stay to meet Lady Mytton." He wished his mother would drop the subject and his voice expressed that wish.

"And all those clothes designed especially for her—she took none of them with her. I can't understand why?"

"I think I do."

"Do you think she plans to return then?" Lady Chalmsforth asked, examining her son's impassive expression.

"No, Mother. It's just that Fiona Guthrie is a very proud woman."

"I see. Well, I always supposed you paid the bills for her brother, for it's no secret he hasn't a sou. Perhaps I should have them sent to her."

"I don't think she would want that—but do as you wish."

His mother paused before pressing quietly, "Peter, nothing happened between you two after I had gone, did it?"

"Of course not, though I'm not quite sure what you mean by that question."

"I mean was . . . was there any feeling between you . . . any feeling other than that of friendship?"

"If you are asking whether I was in love with her, the answer is no." His reply was sharp.

"Well, don't get angry. It's just that people keep asking me if she left because of you, and though I assure them that such was not the case, they seem to think that . . ." She stopped, as though unsure of herself.

"That what?"

"That she was in love with you and you . . . you turned her away."

He laughed, though there was little humour in his laugh. "You can assure those busybodies that that is completely untrue. I've never been less loved by any woman than by Fiona Guthrie."

"That is not completely true, Peter. I know she had a high regard for you."

150

"What makes you say that?" He was unable to keep the interest from his voice despite his desire to preserve an attitude of insouciance.

"Well, she once told me that she thought you had greater understanding than any man she knew. She admired your mind and thought you put your God-given gifts to better advantage than most men in our circles by collecting, preserving, and appreciating knowledge. In general, I know she found the activities of people in society trivial and felt they wasted their lives. I think that is one reason why she appreciated you."

He eyed his mother in amazement. "Did she really say that?"

"Certainly she did. I think the happiest time of her stay here was toward the end when you came to see us more often. She didn't say a great deal, but I know she looked for you and I noticed her expression whenever you entered a room. She liked the things you planned for us so much more than our usual visits and shopping." Lady Chalmsforth paused for a moment before asking, "I take it that she refused Elton's offer?"

"Yes, she did. I've often wondered, Mother, why you didn't convey it to her yourself. You could have, despite all your explanations to the contrary."

"Well, now she's gone, I must confess to you that I was secretly hoping you might propose to her yourself and that Elton's offer might prompt you to do so if it was at all on your mind. You see, I noticed that you objected first to Gerald's intentions and then Elton's, and I deduced you had chosen her for yourself. I see I was mistaken, but I don't think any harm was done. I hope you'll forgive me, for I've tried not to be a contriving mother. It was simply that I really liked Fiona."

Chalmsforth said nothing and left soon after to mull over his mother's words. Had Fiona really liked him after all? If so, he thought bitterly, she had had a strange way of showing it. To allow Newlyn of all men—no, he refused to dwell on that. But he did. He could not get her or that incident from his mind. Thus, one afternoon when he ran into Neill Guthrie at White's, he insisted on his returning to Grosvenor Square to dine with him. Neill was only too pleased. He had a high regard for Chalmsforth, he was the one man he most wished to emulate, and he regarded it as a distinct honour to be asked by him to dine.

In the course of dinner, Chalmsforth casually asked after Fiona.

"My mother misses your sister a great deal, you understand," he said, by way of explanation for his enquiry.

"I expect she does, and I'm sure I don't know why Fiona returned to Cambridgeshire just now, for there was no need of it. Christmas was dismal and you know Aunt Agatha doesn't at all mind being on her own. She dozes a lot now and doesn't want to move around a great deal. I think when Fiona's there she fusses more and doesn't like to go off to lie down and snooze as she does when she's alone."

"Is she quite well?"

"I think Aunt Agatha's fine. She sleeps a lot because she's getting up in years."

"I meant your sister."

"No, as a matter of fact she's been moping around the house ever since she got back, not at all the thing."

"I suppose she misses the excitement of the parties and the round of entertaining that went on here."

"I don't think that's it, because she's not a great one for that sort of thing as a rule; not that she didn't enjoy it here, but she's rather serious you know, she thinks a lot. I suppose, truth to tell, she's got a better mind than I have, though nothing was ever spent on her education whereas I had Harrow and two years at Cambridge—not that it did me much good. Fiona would really have profitted by it, but that's the way it is: we never get what we want in life, I suppose."

"But she's not ill, is she?" Chalmsforth persisted.

"That's it, I'm not sure. She certainly isn't well, she's frightfully pale and her appetite is awful. I've asked her to eat more, but she says she feels nauseated much of the time. Not like her at all."

"Probably the change of air," Chalmsforth remarked, and turned the direction of the conversation from Fiona, though he could not dispell a pang of uneasiness at the symptoms Neill described.

Over port, Chalmsforth asked Neill what he wanted to do with his life.

"I don't suppose there's much I can do. We're awfully strapped financially, you know. If I had the money, some of the money I've squandered since I came into the title, I think now I should have purchased a commission with it. I think I would enjoy a military life. At least it would give me a direction to move in. But now it's out of the question."

"Not necessarily. You know I had a commission in the Tenth Hussars and I must say those were among the happiest days of my life. I know that Farendon mentioned that Bucky Wynne is going to sell out and return home. He's not been the same since he received that wound in his leg at Salamanca. How would you like to be part of the Tenth? It's a crack regiment and a finer bunch of men you'll not find anywhere."

Neill flushed. "It's not a question of whether I'd like it. Of course I'd like it, but the fact of the matter is, it's simply not possible. Even if I could scrape together the money to buy the commission, there would be the uniforms, horses, and all the gear that's required, plus the money I'd need for the men. There are loads of expenses and I'd need something to get along for myself besides. No, I'm afraid the army is a rich man's province."

Chalmsforth leaned back in his chair. "I like you. I can't go and Gerald doesn't want to go. I'd like to stake you and I can afford it. You could think of it as doing it for me because I'm tied into managing things here."

Neill flushed with pleasure at the thought of doing anything in Chalmsforth's stead, but he shook his head. "I'm sorry. I really couldn't accept it. We Guthries have never taken anything as a gift."

"I'm well aware of that," said Chalmsforth dryly, "but this is not so much a gift as that you would be doing me a service. Farendon will be out soon, and as I said, Bucky Wynne is selling out. I'll have few close friends left in and I like to keep my hand on the military pulse. Call it living vicariously, if you please. I'd like you to be there in my stead. I've observed you. You have the makings of a fine officer, you're alert and resourceful, and you know how to take orders as well as give them—that's not true of all young men of our rank, you know."

Neill looked thoughtful, then he said slowly, "Well, even if you can convince me to believe it's not a gift, I shall never be able to convince Fiona, so it won't serve."

"But need she know?"

"She knows I could never raise the money it would demand to purchase a commission in a crack regiment like that."

"Could you not tell her you won the money?"

Neill laughed. "I'm afraid she is all too aware of my skill at cards. Besides, I've sworn off since . . . for quite a while now."

"That does make it difficult, but surely it's not an insurmountable problem."

For the rest of the evening they put their heads together concocting stories which grew less and less plausible as the port in the decanter on the centre of the table diminished.

"I've got it," Chalmsforth said suddenly. "You can say your uncle popped for it. I don't think Fiona would be likely to come up to check or even write to ask. She doesn't care for them too much from my observation."

"But she knows enough of my uncle to know he'd never pop for that much," Neill replied lugubriously.

"She might suspect he wouldn't, but if it's already an accomplished fact there's little she can do about it. If you'll take my advice, go to Weston's for your uniforms—the cut is superior—and send the account to me, and I'll get Nicholson to get on with the commission purchase in the morning. You'll make a splendid hussar. Go and see your sister in uniform and she'll be so overcome with your handsome appearance she won't have breath left to argue."

He was right. Fiona was breathless when Neill appeared at Culross Abbey some three weeks later in full hussar garb of red shako, grey fur-lined pelisse, silver lace-trimmed jacket with the lace formed into three loops to designate the Prince of Wales' feather, that gentleman being Colonel of the Regiment. To top it all, in the continental fashion, he had grown a moustache.

"Oh, Neill—a moustache! And who on earth did you get that uniform from?" she gasped.

"I didn't get it from anyone, it's mine. I am now a commissioned member of the Tenth Hussars." He lifted his chin slightly as he spoke, already filled with pride at his new position in life.

"But you can't be, it would cost thousands to purchase such a commission, don't be silly. You look very handsome, I must admit, but I won't believe that it's your uniform."

"But it is, I assure you it is." Neill often wished that sisters were not quite so scornful. "I expect I'll be going over to the continent soon. Honestly, Fiona, I've never seen a finer bunch of chaps. I can't wait to be fully a part of them and be with them in action. Oh, Fiona, I'm enjoying it so."

His face beamed, she'd never seen him looking so happy, so sure of himself, yet she could not but question, "But where did the money come from?"

"As a matter of fact, Uncle James popped for it," Neill said sheepishly.

As he thought, Fiona gave him an incredulous look.

"Uncle James! Don't sham, Neill, that's impossible. He'd no more give you the money for such a commission than he would dance a minuet. Do be serious."

"But I am being serious." Neill suppressed a smile at the idea of Uncle James in the complication of the minuet. He had thought Fiona would never believe that story. He wished Chalmsforth had been there to argue in his stead.

Fiona looked at him for a moment, then her eyes narrowed.

"The Tenth Hussars. That was Chalmsforth's regiment, wasn't it?" she demanded.

"I think it may have been," he agreed reluctantly.

"You know very well it was. And it is he who has bought your commission, isn't it? Be honest with me."

"Now, Fiona, don't go telling me to give it up, because I won't. It's the only thing I've ever done that's meant anything to me and I won't relinquish it, say what you will."

She squeezed his arm. "I've no intention of making you give it up, Neill. I just wish we'd thought of it before, that's all. I can see by the way you wear that handsome uniform how you feel about it. I wouldn't rob you of that for the world. It's just that if Chalmsforth has paid for it, we must return the money to him." She paused for a moment before continuing, making an effort to keep her voice light. "I think we should sell the abbey."

"Sell Culross!" Neill was astounded. "Did I hear you aright, Fiona Guthrie, you, who have spent your whole life fussing over this place? Did you suggest we sell it?"

"I think we should. It is ours, after all, to do with as is best, and I'm aware you have never cared for it, at least not in the way I have. But these past few weeks I've come to realize how ridiculous it has been, risking our lives practically to hang onto the place and for what? It is falling apart, we can't afford the most basic repairs, all we will have to hand on to your heirs, if you have any, is a pile of rubble. I think it would be as well to sell now, before its condition gets any worse."

"But what would you do?"

"Well, with my share of the proceeds, I would like to try my hand at teaching young girls. Anne and I have often talked of starting such a school, a school where girls could really learn. This could provide just the impetus to make us do so and give our lives some direction also."

"Gosh, I never thought you'd say so, but quite honestly it would be a relief to get rid of the place. The army is all I want, I'm sure I've found the life for myself, and if you will be happy with a school, things could work out for both of us. I'll stop and talk to our agent in Cambridge on my way back to London and arrange for him to sell it."

"Yes, do that, dear." Fiona kissed her brother lightly on the cheek and then turned away to prevent his seeing the tears which sprang to her eyes at the thought of no longer calling the abbey home.

XVII

Neill returned to London the next day and life resumed its slow pace at Culross Abbey, except that now Fiona found herself lingering over her daily tasks and looking anew at all the familiar rooms and offices as if to indelibly engrave them on her memory. She talked to Anne Robarts of starting a school and Anne, still not entirely over her rejection by Gerald Chalmsforth, greeted the idea of such an engrossing project with enthusiasm. Nothing, however, could be done until a buyer was found for the abbey.

Neill wrote to say that the agent was not overly optimistic for a quick sale; it would take a very discerning buyer to want such a place. "By discerning, I think he meant stupid," wrote Neill, "but he was too polite to say so to my face. Anyway, it is done, and we must sit back and wait. Be assured that when the sale goes through I shall return every penny to Chalmsforth, you need have no more worry on that score. It went against the grain with me also to allow him to buy the commission, but he was very persuasive and by the time he was finished, I was convinced I was doing him the greatest favour in the world by letting him purchase it."

Undoubtedly, Fiona thought wryly, it would probably suit him for us to be indebted to him again. It had been well nigh impossible to repay the last amount; it would not happen again. She had not wished to think of the manner in which that last repayment had been accomplished. For long after she had had nightmares of that stabbing, horrible dreams from which she awoke soaked in perspiration, terrified, feeling Newlyn's breath on her face in the dark so that she had had to get up and light a candle to convince herself that she was alone in her room. She had asked Neill whether he had seen Newlyn, wishing to know whether he was seriously wounded, and had been distressed to learn that he was no longer in London but immured on his estate somewhere in Wiltshire.

At least he wasn't dead, she thought, deriving some comfort from that. Despicable he might be, but the thought she might have killed him was far more abhorrent to her.

Nor had she wanted to think of Chalmsforth, yet again and again her thoughts insisted on turning to him, remembering sometimes that last deplorable interview, but more often thinking of the day they had spent together in Richmond, his empathy as he had listened to her, his thoughts on his own life, and, despite her wish to put it from her, their shared embrace, so that although their last meeting had been one of recriminations and anger, she longed to see him again.

Yet one afternoon, as the snowdrops beneath the trees in front of the abbey signalled the arrival of spring, and as Fiona sat in the library reading while her aunt dozed in the pallid sunlight streaming through the windows, when sounds from the hallways foretold the arrival of a visitor and the door opened to reveal Chalmsforth's tall, elegant figure, as handsome as the day she had first seen him in that room, while her heart raced in confusion at the sight of him, her pride forced an outward indifference.

For his part, he immediately took in her pale complexion, so unlike her former robust self, giving her an ethereal air, and his concern deepened.

"I was passing through Haddenheath and thought to stop and see you," he said after his initial greeting. Fiona merely nodded, overlooking the prevarication, for the village was not situated on the main road. Aunt Agatha had awoken with a start and Chalmsforth enquired briefly after her health. A few minutes passed in desultory conversation and Chalmsforth, fearing the whole afternoon would pass in like manner, turned to Aunt Agatha and asked directly,

"Would you mind if I have a few words alone with your niece? With your permission, there are some matters I should like to discuss with her."

"Of course," Aunt Agatha arose in a flurry, dropping her knitting from her lap, and Fiona came over to rescue it.

"Please don't move, Aunt. I'm sure Lord Chalmsforth will not be here long. I cannot think of anything he has to say which can make for any lengthy discussion. We can walk out in the sunshine, for I would enjoy the air."

"That would be admirable," he agreed, following her from the room.

"How are you feeling?" he asked as soon as they left the

house. "You look pale. And your face is thinner than it was. You do not seem yourself at all. Is anything wrong?"

"Nothing at all. I think I ate overmuch in London, which may be why I appear thinner now. I feel quite well, I assure you."

"But Neill has said you have not been at all yourself since your return to the abbey," he pursued.

"A temporary indisposition," she assured him, "nothing more."

They continued walking in silence along the path which led to the sloping pastures beyond the cloistered north wing.

"Your brother tells me the abbey has been put up for sale."

"Yes, that is so."

"And whose decision was that, his or yours?"

"Let us say it was a joint decision."

"But how on earth can you sell it after all you have done to save the place? Doesn't it seem ironic to you to sell now that there is no pressing need to do so?"

"But I believe there is a pressing need now. I want to thank you for assisting Neill to purchase a commission in the Tenth Hussars, but you can't for an instant think we can again be in your debt."

"But you are not indebted to me at all," he insisted. "No more is your brother. If I have been able to help him in this instance, it is a matter between the two of us. We agreed it would be so. Why must you insist on the abbey's being sold?"

"Neill has no real interest in keeping the abbey. It is foolish to attempt to hold it. It is in disrepair and every day becomes worse."

"But you know you love the place. It has been shown in everything you have done to save it."

"Whatever I did in the past is done and forgotten," she said curtly.

"Is it?" he asked, scrutinizing her face. "Is it all really forgotten?"

She felt her face flush, remembering again that night at Newlyn's, wondering how much Chalmsforth knew or might have guessed. His next words answered that doubt.

"I saw Newlyn the day you left London."

"Did you?" Her tone was noncommittal.

"He told me everything."

"Everything?" she faltered, unable to look at him.

"Yes." She glanced up and caught the anger in his eyes, which made her reply defensively,

"Then I do not know why you wish to discuss it with me."

"Fiona, why did you do it? Why did you let a rogue like that come near you? You must know the kind of man he is from your own observation, even if you wished to ignore my warnings."

"I don't deny he is detestable, but it is all in the past now."

"And you can shrug it off as easily as that. I assure you it has not been that easy for me to bear. Did you stop to think what you were doing to yourself, to your reputation? Did you hate me so much that you would prefer to ruin yourself rather than owe me something, something for which I cared not at all?"

"I had not thought of it in terms of ruining myself."

"But surely you knew he would not keep quiet. That tongue of his would wag all over London."

"Oh! So it has become the lastest *on-dit*, has it?" she paused. "Does Lady Chalmsforth know of it?"

"No. I succeeded in persuading him not to spread his tale. I doubt that anyone will hear of it, otherwise it will be the worse for him."

"I suppose I should thank you," she said reluctantly.

"There is no need of that, I assure you."

After a pause she asked hesitantly, "Is Newlyn all right?"

"Are you worried about him now? You don't mean to tell me you went to him because he appealed to you." He made no attempt to hide his anger.

"No." She became angry in turn. "I went because he happened to supply the avenue of escape from a situation which I found intolerable."

"Which was?"

"My indebtedness to you. Now I owe you nothing. Whatever happened is past."

"Your indebtedness! As if I cared a fig for that money. You knew I did not."

"That is true," she turned on him fiercely, "but I did. I have my own pride. I did not wish to live my life indebted to you. Whether you acknowledged the debt or not, I was aware of it. At least now I am free."

"But I did not care about it."

"And I did."

"Sobeit," he said quietly. They stood facing one another,

each wanting to talk of matters other than the one under discussion, yet neither daring to say what was nearest to the heart.

"If you have quite finished berating me, I think we might as well return to the house. You have said you are bound for somewhere else."

She turned back, but he caught hold of her arm.

"If you are determined to sell the abbey, then I am determined to buy it. Does that not make you change your mind?" he asked grimly.

"You . . . buy Culross Abbey! Do you not already own enough of England as it is?"

"You do object then?"

The indignation faded slowly from her face.

"How can I? It is for sale on the open market, you may buy it as well as anyone else." Then she added thoughtfully, "You would probably be a good owner after all, for at least you have a sense of history."

He bowed gravely. "I accept the compliment. But tell me, if there were a way for you to keep it, would you not wish to do so?"

"There is no way that is possible," she said firmly. "We will accept financial assistance from no one outside the family, and there is no one within the family who will render it."

"Doesn't your pride strike you as being somewhat short-sighted? You will not let those who wish to do so, help you. You narrow your sources of possible benefit to those whom you are well aware will not aide you, while refusing all other assistance."

"I respect family pride. I hold it to be connected with some of the noblest feelings in our nature. Are you not proud of your own family? Would you consider borrowing money outside it? But it is foolish to ask you, for you have never been confronted with such a situation. Let me assure you that while poverty is awful, the sense of being indebted to others is worse yet."

"I must acknowledge what you say to be true, yet I wish you would allow me to do something for you."

"I thank you," she replied with dignity, "but you have already done much. You were right in securing that commission for Neill. I can see it is what he needed. But now you must see that having taken action—action that has caused me some pain—to clear myself of indebtedness to you, I can incur no further obligations."

He saw they were now approaching the entrance to the abbey and again he took her arm to detain her.

"Fiona. I must confess I have not yet spoken of the true reason behind my visit. I had a question and I must ask it before I leave." He was silent and she looked at him in puzzlement. "I meant to ask you in the beginning, but as happens so often you made me forget my usual orderly manner and say things I had not intended to say while leaving unsaid those uppermost in my mind."

"I'm sorry." She smiled for the first time that afternoon and he thought how lovely she was despite her plain bonnet and wan visage. "Do I really do that?"

Yet still he did not speak and at last she prompted him gently, "Well, what is it you wish to ask me?"

"I wondered . . . I wanted to know whether . . . Will you consent to marry me?"

She caught her breath. The smile faded from her lips and her eyes filled with troubled incredulity.

"Marry you?" she questioned, her pulse quickening, scarcely believing she could have heard aright. "Marry you? But what can be your reason for asking such a thing?"

"I had not expected my proposal to be greeted in quite those terms, though I had wondered how you would receive it."

"I'm sorry. I did not intend to be rude. But you must forgive me, for it was hardly to be expected after all that has passed between us. This afternoon you led me to believe you held me in contempt for my past actions, and then you ask me to marry you. Please don't pretend it is from reasons of affection, for I would find that hard to believe. And we both know I have no money. Now, even my name is tainted, so why in the name of heaven would you suggest I should become your wife?"

"You make it very hard for me to say anything, having disposed of all possible reasons in your eyes, yet what, after all, do you know of my affections?"

"No, sir," she replied quickly, "that will not do. I know enough of them to know they are not engaged in my direction. Were you not to offer for Annabel Telford?"

"That was merely a matter under consideration. I do not believe that she and I would suit."

"And I do not believe that under these circumstances you and I would suit. I have already spoken of my views on marriage. I base them on the marriage of my own parents; perhaps I place my ideals too high, but nevertheless, there it is. You obviously do not love me, so I find your wish to marry me mystifying." She paused briefly. "Do you ask out of consideration that I shall have to move away from my home? If so, your generosity is appealing but misplaced."

"That was not the reason, though it is true I do not wish you to leave. I feel you have never considered me sufficiently to know anything of my affections or where they lie. But be that as it may, I fear this discussion is abhorrent to you and I will discontinue it and never mention it again if you will give me your assurance that you are not . . . in need of a husband."

"In need of a husband?" She looked at him without comprehension. "What can you mean?"

"I mean . . . would it ease your present situation at all if you were married?" He was clearly uncomfortable yet he knew he must have her answer.

"You don't mean you think that I am . . ." She was unable to finish.

"Forgive me if my fears are unjustified. It was simply that Neill has told me how sick you have been since your return from London, and I know that is not like you. I only thought that perhaps after what had occurred with Newlyn that you found yourself in a difficult situation and that perhaps I might be able to relieve you of at least part of your burden." He spoke slowly, with difficulty, as though it hurt him to discuss the matter at all, and she stopped him from going further.

"I assure you that your suspicions are completely unjustified. I don't know exactly what Newlyn told you of all that passed between us, but if you fear that as a result of that evening I . . . I. . . ." She found herself on the point of tears and could not continue.

He grasped her hands. "Fiona, forgive me, but I had to ask, I had to know. I knew you would not confide in me and I could not bear to think you might be alone and in such difficulty." He stopped, then continued hesitantly, "It was not my sole reason for asking you to be my wife."

"I must thank you, though I did not till now realize how far you thought I had fallen."

"Fiona! Fiona! Forgive me. I would not knowingly cause you pain. I only wished to help you."

"I know. I realize that. It's only. . . ." She blinked to keep back the tears. "I must go now. It is cold."

"But what will you do?" he asked, not wanting to part from her.

"Anne Robarts and I are hoping to open a school for girls. Some of the money from the sale of the abbey will be mine—enough, I believe, to suit our purposes. We both have perhaps grandiose ideas that women should be taught just as men are taught and that, given the opportunity, they can use their knowledge to the advantage of all."

"From all I know of you I find nothing grandiose in that expectation. And will that make you happy?"

"I don't know," she replied. "But with Neill and the abbey gone, it will provide a direction for my life."

"Where will it be, your school?"

"In Cambridge, I expect."

He was loathe to part from her and still lingered before the front steps.

Suddenly he remembered something and reaching into his overcoat pocket he drew out a miniature for which she had sat at Lady Chalmsforth's home.

"My mother asked me to give you this. She misses you a great deal."

Fiona took the painting and looked critically at the fashionable face which smiled back at her from the small gilt frame. Had she really been that elegant, calm creature so little time ago?

"I miss your mother also," she said, handing him back the miniature. "I really have no use for my own likeness. I wish your mother would keep it. Please tell her I shall write to her and I hope we shall always be friends. I shall never forget her kindness to me."

He stood before her, making no attempt to leave, and she thought again of his astonishing proposal, suddenly appreciating the fact that he had offered to marry her even though he thought she might bear Newlyn's child, one he would have had to bring up as his own if she were his wife. Newlyn, the man he detested so much that he had said he would never allow any horse he had handled in his stable, yet he had offered to marry her while believing Newlyn had despoiled her. It was an act of such generosity that it could not be overlooked, though she knew not how to acknowledge it properly.

"I am sorry if I appeared ungracious about your . . . offer.

I do appreciate your generosity in . . . in wishing to retrieve me from at least one predicament which I escaped. It was quite a magnificent gesture."

"Perhaps it was not merely generosity which prompted it."

"Well, whatever you wish to call it, it was a gallant act and I shall so remember it always. Now I wish you a pleasant journey, for I must go in."

He could think of no other reason to delay her, so, returning the miniature to his pocket where it remained until he returned to London to put it in a drawer with his handkerchiefs, each day thinking he must take it to his mother but somehow forgetting to do so, he bade her goodbye. "I hope our paths may cross again," he said as he bowed to her.

Fiona smiled. "When you have daughters whom you wish to receive an education instead of a smattering of useless accomplishments, perhaps you will send them to me." Then she turned and walked up the steps and entered the abbey without looking back.

XVIII

By the middle of April, Fiona was able to write to Lady Chalmsforth to announce that they had at last found a house in Cambridge for their school.

"We were so lucky," she wrote. "We had been quite in despair, for all the houses we had seen were much too small or much too expensive. At last the agent showed us one close to Castle Hill which was quite perfect in all respects, in the number and openness of the rooms, in the size of the garden, in all the domestic offices, and all to be had at a reasonable rent, but he doubted that the owner would want to rent it other than as a private residence. He informed us the following day that Mr. Lane, the owner, had adamantly refused to allow its use as a school. I asked whether I might talk to Mr. Lane myself, but he told me it would be to no avail. In this he was wrong, for when Anne and I at last spoke to Mr. Lane, explaining our purpose and assuring him that no damage would be done to his property, he was most reasonable. He invited us to stay for dinner and we talked over the manner in which we planned to use the rooms. He was so kind that he offered to make any alterations we might need and at no cost to us. We were elated.

"Anne, Aunt Agatha, and I are now in residence and liking it very well. We are acquiring extra furnishings which will be needed and, while we have hired some domestic help, we are keeping our staff small until we see how many pupils we may expect. It is our plan to advertise next week after Anne and I have made final decisions on the curriculum.

"We are most fortunate to have the help of a Cambridge tutor, Mr. Hadley, a King's man. He will be joining us to teach Latin and Greek, languages of which I deplore to admit I am totally ignorant and of which Anne feels her knowledge to be too limited, though we feel our French will suffice. We are both anxious that the education we offer to our pupils will be as far as possible like the education a boy of similar years could expect to receive were he enrolled in a similar school. It will be limited on so-called accomplishments but balanced in favour of those subjects which make for an enquiring mind—languages, mathematics, geography, history and, perhaps most particularly, discussions of current events of the world in which we live.

"I do hope you are well, my dear Lady Chalmsforth. I think often of our days together and your many kindnesses to me. They will never be forgotten. I hope that one day you will do us the honour of visiting our school. You will, I hope, not be disappointed."

Lady Chalmsforth gave this letter to her son to read when he called on her the following morning. He read it and handed it back to her without comment.

"I can't help but feel it strange, Peter, that Fiona should choose to slave away in a girls' school when she could have been Lady Elton. She could have practiced her educational ideas on Elton's daughters and lived a life of luxury. And that such beauty should be hidden away in a schoolroom is a shame. I hope she won't waste herself on someone like this young tutor."

Or Mr. Lane, thought Chalmsforth, privately considering that gentleman's intentions. Yet Fiona's enthusiasm was evident and he wished her to make a success of her venture. Therefore the following week when he saw the advertisement for their school in the *Morning Post*, he went to call on his sister-in-law, Kitty.

"This is an honour, Chalmsforth, you come so seldom. I wish you would look in on us more."

"You look well, Kitty. And how is Susan?"

"She is quite well, but she still mopes after Miss Guthrie. I must say she took a great liking to her while she was here. Have you heard anything of her?"

"Actually, apart from seeing how you are, that was one of the reasons for my visit. I noticed in this morning's *Post* that she is opening a girls' school in Cambridge and I wondered whether you might care to enroll Susan. You know she has quite outgrown that governess of hers."

Kitty eyed him sharply. "Oh, dear me, no. I don't approve overmuch of education for girls. Of course, had she been a boy I would have insisted on Eton and Oxford, exactly the same education as you and George received, but schooling for girls is a waste, don't you know. Besides she thinks and reads far too much already. I would rather not encourage it. Miss Dudley is quite satisfactory. If I were to enroll her in any school it would be Miss Bates' in Kensington, for that is where the daughters of most of my friends are enrolled. Mary Castlewick's piano playing has improved so much since she has been there. She is so plain, you know, that she needs all the help she can get. Such is not the case with Susan."

She smiled at Chalmsforth, and he replied as she had hoped,

"But, of course, Kitty, she takes after you, how could it be otherwise. However, I rather think that the rudiments of an education would benefit her, something a little more than she is now getting from Miss Dudley. I also feel she would benefit by a period away from home, being with other girls of her age. She is growing to be a young lady, being with others of like age and experience would enable her to make more friends. She is rather inclined to be shy, you know."

"Since when, Peter dear"—Kitty handed him a glass of sherry and then tapped his hand softly—"have you taken such an interest in Susan? Is it because it is Miss Guthrie's school that you wish Susan to be there?"

Chalmsforth's gaze was direct. "I think Susan would benefit from it. She is my niece, and I would be willing to pay the fees and her clothing allowance and any other expenses she incurs. It is merely a suggestion, nothing more, and you, as her mother, are free to reject it."

Kitty was thoughtful. Whatever Chalmsforth's motives, the financial benefits she would derive could not be overlooked. She could dismiss Miss Dudley, for whom she had never cared, and it was possible that if Chalmsforth were paying the dressmakers' bills he would not care particularly who the gowns were for. Then, quite frankly, Susan was getting so grown that she was beginning to hate to introduce her as her daughter, it made her feel old, though heaven only knew that was hardly the case. And she always felt Newlyn was put off by Susan, who made no attempt to hide her dislike of him. Perhaps he would call more often if she were out of the way.

"Your offer is generous, Peter."

"Well, then, think it over. If you decide, you can take her down and enroll her. I shall reimburse any monies you pay out and you can forward your bills to me."

So it was that the following week Susan and Kitty journeyed to Cambridge, the coach loaded with Susan's boxes and books.

"I don't think you need all these books," her mother had protested. "After all, you're going to school, surely they'll have enough books there."

"But these are my friends, Mother, let me take them with me."

So it was that when Fiona saw the mass of belongings Susan had brought she hoped it would not be so with all the girls, otherwise their closet space would never suffice. But she laughed with delight to see Susan again and was almost as happy as Susan to renew their acquaintance, so much so that Fiona had to remind Susan to kiss her mother good-bye when Kitty was ready to leave.

Susan was their first pupil, but she was shortly followed by Lord Elton's three daughters, together with the daughters of several of his friends, two girls from Cambridge who had been recommended to the school by Mr. Lane, along with four responses to their advertisement in the *Morning Post*.

Classes began in earnest and Fiona found that the days and weeks flew by. At night she was exhausted when she at last reached her bed, tired not only with her own share of the lessons and correcting homework but also with managing the domestic arrangements for such a large group. She tried to keep their expenses to a minimum, but she had not counted on the appetites of growing girls, so that their bills for provisions were far higher than she had anticipated, nor were they able to grow their own supplies to augment those purchases as they had at the abbey. She wondered what was happening with all the apples and pears there. The trees must be full and, could she have borne to look upon the place again, she might have been tempted to go and see whether they were being picked.

Shortly thereafter, several large boxes arrived, filled with this self-same fruit, simply bearing the direction "For the girls of Miss Guthrie's." She knew they must have come from the abbey and wondered whether Chalmsforth had sent them. She had not seen him since he had taken possession of the place and had no idea whether he spent any time there or not. If he did, she thought, he must pass through Cambridge, but of course he would have no reason to call.

In this, however, she was mistaken, for some days later as she was wondering how on earth they could owe the grocer the enormous sum of eight pounds and vowing that she would have to check in all the provisions received herself next time, Lord Chalmsforth was announced.

She greeted him, aware of his elegance contrasting with her plain, even drab attire. She had found it necessary to dress without any adornment and to do her hair in the plainest style, for she had already lost one pupil whose mother had removed her complaining of her husband's too frequent visits to the school. She had no wish to incite jealousy, and she could ill afford to lose any more pupils. But if Chalmsforth noticed her plain appearance he made no comment on it, greeting her with every evidence of pleasure and saying that since he was passing through Cambridge he had decided to break his journey there and wondered whether his niece could dine with him that evening.

"I am staying at the King's Arms. I have arranged for a private parlour. Perhaps you could accompany Susan and dine with us, as a chaperone or as a friend."

"That would be delightful." Fiona smiled. "I know that Susan will be so happy, and in truth I have not dined out since we came here. I shall also enjoy the experience."

"Then I shall expect you at six," he said without further ado. "I shall send my carriage."

Thus that evening Fiona found herself seated across the table from Chalmsforth in an upper parlour at the King's Arms.

"Oh, it's so good, Uncle," said Susan, savouring the sweetmeats which had followed the roast pheasant.

"I'm afraid the girls find our fare rather Spartan," said Fiona. "We really have little to spend on luxuries and I am sometimes at my wits end to make sure that they have enough to eat. I know that most of them are used to much more luxurious food than we can afford, but they bear with our restricted diet very well."

"Oh, Miss Guthrie"—Susan's face was stricken—"I in no way meant to infer I did not enjoy what we have at school, I do, I love everything about school."

"I know that was not your intention, Susan. You are one of my star pupils. You should be proud of your niece, Lord Chalmsforth, her intelligence at times astounds me."

"I expect you say that to all the visiting relatives," Chalmsforth said with a grin.

"No, that is not so." Fiona smiled back at him. "Only to those who are deserving of it."

"You see, Uncle, I am really trying hard, for I want to learn. And I doubt Miss Guthrie can say that to Lord Elton, for though I know Mary likes her lessons, Katy and Maud really hate anything unless it is dancing or playing the piano, and that, they complain, is always out of tune."

"I think they are probably perfectly right, Susan. I had that piano when I was little and I must confess I never practised as I should, so years of disuse after my mother died have undoubtedly taken their toll on the instrument. Mr. Cardwell says there is little he can do."

"Does Elton come often?" Chalmsforth interceded casually.

"Oh, he's always calling to see his daughters," Susan prattled. "I became quite jealous for no one came to see me until today. And he's always bringing things for them or for the school."

"How very generous of him!" Chalmsforth's eyes mocked Fiona, who hastened to assure him, "Lord Elton's estate is in Lincolnshire, so of course Cambridge is directly on his road. Since he has all three of his daughters enrolled, it is only natural that he should wish to see them."

"Of course," he replied. "It is just that I hadn't realized until now that Elton took such an interest in their education."

"Oh, but he does," she assured him. "He often brings books he feels will augment our curriculum and is most helpful in every way."

"I don't doubt it," said Chalmsforth in such a wry tone that Fiona would have protested its implication had Susan not been present. However, she changed the subject to ask him about his own days at Eton and soon had him regaling them with tales of his exploits which amused them all, himself included.

"You surprise me," said Fiona, still laughing over the vision Chalmsforth had just conjured up of a highly pompous tutor being doused by a tub of very cold water while he, who had administered the dousing from the chapel tower, became hopelessly enmeshed in the bell pulls. "I would have thought you to have always been a very quiet, obedient boy. It seems you did not always have the same sense of decorum we see today."

"I assure you, if I appear decorous it is only because I rarely find life amusing, unlike this evening when you have brought back memories even I thought to have forgotten."

"We enjoyed it also, I can't say how much. But now we really must leave. The girls have to be in bed by ten and Susan probably has matters to attend to first."

"Oh, can't I do my homework in the morning? This is such a special evening," Susan pleaded.

"Even so," Fiona reminded her gently, "did you realize that it is now after nine? By the time we get back there will be little time for anything, so your homework will undoubtedly have to be left till the morning."

Chalmsforth arose. "I shall see both of you back. And don't look so sad, Susan. I shall come again soon, I promise. I often pass this way and I have thought to stop before but I doubted. . . ." He looked at Fiona without completing that doubt. "I shall be in Cambridge next Thursday. Would that be too soon for us to repeat this adventure?" Fiona found two pairs of eyes fixed upon her, one beseechingly, the other earnestly.

"I would also enjoy it," she admitted. "So we shall say till next Thursday then."

Thus began an almost weekly ritual of dining with Chalmsforth at the King's Arms. He punctiliously adhered to the school rules, always seeing that they were back before ten, though often he inwardly chafed at this restriction, enjoying their company so much and not wishing the evening to end. It was certain that his niece shared his opinion, and though Fiona said little openly, the fact that she continued to join them week after week bespoke her own pleasure. She came to look forward to his visits almost more than did his niece, for Susan sometimes felt that the grown-ups talked so much together she had difficulty to get a word into the conversation. When the weather was warm, they eschewed his carriage to stroll along the Backs, which bordered the colleges on the banks of the Cam, Fiona and Chalmsforth strolling with the gentle flow of the river while Susan ran ahead. The beauty of the scene even made Chalmsforth admit at times he wished he had been a Cambridge man.

Some weeks after Chalmsforth's first visit, a new piano was delivered at the school.

"There must be some mistake," Fiona protested to the carter who had carried it from London. "I did not order this instrument."

"I assure you, mum, it is addressed 'ere and I'm not going

to carry it back to town. Weighs a ton, it does. The 'orses'd never last. They're wore out enough as it is."

"But how can I accept something which I have not ordered and for which I am unable to pay?"

"That is your concern," said the carter, mopping his brow with a large red kerchief. "I was told to deliver it 'ere and deliver it 'ere I will. You are Miss Guthrie, aren't you?"

"Yes, I am."

"Well, then, it's for you right enough. Now I'm going to need at least another couple of men to 'elp me get it 'ere inside."

The piano, made of mahogany, was clear and resonant in tone. The girls gathered around in excitement, anxious to try it. Despite the rigours of the journey, it was still in tune.

"Oh, what delight!" said Maud. "Now I can really practice my Chopin étude."

"But don't forget this is my afternoon to practice," said her sister. "Yours is tomorrow."

"Oh, bother!"

By the time Chalmsforth next called, the piano had become a fixture of the school, though that did not prevent Fiona from accosting him,

"It is a gift from you, is it not? It has to be, for I know of no one else who might have sent it. I had thought it might have been Lord Elton, but he assures me it is not so."

"He's called again, then?" Chalmsforth challenged.

"He stopped in briefly on Tuesday, soon after it was delivered, as a matter of fact. That is why I thought it must be from him."

"He was probably sorry he had not thought of it." Chalmsforth grinned boyishly, while Fiona flushed, for those had been Elton's exact words.

"Anyway, you know I cannot accept it as a gift either from you or Elton."

"I know, I know. But you see, strictly speaking this is not from me. It is a gift to the school from Susan. It is not unusual for pupils to donate to an institution from which they have derived particular benefit."

"It is not unusual to do so in later years, but hardly while they are still in attendance."

"I find that an extremely silly rule, for why should not Susan enjoy the benefits of her gift just as much as girls who will come after her?"

Fiona could think of no plausible reply and she knew that any attempt to remove the piano now that the girls had used it and had been able to compare its tone with that of the old one would produce a small rebellion.

"I shall have to accede in this instance, but I must insist on no more expensive gifts to the school. It places me in a difficult position."

"I am well aware of your scruples and you may trust me not to trample upon them," he assured her gravely. "Now I hope you are not going to hold this against me and refuse to dine with me tonight—and Susan, of course," he added as an afterthought.

Fiona realized how little able she was to refuse him; she had come to rely on his presence, often unburdening her problems upon him while Susan sat curled up in a chair engrossed in some book or puzzle her uncle had brought for her. Though Anne was always at hand, it had not escaped Fiona's attention that a growing interest had developed between her friend and Mr. Hadley, and she had no wish to break into this spell with mundane affairs that at times weighed heavily upon her. Chalmsforth, on the other hand, would listen in that pensive way she knew, often able to resolve a difficulty by simply seeing through the morass of detail in which she had become entangled. Nothing was beneath his notice, so that she could speak to him with equal intensity on Maud's inattention in her geography lesson or the fact that all of the school wash had been sent to King's College by mistake and a set of gentlemen's garments had been received in its stead, an amusing incident in itself, but not so when there were ten girls demanding their clothing. Fiona was aware of how much she waited for Chalmsforth's coming, often savouring little incidents that occurred, the retelling of which she knew would amuse him. She did not ask him why he came through Cambridge so often. She presumed he must often visit the abbey, but they never spoke of it. Anne heard from her father that much work was being done there, but the realization that anything done to it would make it other than the place Fiona had always known as home made her avoid any reference to it in her conversation, and Chalmsforth made no attempt to discuss it with her, keeping always to topics that concerned their present relationship, never speaking of London friends, rarely even mentioning his mother.

But Fiona continued to write to Lady Chalmsforth, and it

was from Fiona that his mother learned of Chalmsforth's frequent visits to the school.

"I do wish you would take me with you some time," his mother complained the next time she saw him, but strangely enough her son did not even want his mother included in his weekly visits to Cambridge. It was a part of his life which belonged to himself alone and one other, for he now made no pretence to himself that he called to see his niece, knowing it was Fiona who drew him there. He had, however, become very fond of Susan, noting the changes in her since she had been in Fiona's care, and he was gratified at the fine young woman his brother's child was soon to become. In her looks she continued to resemble her mother, but her character and mind were so far superior to Kitty's that it was in aspect only that their resemblance lay.

Following the incident of the piano, Susan gave Chalmsforth a small volume as a gift from the school. It was Dodsley's first printing of Gray's "Elegy written in a Country Church-yard," which Fiona had obtained from an elderly resident of Cambridge who had known Gray during his days there. It was to Fiona that Chalmsforth conveyed his delight, though he thanked the girls by sending from London a box of Gunther's bonbons, a token which gratified their sweet tooth though not nearly as much as Chalmsforth's smile had warmed Fiona's heart.

One Thursday, when Chalmsforth was expected, Fiona was surprised to find Kitty ushered into her study.

"Mrs. Chalmsforth, this is a pleasure!" she exclaimed, in greeting her guest. "I had not known you were coming. You will, no doubt, wish to see Susan."

"Yes, Miss Guthrie, and if you don't mind I wish to see her alone."

"Of course," Fiona responded, puzzled at Kitty's impatient tone. She could think of nothing that had occurred that might have incurred her displeasure. "Susan is doing very well in school. We are all proud of her."

"Yes, yes," Kitty replied without interest. "But you must know it was not my inclination to send her here, but Chalmsforth's. He was quite set on it. I don't hold with overeducating girls and filling their minds with things that don't concern them. However, since he is paying the bills, I consented to give it a trial."

Fiona might have argued with Kitty's premise had she not

been so astounded to learn it was Chalmsforth who had enrolled his niece in her school, but she could ask no questions
for Kitty tapped her foot imperiously.

"I have little time to spend here. I had intended to write to
Susan and had I remembered how long and boring the journey here was I should certainly have done so. As it is, since I
am now here, would you send her to me immediately so I
may return to London before it is quite nightfall?"

"Of course, please excuse my delay."

Kitty left after seeing Susan, with no further word to
Fiona, but when Fiona reentered her study some time later it
was to find Susan sitting in her large armchair, dissolved in
tears.

"What's wrong?" she asked, hurrying to put her arms
around the girl's slender, shaking shoulders and holding her
close. She stroked her hair and murmured, "Don't say anything for a while. Cry as much as you want to."

Her soft words and gentle manner at first made Susan cry
more freely, but at last she lifted her tear-stained face to
Fiona to say,

"It's my mother. She . . . she's to marry again."

"Well, Susan, that's not so bad. Your mother is still young
and very attractive, so that it is only natural that she should
one day marry again. Besides, you will be gaining a father.
Even though he is not your natural father, it will be someone
who will stand in his stead."

"No, he can't," Susan cried. "This man can never stand in
place of my father. I hate him! Mother is to marry the Earl
of Newlyn."

XIX

Newlyn had stayed away from London for over a month, a fact that did not go unnoticed at the height of the season. Although it was known that both he and Fiona had quit the scene at the same time, since they had gone in different directions their names were not linked together.

During the time Newlyn spent in Wiltshire he had had occasion to reflect on the brevity of life. The attack on him by Fiona, minor though the wound had been, and the threats of Chalmsforth caused him to consider that had either of these proved fatal he would have had to leave this world with no heir of his own to take his title or his estate. All would have passed to a distant cousin, Reginald Percy, whom he considered a simpering, prating fool. The thought that Percy would recline in his bed, enjoy the comforts of his house on Albemarle Street, and be referred to by the world as Newlyn was more than he could stand. He therefore decided that when he returned to London it would be with the purpose of matrimony, much though he preferred his single state.

He ran through the list of women he knew. The woman he chose must have noble blood in her veins, an agreeable disposition yet with some passion, must be understanding of his own wandering eye, and, of course, must possess money. It was, thus, that he decided on Kitty Chalmsforth as meeting all these criteria, for she had not only a fortune in her own right but had inherited from her husband on his death. She was a good hostess and she was by no means indifferent to him.

Thus, he hurried to press his suit on his return and, as he had surmised, it was well received. The only deterrent to the ceremony was that Chalmsforth refused to attend the wedding. He also assiduously avoided him whenever possible, refusing invitations at which he knew Newlyn would be present or, if refusal was impossible, he would bow distantly and leave soon after. Newlyn was not sorry at Chalmsforth's displeasure over the match. He had no wish to satisfy him, but he was galled that the frequent snubs which Chalmsforth administered did not escape society's notice and he would have preferred a more amicable arrangement.

Soon after his marriage, it came to Newlyn's attention that Susan was enrolled in Fiona's school at Chalmsforth's request, that he was, in fact, paying her expenses there. In this he saw a means of frustrating Chalmsforth's wishes.

"As her stepfather, I really cannot allow such an arrangement to continue, my dear," he told Kitty.

"But he has really been most generous. I assure you he does not quibble at any of the dress bills I send over. And I really don't think Susan should come back now. It is better that we be alone. You know that she was not always as polite to you as she should have been. I often talked to her of it."

"That's as may be, but I expect she will soon come around. After all, I am head of the house now, not a visitor. That position alone should command her respect. No, I cannot go on allowing Chalmsforth to pay something which is not his by right of law. Nor am I convinced that Miss Guthrie is the person she can benefit from."

"Why ever not?" his wife asked curiously.

"I have reason to believe her reputation leaves something to be desired."

"Why, I never heard anything of the kind. Do tell!"

Newlyn was not anxious to pursue this subject and said rather brusquely, "Apart from that, I think that in your condition it would be as well to have Susan here. You need to have someone around to read to you and whatever."

"No one but you, my love, you are all I need."

Newlyn had not expected his wife to have the possessive streak she was displaying, especially now she was with child. It annoyed him to feel tied to her, to anyone for that matter. If Susan were at home he could come and go more freely, perhaps without the constant catechism he now had to endure. So he was insistent.

"As master of the house, I think it is best that she is with us. I think only of you, my dear, and your health. You know you are precious to me. I shall go to Cambridge tomorrow and bring her back."

Thus it was the following day that, much to Fiona's dismay, Newlyn was ushered into her study. She had wished never to see him again after that night, but following her initial shock, she attempted to be as polite as the situation demanded. Newlyn, however, had forgotten nothing and was not of like mind.

"A new occupation for the card sharp, I see. Pray, how are the girls coming along with their piquet?"

"Oh, our curriculum is broad, but it does not yet include piquet, though I don't doubt much could be learned by its study."

"Well, I learned much from you, that is certain." He took in the plainness and drabness of her attire and her severe hair style. "Quite the little schoolmistress now, I see. Is that the way Chalmsforth likes you? I thought he had a better eye for women than that."

She flushed and ignored his insinuation. "To what, pray, do I owe the pleasure of this visit?"

"Pleasure? It is a pleasure, then?"

"Well, I understand that you are now Susan's stepfather. Allow me to congratulate you on your marriage."

"Just so. It is about Susan that I have come. I wish to take her back to London with me."

"But you can't." Fiona gasped. "The term is not yet over. She is doing so well here. I hope you will read some of her essays. Pray do not take her away unless there is some pressing reason for it."

"There is a pressing reason. It is my desire that she reside in her own home, and her mother's also. Susan's wishes do not concern us; it is we, or I may say, I, who make the decisions."

"But I understand that it is Lord Chalmsforth who has enrolled her here and pays her tuition."

"He is not her guardian and has no say in her affairs. If it suited him to have her here, undoubtedly he had other motives." He smiled as he slowly ran his eyes over her. "Even though you look much plainer than formerly, that is not to say you are less warm-blooded."

"I cannot allow you to take Susan. Only her mother can do that," Fiona insisted, ignoring his insinuations.

"So, you don't wish me to take her. If I were to oblige you, what would you give me in return?"

Instinctively, she retreated toward her desk, wishing to put it between them. He glanced sharply at the desk top as she did so.

"I trust you have no sharp letter openers with which to accost me this time."

Even though she feared him and he repulsed her, Fiona shuddered at the thought of ever using a weapon on him again.

"I suggest you not repeat your conduct then. Keep your distance or I shall summon aid."

"And what aid would there be in a girls' school? Don't tell me that my stepdaughter is living in a house under the same roof with unknown persons of the opposite gender? That would hardly do. I'm sure Elton would not have his daughters here if that were the case. For my part, I saw no one but the old gardener, and he is well out of earshot. Anyway, I warrant he is deaf. Now if you made a fuss, your precious charges would come running only to find us making love. Would you like that? Educational it might be, I understand you have advanced ideas, but not that advanced I'll be bound. By nightfall you would hardly have a pupil left. Only consider."

He had walked over to her while he talked and now he took her hands, though she tried to prevent it. The truth of his remarks struck her forcibly. Any effort she made to draw attention to her plight could only bring discredit on herself and the school.

"Perhaps I spoke hastily just now. Please, let us sit down and discuss the matter. Let me get you a glass of wine. You have had a long journey," she reasoned.

"I will accept your offer, but not now, later. For the moment we have some unfinished business." He laughed softly, pulling her to him.

"You cannot behave this way. Please, I beg of you." Yet he showed no sign of desisting and she added bitterly, "If you take advantage of me, I assure you it will be the worse for you."

"Why?" he laughed. "Why should it matter one jot? You're little better than a governess now, a governess in trade, which is even lower in esteem. Don't try to make a high and mighty lady of yourself. And who is to make me make amends? Your brother, I know, is gone and Chalmsforth is unlikely to call me out to a duel again as he so stupidly did before, not now that I'm married to his brother's widow and she with child. No, society would never stand for that."

His encircling arms pulled her, forcing her body against

his. The more she struggled to free herself, the tighter his grasp became until she could scarcely breathe and stood a prisoner of his hold.

"Come, Fiona. You are a firebrand, but I've plenty of time, though I wouldn't want you to tire yourself and enjoy the loving less."

"It is despicable to talk of loving," she spat at him. "I hate you!"

"Let me see if I can't rectify that." He brought his mouth down on hers swiftly, harshly, bruising her lips which she kept tightly closed to guard against his invading tongue. Then he ran his hands down her body, tearing at her dress. She felt his fingers clawing at her breast and heard him grunt with satisfaction. In desperation, she kicked at his shins, but in response he dragged her, pulling her down to the floor.

Forgetting all her previous scruples of being found, involuntarily she tried to scream for help, but to no avail for his mouth covered hers, gagging her. She felt him pulling at her skirts and forcing his knee between her legs and her struggle became more furious, yet she could feel him against her and thought he must surely have his way, when she heard a man's voice at hand.

"Miss Guthrie! Miss Guthrie! What in the name of heaven!"

Arthur Hadley stood in the midst of the room, his dark expression matching his dark clerical attire to express the horror of the scene before him. Newlyn rose swiftly, adjusting his clothing as he turned away. Fiona pulled her torn dress to her and, barely able to speak, ran from the room, trusting she would see no one in the hall, to seek the safety of her room, where she removed her tattered garment and took water and washed herself in an effort to remove every trace of Newlyn's touch.

Shortly thereafter Anne came to her, Mr. Hadley having informed her of the contretemps. She assured her that Newlyn had left.

"Did he take Susan with him?" Fiona asked quickly.

"No." Anne's expression was sad. "But he said that he and his wife will come for her next week. He said that if any attempt is made to prevent them from removing her he will see that the school is closed forever. Oh, Fiona, he is such an evil man. I feel as much as you do that Susan should not be exposed to him, but we have no right to detain her."

"I know we have no legal right, only a moral one. Something must be done. The man is a monster. It is wrong for her to be in the same house with him now she is growing into such a beautiful young lady, yet it is impossible to explain that to her mother."

Resting her head on her hands, Fiona thought instantly of Chalmsforth. If anyone could do anything, he could. She had been amazed to learn that he had sought to duel with Newlyn over her. She would not have thought it possible. Newlyn was right, Chalmsforth could never call him out again, and for that she was grateful for it would solve nothing. He would know, though, what should be done. She felt suddenly lighthearted. It seemed natural to turn to him in this instance for he was Susan's uncle, though she realized even if he had not been so directly involved it would have seemed natural to turn to him anyway.

"Please, Anne, bring me my writing materials. There is a letter that must be despatched immediately, then I'll be down for my geography lesson."

"I'll take that for you, Fiona. You must rest after that ordeal."

"No. It is far better that I am busy rather than here thinking of it. And, in the event anything had been noticed, I would prefer to appear as usual. I cannot have the girls terrified of being preyed upon by such creatures. Oh, that we had the means to protect ourselves!"

"But we don't, being of inferior strength. If a man behaves without any compunction, as did Lord Newlyn, we have no recourse."

"Our only recourse is our wits. Looking back now, I can see that I could have prevented the situation by never allowing myself ever to be alone in a room with a man I knew to be completely untrustworthy. I can assure you that will never happen again."

Chalmsforth, when he received Fiona's letter, was alarmed to learn that Newlyn had visited her though she gave only the barest outline of that visit, excluding his discreditable conduct and concentrating instead on Newlyn's determination to remove Susan from Cambridge. He would, she wrote, be the worst possible influence upon the child and though she said no more, Chalmsforth wholeheartedly agreed with her. He was, however, in a quandary for he had no legal claim upon his niece and he knew that Kitty would undoubtedly do as her husband instructed her. To plead with Newlyn would be to no avail, not as matters stood between them. It was a predicament which kept him awake late into the night.

The following day he deliberately allowed his path to cross Newlyn's by going to White's, a club he had avoided for some months, at an hour that he knew Newlyn to frequent it.

"Hello, old chap, surprised to see you here," Newlyn greeted him in response to his half smile of acknowledgement. Newlyn felt that even this slight token indicated that Chalmsforth recognized he was not to be trifled with.

"Oh, I felt bored," Chalmsforth replied nonchalantly. "I was looking for a little *divertissement*, but I see there's not much to be found here. I was about to leave."

"So am I." Newlyn was pleased that it was noted that Chalmsforth was conversing with him in amiable fashion and he determined to take advantage of it. "I'll walk with you. Which way are you going?"

"Back to Grosvenor Square, I think." Chalmsforth was pensive for a moment and suddenly extended his hand. "I think I've been rather remiss since you married Kitty. I apologize. I should have congratulated you earlier, but anyway, I do so now."

"Thank you, Chalmsforth." Newlyn was even more pleased that it was Chalmsforth who extended his hand in front of the assembled company. "You know, there is a little matter I would like to discuss with you, perhaps we could do so while we walk. It concerns Susan, Kitty's daughter."

"Oh." Chalmsforth gave no indication in either his face or voice that he was most vitally interested in discussing the very same matter, and Newlyn decided he could know nothing of his visit to Cambridge, or he would never be so composed otherwise.

"I understand from Kitty that you have put her in school in Cambridge, but she is needed at home. Kitty is in the family way and it would be well if she were at hand."

"Well, certainly, if Kitty wants her to leave I can see no great problem. Withdraw her by all means."

Newlyn breathed a sigh of relief to himself. He had never expected it would be that easy. Well, that would show the little hussy. At least Chalmsforth knew where the law lay and, apart from that, he was being entirely reasonable. Probably he didn't care for Fiona Guthrie anyway now that she was so plain and dowdy.

"That is exactly what I thought to do myself, only it seems that some people have different ideas."

"And who could that be?"

"Miss Guthrie. She seems to think you should release her from her charge. It is altogether quite ridiculous. I tried to reason with her, but she was adamant."

"Well, if that's what she thinks, have her write to me, Newlyn. Better still, I'll write myself to set the matter straight." Chalmsforth caught Newlyn's smirk of satisfaction and he went on, still intent on disguising his overeagerness,

"I say, Newlyn, are you doing anything for dinner? I just don't feel like eating alone. Would you care to join me to show that bygones are bygones?"

Newlyn was delighted. He felt suddenly secure in his new position with Chalmsforth, if not directly related then related through marriage. Chalmsforth's attention flattered him after all the rebukes he had administered to him in the past. If he had been in the least surprised, in the beginning, at Chalmsforth's changed attitude, his own good opinion of himself soon outweighed any suspicions that might have arisen. Dinner with Chalmsforth was much preferable to dinner with Kitty. She was pestering him not to bring Susan back and he preferred to avoid her until her daughter was safely under their roof. With Chalmsforth on his side, he would have no trouble now. A note would suffice, though perhaps he would go down again. He would like to see Fiona's face in defeat. Also, this invitation gave him the opportunity to discover for himself whether Chalmsforth's port was really as superior as others had maintained.

An hour later saw them seated across from one another in the large dining room at Grosvenor Square over that very same port which was proving to be every bit as flavourful and aromatic as had been predicted. It was Newlyn, feeling relaxed and secure in his new relationship with Chalmsforth, convinced he knew nothing of what had occurred in Cambridge, who again broached the subject of Fiona.

"I must say I was surprised to find Miss Guthrie had taken to the schoolroom now."

"Yes. I have visited Susan there once or twice. From what I observe, Miss Guthrie seems to be enjoying her new life well enough. It is probably what she wanted all along." Chalmsforth carefully maintained his casual pose, for though he intensely disliked discussing Fiona with Newlyn, yet it was essential to preserve his guest's self-complacency if he were to bring his scheme to a satisfactory conclusion.

"Oh, I don't know about that. You know, one can never tell with women. Mustn't let that calm exterior deceive you."

"Really." Try as he might, Chalmsforth could not keep the edge from his voice, but Newlyn, sipping his port, failed to notice.

"Yes," he said confidently, as though taking Chalmsforth into his confidence. "It's my opinion she wants what all women want."

"Did something occur when you saw her to give you that opinion?" There was now no mistaking the steely tone and Newlyn forbore to press the subject further.

"No, no, of course not, just intuition, that's all, the way she looks at you, that sort of thing. Nothing really. I say, Chalmsforth, what do you say to a game of cards? I don't believe I've played with you. I suspect you play a good game of piquet."

"Not really my game, Newlyn," said Chalmsforth, rising, secretly delighted that Newlyn had, himself, suggested it. "But I wouldn't mind a game or two to pass away the evening."

"You name the odds, then."

"What say to ten pounds a point?"

Chalmsforth noticed the odd look Newlyn gave him and wondered at its meaning. "Not too steep for you, I hope?"

"No, indeed, why not make it twenty while we're about it."

Chalmsforth whistled slightly, but nodded his agreement.

Play began and despite Newlyn's attempts to allow Chalmsforth initially to win, he lost the first four hands in rapid succession.

"You're right, Chalmsforth, this isn't your game," Newlyn smiled as he gathered the cards together. "But I daresay you'll improve. Have you played much?"

"No, it's been some while, but truth to tell I find it quite fascinating and I think I'm beginning to remember it. Let's continue, double the odds again, if you're agreeable."

They played on, Chalmsforth winning a hand occasionally, but Newlyn maintaining a heavy lead. By midnight he was a hundred and ninety points ahead and he was wondering whether he should carry it any farther when Chalmsforth suddenly began to win.

"You seem to be catching on quite well now," Newlyn said edgily after Chalmsforth had taken two rubbers.

"Yes, I find it's coming back to me," Chalmsforth replied languidly.

"Yet you don't play much?"

"Scarcely at all. Cards just don't appeal to me as a rule, though I'm enjoying the game tonight."

"I thought perhaps Miss Guthrie had been giving you some lessons."

"What made you think that?" Chalmsforth tried to keep his awakened interest from his voice.

"Well, she fleeced me. And at this very game. Then she had the indecency to turn around and wield a knife, wounding me in the back." Seeing Chalmsforth's look of amazement, he went on, "I know, you can scarcely credit it, but I assure you it was so, she actually knifed me after winning some seven thousand from me. As you must guess, I have little regard for her. In some ways, I feel she acts more like a man in the way she thinks. Even her strength is amazing for one of her size."

Chalmsforth longed to press him further, but he did not want him to know the astonishment his revelations had caused. So she had won the money at cards! The relief and yet the inward recriminations he felt were enormous, but he was not yet finished with Newlyn and casually he refilled his glass.

"From what you say I should have apologized to you on her behalf the last morning I saw you instead of giving you a facer. That a guest of my mother's should have actually raised a weapon to you is preposterous. How is your shoulder, by the way?"

"Oh, the wound wasn't too deep, thank goodness, though I didn't know it at the time. It hurt like blazes, let me tell you."

"I wonder what could have possessed her to strike at you after winning that way." Chalmsforth studied his cards carefully.

"Well, she sat there tantalizing me all evening and then was unwilling to give me so much as a kiss in return. It was at her suggestion we played. Surely she must have known that by going unaccompanied to a man's house she would be expected to put out a bit."

"I fear Miss Guthrie is not too worldly."

"She may not be worldly, but she's astute enough."

"I think it is my lead," said Chalmsforth, and proceeded with amazing alacrity to take the next four hands.

"Let's see," he looked down at the score. "I think you're down twenty-eight thousand now. I'm getting tired, what about you?"

"It's not fair to quit when you're ahead," Newlyn protested.

"You're quite right," Chalmsforth agreed, taking up the cards and dealing again. "Your lead."

Within a surprisingly short space of time Newlyn was down over forty thousand pounds. He couldn't believe it. He looked with hatred and suspicion at Chalmsforth.

"This may not previously have been your game, but it certainly is your game tonight."

"It does seem so," Chalmsforth replied smoothly. "Suppose we have another hand, and since I am so much ahead I will allow two to one odds in your favour. It will allow you a chance to get even."

Newlyn jumped at the chance, but far from recouping his losses he was soon in debt to the tune of some seventy thousand. It was impossible, and to make matters worse, he was not quite sure how it had happened. It was he who had named the odds, but he had not foreseen such disastrous consequences. He remembered he had led for the first part of the game and now he stared at Chalmsforth with outright loathing.

"You deliberately led me into this, didn't you?"

"What do you mean?"

"Claiming not to know the game. No one could play as you have played those last hands without knowing it inside out."

"I said I didn't play much, not that I didn't know it," Chalmsforth replied evenly. "I used to play quite a bit when I was in the army, though not for such high stakes I must admit. I believe, however, it was you who suggested them."

"You realize I'll have to sell my Wiltshire estate to raise such a sum. Kitty's property alone won't do it."

"Such a pity." Chalmsforth took a pinch of snuff. "Especially in view of the heir on the way. Of course, we might arrange some other means of recompense."

"And what might that be?" Newlyn was antagonistic, but interested.

"I should like to be Susan's legal guardian."

"So that's it! I might have guessed. Little Miss Guthrie got to you after all. The jade!"

Chalmsforth dropped all pretense of civility.

"I suggest you don't talk of Miss Guthrie in those tones now, or ever again. I also suggest you keep your distance from her in the future. If I hear of your visiting Cambridge again, you'll have me to answer to, I want that clearly understood. I have given you your choice. You can sell your estates or give up Susan. I know Kitty will be only too willing to do so, so it is your decision. Settle your debt as you will."

"You know damned well I don't want to sell out."

"Then allow me to become Susan's guardian."

"Very well." Newlyn rose in fury, realizing he was beaten. "I might have known your proffered olive branch would turn into a bramble bush."

As he strode from the room Chalmsforth called after him, "I shall expect some notification from Kitty's solicitor in the morning apprising me that action has begun in this matter, or else I shall not hesitate to broadcast the amount of your indebtedness to me. I'm afraid the size of the debt may cause some of your other creditors to grow rather anxious, especially since they well know debts of honour must be paid first."

"You and Miss Guthrie make a good pair, both bloody card sharps!"

As Newlyn slammed the door shut, Chalmsforth went over to the writing table and pulled out Fiona's note, which he had placed between the leaves of the book he was reading. It was strange that Newlyn, of all people, should concur in what he had always thought, that he and Fiona would make a good pair.

XX

As soon as Chalmsforth received the advice he sought concerning his niece from Kitty's solicitor, he hastened to Cambridge with the news, his heart full of his findings of the previous evening—Newlyn's disclosure that Fiona had gained the money to repay him by winning at piquet rather than as Newlyn had previously intimated. His earlier conversation on the subject with Fiona distressed him, even embarrassed him, though his embarrassment was greatly exceeded by his desire to see her. As he drove he imagined what he would say and how she would reply. The more he thought over the matter, the more he realized its insignificance; he made the startling discovery that he did not really care what Fiona might have been forced to do, he loved her despite anything. She had been right in her assertion that where there was true love nothing else mattered, and he knew it was this that he wanted most to tell her, yet all his plans were for nought, for when he reached Cambridge it was to discover that Fiona had left earlier in the day to accompany home one of the girls who had contracted measles and she was not expected to return until late the following day.

"But surely she should consider her own health," he worried.

"I agree, for she was most fatigued before the journey began," Anne told him, "but she was afraid that we would have a house full of stricken girls. There was really no way of isolating Eleanor, so Fiona felt it best to conduct her home immediately. I assure you that Eleanor was quite well enough to travel."

"It is not Eleanor who concerns me, Miss Robarts, but Miss Guthrie. Surely it is dangerous for her to be exposed."

"She was not worried about the danger, for she believes she had the disease when she was very young. Her concern was all for the others. Yet she was loathe to leave because of Susan. She has been daily in dread that they would send for her."

"It is on the matter of my niece I wished to speak to her. But now it must wait for her return. Please give her this and tell her I shall call on Friday morning."

He handed her a small box in which he had put the gold broach that Fiona had returned to him with the money. Tucked inside the wreath of thistles were three ears of corn tied with straw in the form of a true lover's knot, a symbol of his pledged troth. Now it only remained to be seen whether Fiona would be wearing it when he returned on Friday.

Miss Robarts, Chalmsforth thought as he drove on to Culross, was rather less acute than usual, in fact she had appeared to be quite absentminded and her colour was bright. He wondered if she were coming down with the measles, but when he arrived at Haddenheath and called in to see how Mr. Robarts was faring, he discovered that it was not measles that ailed Miss Robarts, but love.

"I couldn't be more pleased, Lord Chalmsforth, for Anne is to be the wife of Arthur Hadley. You must, undoubtedly, have met him. Apart from instructing Miss Guthrie's pupils in Latin and Greek, he is also a tutor at King's. Now, it seems, he has been offered a living in the north of England, not a handsome stipend, but nevertheless it will provide a satisfactory income, enough for him to marry on. He is anxious that Anne should accompany him when he leaves. I'm afraid it all makes for rather a rush."

"But what about Miss Guthrie?"

"That's it, to be sure. It was the first thought that occurred to Anne and she was determined to wait and join Arthur later, but Miss Guthrie would not hear of it. I believe she has already advertised in the London papers and hopes to find someone suitable soon. I fear the girls have had rather a time of it making ends meet as it is, so I don't know what kind of salary she will be able to offer. It may make it difficult for her."

"Miss Guthrie has never mentioned her difficulties to me," Chalmsforth protested.

"Miss Guthrie was never one to complain. She always sets to and one way or another gets things done no matter what difficulty it may entail. A wonderful woman, so like her dear mother."

Chalmsforth agreed with such fervour that Mr. Robarts could not help but wonder whether another wedding might not be in the offing.

Before he left, Chalmsforth extracted a promise from Mr. Robarts that the wedding, fixed for the following week, should be followed by a wedding breakfast at the abbey. It would, Chalmsforth realized, be the first time that Fiona had seen it, and he was anxious that she should, for its restoration had been the matter of his major concern for some months. The lawns surrounding the abbey were now plush and green with the abbey itself standing out like a rock in the midst of the neatly clipped verdure. As Chalmsforth crossed the hall with its glowing stone flags covered with thick oriental rugs, the walls adorned with Guthrie portraits he had at great expense reclaimed, he wondered what Fiona would say. He entered the great library to see that Nicholson, already proving as invaluable as Trevor had been, had sent the volumes he had acquired, many of which had originated there, for the glass-covered bookcases were now filled. A fire burned brightly, casting bright lights and shadows on the bust of Robert Burns which rested on the high mantle. As Chalmsforth sat down he wished, as he so often did, that Fiona were there to share the warmth and comfort. Now that she had turned to him in the matter of Susan, he was sure that she trusted him. When he saw her on Friday, if she wore the broach he would know she wished to be his wife.

By Friday, however, Chalmsforth was to find himself astonishingly and distressfully engaged in marriage to another.

In London, Newlyn fumed at his loss. His temper was not assuaged by Kitty's greeting with pleasure the news of Chalmsforth's desire to become Susan's guardian; it would solidify their own family, she maintained, and she could still see Susan as frequently as she wished. After all, she pointed out, it would not be long before Susan would have to be presented, and then there would be the matter of a settlement on her marriage. These expenses would now all be borne by Chalmsforth, leaving them to devote their resources to their own needs.

But Newlyn, though he supported the sentiment of Kitty's

remarks, was furious that Chalmsforth had once again out-witted him. There could no longer be any doubt that he still doted on Fiona Guthrie and Newlyn had little doubt that she would be infinitely more amenable to Chalmsforth's advances than she had been to his own. He longed for a means of even-ing the score.

That means came in the form of the Marquess of Orbury whom he ran into at White's later that day while his fury at Chalmsforth still rankled. He remembered the match which had been proposed between Orbury's eldest daughter and Chalmsforth that had never transpired; and he drew Orbury aside to question him about it.

"It just didn't happen, Newlyn, that's all. I wanted it and certainly my mother had her heart set on it." Orbury's face grew long at the thought of just how much his mother had been set on it. "It is my belief that Chalmsforth got taken in by that young guest of his mother's. After she arrived he paid little attention to Annabel, though I can't say he had ever done or said anything that could be construed as binding. Anyway, Annabel has caught the eye of Lord Alving now. She seems quite happy with him and I'm sure his intentions are serious, though he has not yet spoken."

"Alving!" Newlyn did not hide his contempt. "Hardly the match of Chalmsforth, is he? Less than a quarter of his es-tate. Serious, but definitely a weak young man, wouldn't be surprised to find that lung disease ran in that family. Didn't he have a cousin who died of it?"

Orbury's dismal countenance deepened. It was just what his mother had said more than once, though he'd reminded her the cousin was not on the Alving side of the family. But he wasn't a great catch, not one you'd boast of like Chalmsforth.

Newlyn saw his advantage and pressed it home.

"I don't know why you are of the opinion that Chalmsforth has no serious intentions toward Lady Annabel. I can assure you such is not the case. As you know, I am related to him by marriage and though in the past we have had our differences, lately these have been reconciled and I now count myself among his closest confidants. Why, I was dining with him at Grosvenor Square last night and he talked of practically no one else. Many call him an arrogant man, but in truth he is shy." Orbury's eyebrows shot up in astonishment. "I know it is hard to believe, but it is so. And it is this shyness, coupled with your daughter's aloofness—I mean no harm, Orbury, she is an admirable young lady, but you must admit she is aloof"—Orbury nodded, and there was a gleam of interest in his eye—"this, together with the fact that he was momentarily swayed by Miss Guthrie, more because of the stir she created than any deep sentiment on his part, which combined to cause what you consider a falling off of his attention. That all his intentions are serious, I can assure you, he told me only last night. But he is of the opinion, now, that she might refuse him."

"If what you say is so, perhaps it will happen after all."

Newlyn knew he must strike now, before Orbury had time to consider further.

"Were I her father, Orbury, I would put the happiness of my daughter foremost. I would not simply stand by and wait for it to happen. All of London has expected the announcement for months. To let the season end without it casts an unnecessary blight on Lady Annabel's future chances. Were I her father I would publish what is already a foregone conclusion and what, I can assure you, would conform to Chalmsforth's dearest wishes as he expressed them to me only yesterday."

Orbury gasped.

"Publish before he has officially spoken, before consulting him?"

"You will be doing him a service by it, I assure you. I happen to know he has gone away to think the matter over, to devise a means of getting back in Lady Annabel's good graces in order that he can propose. If it were already a published fact, it would save his turmoil. Besides"—Newlyn glanced thoughtfully at his fingernails—"it would prevent any possible further interventions."

No one but a man so heartily imbued with his own desires to the exclusion of common reason, no one but a man whose mother daily accused him of losing a connexion she had made with great difficulty, would have been gulled by such an outrageous suggestion, but Orbury, apart from desiring the match almost as much as his mother, was sly enough to realize that once published Chalmsforth would be forced to go through with it. To publicly jilt a lady, especially one of his daughter's rank, would bring discredit on himself and his

193

family, as well as the lady herself. Orbury knew enough of Chalmsforth to know that he would never do that. He did not believe he was shy, but he knew he would never act with dishonour.

The next day's *Morning Post*, therefore, contained an item concerning the forthcoming marriage of Lord Peter Chalmsforth of Perrynchase, Hampshire, and Grosvenor Square, London, to Lady Annabel Telford, eldest daughter of the Marquess of Orbury, the date and place to be announced.

The item sent London tongues wagging, the Dowager Marchioness into high glee, Lady Annabel Telford into tears, Lady Chalmsforth into dumbfounded astonishment, Lord Newlyn into transports of delight, and Mr. Robarts into surprised justification that his prediction of another wedding was correct though the bride was not the one he had envisaged.

Lord Chalmsforth, reading it over his morning breakfast at Culross Abbey, choked on a morsel of smoked haddock he had just put in his mouth, read the item again, flung down his serviette, and rose from the table, his face white with rage.

Fiona Guthrie had returned to Cambridge after a journey of some eighteen hours, half of which had been spent with a sickly, overwrought child, to be met at their destination by distracted parents who had pressed her to stay but whose kind invitation she had refused because of her anxiety to return immediately to Cambridge in case others might have contracted the disease. Besides, she was losing both Anne and Mr. Hadley in one fell swoop. They had been the mainstay of the school and though she had found a replacement for Mr. Hadley, she had no other schoolteacher, which meant she would have to be prepared to teach the entire curriculum until one were found.

She was exhausted when, at last, she climbed down from the post chaise, but she was cheered by the news that Chalmsforth had called and would return that morning. Without him she now believed she could no longer exist, he had become everything to her. Thus when she opened the box he had left for her and her eyes fell on the broach it contained with the promise of its knotted corn centrepiece, her heart jumped wildly and she gasped with joy. It was more than she had dared hope, that he would propose again after all that had happened, yet this could have no other meaning. She well remembered Anne's explaining to him this ancient

Cambridgeshire custom. Life was suddenly bright again and her fatigue melted like dewdrops under the warmth of the sun in her newfound ecstasy. She hugged Anne, who had given her the box, wishing to hide the tears of joy which had come to her eyes, but she said nothing except to insist that they breakfast together as soon as she had changed. She took the stairs two at a time, more like schoolgirl than schoolmistress. Nothing mattered now, for whatever occurred she would no longer face it on her own, there would be a companion always at her side, one whom she knew she had always loved even in their most serious differences.

She peeled off her dusty garments and stood in her shift, stretching and examining herself in the looking glass, wondering what she should wear for him. She rarely thought of her appearance, but now it was of the utmost importance. Suddenly she laughed out loud and spun around still laughing at everything and nothing.

She walked over to her bed and picked up the previous day's *Morning Post* which the maid had left on her night table and glanced through its pages without particularly caring about any of it until her eye caught sight of a name known above all others to her, one which she expected soon to be her own.

At first she could not believe the announcement. She read it again, and then again. Then she crushed the newspaper between her hands and stood perfectly still, staring down at the crumpled paper which at last she threw on the floor before falling full length onto the bed and burying her face in the pillow as though to immure herself from the entire world.

When Anne called her down to breakfast she pretended to be sleeping and Anne left her, creeping quietly from the room. She lay there without moving until Anne knocked softly at the door to say that Lord Chalmsforth was below and wished to see her. Only then did she get up to look into her pale, drawn face in the mirror, longing to refuse to go down, yet knowing it must be done. As she dressed she told herself that he could not be capable of so cruel a joke, it must be that he had forgotten the significance of the knotted ears of corn, remembering only that it was a Cambridgeshire custom. Perhaps he thought it was a token of friendship, given in consolation for the fact that he would see her less often from then on.

If Fiona was loathe to see Chalmsforth, Chalmsforth had been even more reluctant to call. Ever since reading the announcement of his own betrothal, Chalmsforth's spirits had been in a turmoil. His first reaction had been to publish an immediate denial, yet no sooner did he begin to word it than he knew it was impossible for him to publicly disown a lady; a retraction could only come from her. He thought to return to London directly without stopping at Cambridge, yet he had promised to do so; he had to ease Fiona's mind about Susan. He found himself, however, in an impossible dilemma—publicly engaged to one woman, privately pledged to another.

What would Fiona think of him? What could he tell her to explain a situation he himself did not understand? In desperation, he hoped she might not yet have read of it, that he might be able to solve the puzzle before she did so. He was, therefore, greatly relieved to learn from Anne Robarts on his arrival at the school that Fiona had only that morning returned. If she said nothing, he vowed to leave the matter in abeyance until he had learned the truth of the matter and forced a retraction from Orbury.

The first thing he looked for, as Fiona greeted him, was a sign of the broach or token; she was wearing neither. Had she opened the box, surely she would have mentioned it, surely she would at least be wearing the broach, her favourite broach with its memories of Mary of Scotland.

Very briefly he gave her the news of Susan, news she accepted thankfully. Delighted though she was to know that Susan was freed from Newlyn, she was unable to show her usual enthusiasm. When he married, she wondered, would Chalmsforth leave Susan with her? Probably so, until Annabel might decide to have her as a companion.

All the things that had been on Chalmsforth's mind, Newlyn's revelations, his own discovery of the great depth of his feelings for Fiona, none of this could be spoken of until the Orbury matter was resolved. Instead he spoke of Anne's wedding, of the breakfast to follow at the abbey, that his mother was invited to attend, yet even this discussion concerning, as it did, weddings, he could ill abide, so he turned to ask her how she would be able to manage without Anne and Mr. Hadley. She told him she had had three promising responses to her advertisement for a teacher and she had already found a tutor to take Mr. Hadley's place, a friend of his, Mr. Vernon.

"What is he like?" Chalmsforth asked, more by way of conversation than for information.

"He is a tutor at Trinity and very well thought of by Mr. Hadley and others. He seems to understand what is needed and to have both patience and good humour."

"He sounds a veritable paragon," Chalmsforth retorted in sudden annoyance that she should speak well of another. "Is he young?"

"I believe he is somewhat older than Mr. Hadley."

"And is he married?"

"I really didn't ask. It seemed to have no bearing."

A silence ensued during which Fiona felt she should congratulate him on his engagement, but could not find the words to do so, and he felt he should speak to her on the same matter, especially since when she did open his box with its symbolic message, she would wonder that he had not done so. They both found courage to speak at the same moment.

"Allow me to convey——"

"There is something I must explain . . . oh blast!"

This last exclamation was caused by a knock on the door which immediately opened to reveal a tall gentleman in his thirties, clad in clerical garb, possessed of a head of dark, waving hair, a handsome face with a straight, slim nose and forthright chin, and an expression of extreme pleasure as his dark eyes fell on Fiona.

"Mr. Vernon," she greeted him. "I was just speaking to Lord Chalmsforth of you," and turning to Chalmsforth, she introduced them.

As the two men bowed, Chalmsforth felt an instant and completely unwarranted dislike of the new tutor.

"I am sorry, perhaps I am interrupting," Mr. Vernon began to withdraw.

"No, please," Fiona said quickly, "unless you have anything more to say, Lord Chalmsforth?"

"Nothing, it would seem," Chalmsforth arose and started to pull on his driving gloves. Fiona saw what she could only construe as an expression of hurt in his eyes and she was suddenly mortified at the offensive manner of her dismissal. He had every right to marry where he pleased, she had already known his name was linked with that of Lady Annabel. He had already done all he could and more for her, especially in this instance in the matter of Susan. She was an ingrate. She rose from her seat as Mr. Vernon withdrew to bring in the books he was going to use, leaving them momentarily alone.

"I thought you said Mr. Vernon was old," Chalmsforth accused.

"I said older than Mr. Hadley," she corrected.

"In point of fact, I suspect he is scarcely older than I."

"You may be right. His age is really unimportant. It is his ability to hold the girls' attention that matters."

"With his appearance and manner he should have little difficulty," Chalmsforth replied caustically before withdrawing.

"I think he will suit very well."

Her reply rankled.

All the way to London he found himself thinking as often of the intimacy that might develop between Fiona and the handsome new tutor as of his own entanglement. He wished he were of a character to ignore the harm that would surely befall Annabel Telford should Orbury refuse to retract the announcement, and he publicly deny it. That he could never do. The affair had publicly linked his name with that of a lady; his honour demanded that he act circumspectly towards her however difficult or undesirable the situation might be. He considered his unspoken promise to Fiona had been made in all honour and sincerity; yet it remained a private matter. She would not be publicly dishonoured should he be forced to marry Annabel Telford. But he would not think of that. There might, perhaps, be some logical explanation, some misunderstanding. There must be.

He found it difficult, however, to contain his ire when in calling on his mother before going to see Orbury, she expressed her regret that he had not confided in her.

"I thought that was all over, until I read of it in the paper. Why didn't you tell me, Peter?"

"I did not tell you, Mother, because I did not know," was his irked response.

"What can you mean, you did not know?" she asked in astonishment.

He wondered whether to apprise her of Orbury's duplicity, but he had no proof of that, not yet. The Dowager Marchioness was, too, his mother's friend. It would be bound to upset her to know that such an announcement had been made without his consent. He would say nothing, not until he knew the truth.

"Just that I had not expected it to appear—at this time."

"You don't seem very happy about it."

"Perhaps after seeing my bride-to-be and her dear papa my humour may improve," he replied grimly. "If you will excuse me, that is just what I am about to do."

XXI

The Marquess of Orbury raised his pale, puffy eyes at Chalmsforth's entrance and, noting his harsh expression, hastened to lower them again. He had been dreading this interview. But his voice was hearty enough as he spoke, perhaps unnecessarily so.

"Chalmsforth, my dear fellow. How delighted I am to see you."

"I may take it you expected me."

"Why, of course, you have undoubtedly come to . . ." Words failed Orbury, an unlikely occurrence, but true nevertheless.

"To receive your congratulations?" Chalmsforth hazarded in dry tones.

"Indeed, my dear fellow, I do congratulate you, most heartily I do." Perhaps the interview would not be as difficult as he feared.

"And now for your explanation," Chalmsforth pursued remorselessly.

No, Orbury thought, it was going to be every bit as difficult as he had feared.

"Well, sir, I presume you refer to the announcement in the *Post.*" He paused.

"I do." Chalmsforth fixed his steely gaze upon him and Orbury rose and then sat down again. His legs felt unsteady.

"Chalmsforth, I want you to understand——"

"I want to understand; please explain, for it is totally incomprehensible."

"Chalmsforth, if you had a daughter pining away, moping around the house, making herself ill, a shadow of her former self, would you not be wishful to do anything you could to ease her distress?"

"You cannot, I am sure, be referring to Lady Annabel."

"But I am, sir, I am."

"I have seen her several times in these past months and at no time has there been the least suspicion that she was fading away."

"There you are wrong. Publicly she has been courageous, but in private, sir, in private, ah"—he sighed heavily—"only a father can know."

"Know what?" Judging by Chalmsforth's tones, there was no respite in his anger.

"Why, that she has been dying for love."

"For love of whom, Orbury? Pray do not tell me that she has been dying with love for me." Chalmsforth snorted.

"But that is so, Chalmsforth, just so. Ever since you dined with the family that night, no, even before that, long before that, she loved you from afar, but that night when you came, she believed you returned the affection which had so long been in her heart."

"The last time I saw Lady Annabel," Chalmsforth put in dryly, "was at the debut of Sir Horace Wakeley's daughter and she seemed to be doing very well, very well indeed with Lord Alving, as, I might add, was he with her."

Orbury fidgeted in his chair. He remembered the occasion and how pleased his wife had been that Annabel had found someone to her taste. But Newlyn was right, Alving wasn't a patch on Chalmsforth, not by half.

"A front, Chalmsforth, merely a front. She saw you there and not for a moment would she have you know how she really felt, but when she got home, how she cried. It is hard to pretend."

"That I can well believe," Chalmsforth replied with sarcasm. "How could you, Lord Orbury, give such a false announcement for publication, without one particle of truth in fact. Never, at any time, did I propose to your daughter. I don't believe I have exchanged more than a dozen sentences with her in the past three months, nor she with me. She is hardly a talkative lady."

Orbury grasped at a straw. "Ah, there you have it. She is not. Nor are you a talkative man, just so, just so. That is what is behind it all. I would never have done such a thing on my own recognizance had I not been assured it was your wish. I knew it was hers. I understood you felt that a rift had developed between you and were anxious to approach her. Forgive me, but as a doting father and your friend I saw one means of solving it all in one coup, the announcement, and it was done."

"It was indeed!" The reply was grim. "But who could have been so base as to lead you to believe that I was dying with love for your daughter, or was it your own fancy?"

"No, indeed." Orbury drew himself up in high dudgeon. "Do not accuse me of coercion, sir! It was your friend Lord Newlyn who assured me such was the case and that I would be doing you a favour by taking such a step. Without his word, I never would have done so."

"I see. I see it all." Chalmsforth sat down and rested his brow in his hands for a moment. That explained everything.

At last he raised his head. "What you were told is false, completely false. I admire your daughter, I respect her, I do not love her. My affections lie elsewhere. I ask you as a gentleman to retract that announcement."

Orbury shrugged and held out his hands helplessly. "Chalmsforth, I cannot. Now Annabel is convinced it is to be. I cannot break her heart."

That left only one hope—Annabel. Chalmsforth was convinced that she liked Alving, if only she would admit it.

"Then may I see her and talk to her?" He sensed Orbury's reluctance. "I should at least be permitted to see someone the world views as my bride-to-be."

"Of course, of course." Orbury rose, heartened by the phrase, and summoned a servant to fetch his daughter. He hoped she would abide by her decision now that he had got Chalmsforth around. She had been more difficult than he had supposed, saying that Chalmsforth was too severe, that she preferred Alving, but he and his mother had both talked to her until, at last, she had proved tractable.

Lady Annabel entered and greeted Chalmsforth formally, though he detected a blush that deepened as he asked to be left alone with her. It did not escape him that Orbury paused to catch his daughter's eye before quitting the room.

"I understand we are to be married, Lady Annabel; at least that is what I read in the newspaper." He did not hide his dislike of the idea, but she replied coolly enough,

"Yes, Lord Chalmsforth, that is so." She might have been discussing the price of apples, he thought bitterly.

"Do you want it?" he questioned bluntly.

"Well, of course," she replied without any particular enthusiasm.

"Are you quite sure there is no one else you prefer?"

"No."

"Lord Alving, for instance?"

She paused before replying, and he caught his breath hopefully, but she replied, "No, I wish to marry you."

"Why?"

She was nonplussed. She had been angry with her father for taking such a step, but it was done. She would have preferred to marry Alving, but perhaps it didn't make much difference. Men were much the same and her life after marriage would continue much as before.

"Since you do not reply am I to assume, as your father tells me, that you are desperately in love with me?"

Annabel was quite sure she would never be desperately in love with anybody—it hardly sounded ladylike—yet to deny it would cause further comment. She nodded.

"Then I believe it is normal on such occasions to kiss."

She held up her cheek, but he took her in his arms and kissed her lips. It was like kissing a porcelain doll. He thought of one he longed to be holding, of how she responded. No he must not do that.

"You must excuse me," he said releasing her, "but you do not kiss as one in love."

"Lord Chalmsforth, please!" Lady Annabel drew away from him in dismay. "We are engaged to be married, but that does not allow you to take liberties with me."

"Liberties?" he questioned.

She flushed at his look and the insistence with which he repeated, "Liberties, Lady Annabel?"

"That—that sort of thing comes after marriage, not before," she asserted primly, though with some asperity.

"That sort of thing, as you call it, is a very important demonstration of love where it exists."

"Well, I shall do all that is proper at the appropriate time, after we are married, when it is quite lawful."

"Proper! Lawful! Allowable! Lady Annabel, answer me directly and honestly. Are you in love with me?"

"Yes, Lord Chalmsforth," she affirmed, though forced to turn away from his scrutiny; "yes, I am."

"And you had expected this marriage?"

"I had, sir, and so, now, does the world."

"I see."

His gloom deepened. She was as unrelenting as her father.

Yet he was a Chalmsforth, he could not publicly disown the lady, only she could release him and he vowed that somehow she would.

"Have you picked a date for the wedding," he demanded, "or should I read the newspapers to discover that also?"

She blushed. "I presume it is for you to decide."

"I am glad to hear I have some say in the affair." He was thoughtful for a moment. "You may have heard that I have purchased Culross Abbey in Cambridgeshire."

She nodded.

"When we marry I shall expect you to reside there. I, of course, shall have to come to London from time to time on parliamentary matters, but that will be my residence and I shall expect you to stay there. We may occasionally entertain, but I do not intend to have a great many people down. I prefer the solitary existence."

"Do you mean we shall not stay in London, not even for the season?" Annabel was horrified.

"No. I shall, very likely, give up Grosvenor Square. But I expect you will find the abbey entirely to your taste. The solitary nature of the fen country is particularly appealing to those of a passionate nature."

He noticed Annabel's slight shudder and took heart.

"I am holding a wedding breakfast there for the rector's daughter on Friday. I would like you and your family to attend so that you may become acquainted with your future home."

The altar of St. Matthew's was decorated with autumn foliage and sheaves of corn for the wedding. Chalmsforth, sitting in the front pew beside his affianced bride and her father and mother, the Dowager Marchioness, and Lady Chalmsforth, realized it was almost exactly a year since he had first seen the interior of that church. How much had happened in that year. He tried to keep his eyes from Fiona, attending the bride at the altar but, try as he might, he could not. And to see her he had to look past Mr. Vernon, who was serving as best man and whom, he found, he disliked even more for his present close proximity to Fiona. It detestably gave the appearance of a double wedding, causing him almost to jump to his feet when Mr. Robarts, in conducting the service, gave the usual warning on possible encumbrances to the ceremony. That was ridiculous. Were it even as he feared, grounds of love were no grounds at all, particularly when the lover, himself, was due to be the bridegroom of another. He watched the altar candles flicker across Fiona's expressionless face as she stood, never once glancing in his direction. She had hardly spoken to him at all. She doesn't care, he thought savagely, and now I can never tell her how much I do. She was not wearing the broach, he had noticed as soon as she arrived. The token he knew she must have removed and probably thrown away, but the broach she treasured. He half expected, since it was not pinned to her dress, that she planned to return it to him as she had done once before. He wished she would so that he might have an opportunity to talk to her, to explain the inexplicable. Despite a deliberate attempt on his part to thwart any enthusiasm Annabel might hold for the abbey, even to the extent of assuring fewer fires were lit so that it was cooler than usual and conducting her to the most deserted parts of the surrounding country, her father and grandmother more than made up for her lack of comment by becoming effusive in their praise. Annabel only nodded in assent. He was convinced that she did not want the marriage but she was a dutiful daughter. Her father and grandmother did and would see to it that she did not give him up. Newlyn had had his revenge.

It had been arranged that Fiona should stay the night at the abbey. She had not wished to, but Lady Chalmsforth had written especially asking her to do so; it was so long since they had seen one another, Fiona had felt unable to refuse. Since Mr. Vernon had driven Fiona and Susan from Cambridge for the wedding, he was also invited to stay, as was Colonel Farendon, who had come with the London party, so that even after the wedding group left, the party was still quite large.

Fiona had been upset from the outset. Though Chalmsforth might have thought her cool and uncaring, throughout the service she had been unnerved by his presence, but more particularly by the presence next to him of the beautiful Lady Annabel who would soon be his wife, for Lady Chalmsforth had said in her letter that the Dowager Marchioness was predicting an early wedding. That would be one that no amount of pleading on the part of Lady Chalmsforth could make her attend, she thought, as she listened to the familiar words of the marriage service, clenching her fists so tightly that her nails bit into her hands.

That morning had seen her first visit to the abbey since it had ceased to be her home. She had always thought she could not abide to see it changed. Now she discovered that it was unbearable to find it completely unchanged, only restored. So many things she remembered as a child had been recovered from the four parts of the world to which they had been scattered and were once again back in place, almost as though by magic: the portrait of the earliest Guthrie who had received the abbey from James was back in the hall, her father's favourite chiming clock was in the room which had always served as his study, her mother's Louis quinze writing desk was again under the window in the library. It had been almost too much to bear. She had seen it only briefly before starting for the church, but it had been enough to make her catch her breath and bite her lower lip to prevent herself from crying. Chalmsforth had seen that, too, as he was helping Lady Annabel with her fur wrap. It was as much as he could do not to run to her, to hold her, to kiss her, not passionately as before but as a father might kiss a sorrowing child. But he had not, and at that moment Mr. Vernon had taken her arm for, since they were part of the wedding, their presence was required before the others at the church.

How she had managed to survive the wedding breakfast she did not know, except that she knew it had to be done for Anne; nothing must mar her wedding. But as soon as the wedded pair left, she had straightway left the others and made her way to the east wing, to Mary Stuart's room, and there, sitting in her favourite chair still in its place by the window, touching the etching on the window pane, *"Ne crie point pour moi"*—Don't cry for me—she had burst into tears. She did not cry for Mary Stuart but for herself, for the husband she could never have, for the home that was no longer hers. How she envied Annabel Telford. For the first time in her life she truly envied another woman and she cried for that also, for envy was a sin.

So distraught was she, she heard nothing of the tap on the door nor the footsteps crossing the room, nothing until she felt the light touch on her shoulder.

"Fiona?"

"Lady Chalmsforth!"

"Peter said I might find you here. I want to talk to you. You are unhappy. I saw it in your face, in your eyes, as soon as you arrived. What is the matter?"

Fiona tried to dry her eyes, but then she threw herself into Lady Chalmsforth's arms and gave way to tears until at last those soothing arms quieted her sobs.

Lady Chalmsforth wiped her brow. "Come, Fiona, talk to me."

But Lady Chalmsforth was the one person above all she could not tell what truly troubled her. She dried her eyes and tried to smile.

"Forgive me, but I do cry at weddings and at this one I had to hold my tears back for Anne's sake. When she left I just couldn't prevent them any longer. I came here because I didn't wish to cast a pall on the party. It's foolish of me to behave so."

"Is that it? Is that all? Because Anne is married and gone?"

Fiona nodded, not trusting herself to speak.

"Are you sure it is nothing more, Fiona?"

"No . . . no, what should it be?"

"Forgive me. It is just that I thought perhaps . . ." She did not say what she thought but took Fiona's hand in hers.

"I love you, Fiona, as a mother loves a daughter. I want you to know and remember that. You are as dear to me as Sarah would have been had she grown to womanhood. I had always hoped . . ." Again, she did not say what it was she had hoped, unless that hope was contained in her next remark.

"It is almost time for dinner and we must change. Annabel Telford's room is opposite yours. I know you don't know her well, but I wish you would talk to her. She seems not altogether happy."

"Lady Annabel not happy!" Fiona's voice filled with incredulity.

"Perhaps you can discover whether I am right in my surmise that she does not wish to marry my son, for I cannot get her to talk to me."

"But that is impossible!" Fiona protested vehemently. "She must be honoured to marry him. Anyone would be."

Lady Chalmsforth gave her a half smile.

"So it would seem."

She knows, Fiona thought, turning away in confusion.

"Promise me you'll talk to her. I know she will never tell me truly how she feels since I am Peter's mother. But you are of her age, she may talk to you."

Annabel Telford was trying to decide whether to wear the

rubies Chalmsforth had given her or her own lapis lazuli necklace which Alving had always favoured when Fiona came in. The arrival of this uninvited guest surprised her; they had barely spoken together and there was certainly no intimacy between them to warrant such a visit.

Fiona, wondering how to begin, saw the rubies and exclaimed at their beauty.

"They're from Chalmsforth," Annabel replied without any particular enthusiasm. She found him even more cold and severe at the abbey than in London. She thought of being alone with him and no one else. The rubies were beautiful, but with no one to admire them, what good were they? She felt miserable.

"I'm sorry, I fear I am late in felicitating you." Fiona held out her hand. "You must be very happy."

She looked closely at Annabel. She looked no happier in receiving Fiona's congratulations than Fiona felt in giving them. Fiona was, in fact, sure she saw her lip quiver.

"You will come to love this abbey, I am sure, every bit as much as I do, if you don't already."

Now it was more than a quiver, it was a tremble. The corners of her mouth turned down and she began to cry.

"No, I won't. I'll never love it. I hate it now and I'll always hate it. And Chalmsforth says we must live here—always, not just for a week or so in the summer, but all year, every year. It's old. I like new places. It's cold. I like warmth. But worst of all it's desolate, miles from anywhere. The people here are dowds like those at that wedding today, not a soul worth knowing. What good are rubies to me here, tucked away from everything in the world that is happening; no one will see me wear them."

"Chalmsforth will," Fiona said quietly.

"He is cold to me. I know he doesn't want to marry me. It was father's doing, father and grandmother, though I think the Earl of Newlyn led them to believe Chalmsforth wanted it. Anyway, they published it without his knowing. Now he will go through with it because of the shame it would cause if he did not, but I know it will be awful. I'm convinced he doesn't like me. He frightens me a little. I would much prefer to marry Alving; at least I know he enjoys the sort of life I do, parties and people, not mist and desolation. He wrote me such a sad letter when he read of my engagement in the paper."

"Can it possibly be true that it was published without Chalmsforth's knowledge?" Fiona was astounded.

Annabel nodded.

"And he would not repudiate it?"

"Of course he could not; my reputation is at stake."

"Perhaps, but how ridiculous it seems for both you and he and—and others—to live unhappily for such a reason."

Annabel tossed her head slightly. "But a lady's reputation is important. If it is tainted in any way, she may never marry."

"Of course, of course," Fiona might not agree, but her thoughts were overcome by her discovery, and the knowledge that Annabel could set matters to rights if she would.

"Annabel, I shall tell you what I have told no one. I love Peter Chalmsforth. I have done so for a long time. Before this announcement appeared, I had reason to believe that he loved me, that he was even about to propose to me. You have told me that you care for someone else who apparently cares for you. Does it not seem foolish to you that we should all suffer because of some desire of others who are not directly involved?"

"I suppose so."

"You could set it all right."

"But how?"

"By renouncing Peter."

"Me, renounce Chalmsforth! Oh, but I couldn't."

"Why not? You don't want to marry him, but I do. You must release him, for as you have said, he cannot renounce you."

"Oh, but I couldn't. There's Papa—but more especially there's Grandmother." Annabel shuddered slightly.

"There is also the rest of your life, Annabel, and not just yours but Chalmsforth's and Alving's, not to mention mine. Think about it, do. If you don't act, all of us must suffer. You would not enjoy living here, you have told me. You do not care for Chalmsforth. If you renounce him, you will not suffer, and you can accept Alving without fear of society's retribution."

She saw Annabel begin to waver.

"I believe you are strong, just as strong as your grandmother if you choose to be. You have her nose, her eyes, and I don't doubt you have her strength of purpose, if you set your mind to it."

Annabel stared at her image in the mirror for a moment, then she turned back.

"No, I couldn't," she whispered.

"Yes, you can." Fiona picked up the lapis lazuli necklace and fastened it round her. "I know you can."

XXII

The party was all assembled by the time Fiona came down, and had been for some time. It was unlike her to be late and Chalmsforth had glanced at his watch more than once wondering whether she was still upset at seeing her old home. He had counted on her having her first sight of the abbey and all that had been done to it under totally different circumstances; with the large gathering he had had no opportunity to speak to her. Things being as they were, perhaps that was as well, yet it must be painful for her to see the abbey restored.

Just when he had decided he should ask his mother to go to her, she came, and he caught his breath. It was not the lilac silk dress she wore of the self-same colour as her eyes, nor the fact that her hair was arranged in a particularly intricate fashion, nor even that her eyes, completely recovered from her earlier tears, gleamed with a brighter light than usual. All this he noticed, but what transfixed his gaze was that she was wearing his broach. The gold wreath was pinned over her heart. It still contained the courtship token of corn, and she had carefully pointed the ears of the corn to the right, a sign of her acceptance of his proposal. He stared first in astonishment, then in perplexity, at last in anger. What right had she to tease him in this manner? Did she not realize how much it hurt him, this acceptance of his suit when he was so hopelessly tied elsewhere? But in response to his questioning frown, she gave him an encouraging smile and went over to speak with Colonel Farendon, receiving with great satisfaction his reports on her brother's progress.

"He's a brilliant soldier, Miss Guthrie. You have every reason to be proud of him. Already promoted to captain and I have no doubt he'll go much farther. I wish I had ten more like him—not even ten, five would do—we'd have Boney on the run." His eye fell on the broach as he spoke. "Might I ask the significance, I presume it has some, of the spray of corn you are wearing?"

"Why, of course." She smiled again at Chalmsforth as she answered. "It is an old Cambridgeshire custom. You have seen it before, have you not, Lord Chalmsforth?"

"I have." His reply was terse. She was teasing him. He turned away.

"But it must have some special significance," Farendon pressed.

"It does, of course it does."

"But what is it, good luck?"

"Yes, very, very good luck," she replied fervently.

The dinner gong sounded to cut short the discussion.

Fiona sat between Colonel Farendon and Mr. Vernon, and Chalmsforth, though removed from her at his place at the head of the table between Lady Annabel and her grandmother, found it difficult to concentrate, his eyes constantly wandering back to the corn token Fiona wore. Why had she done it now, why, why? He could hear Orbury's voice recounting some long tale to his mother who sat opposite him, while the Dowager Marchioness kept up a monotone similar to that of her son in his ear. He spoke little, and Annabel said not a word.

As soon as the ladies withdrew, leaving the men to their port, Fiona drew Annabel aside.

"When will you speak?" she asked quickly, in an undertone.

Annabel shook her head. "I can't." She motioned toward her grandmother. "I can never do it. She would not wish it."

Fiona was exasperated. "Annabel, I thought you had more stamina than that. Are you willing to spend your life in misery for fear of the temporary displeasure of your grandmother? No, I cannot believe that of you. You are brave and can do what must be done."

But Annabel merely shook her head.

Fiona had believed Annabel would speak. She must be made to speak. She was the only one who could release Chalmsforth. She would speak.

When the gentlemen rejoined them, Fiona went over to the Dowager Marchioness to ask whether she had not enjoyed the wedding.

"Yes," she condescended. "It was a pretty thing, a small, country wedding. But, of course, that won't do for Annabel.

212

It must be St. George's, Hanover Square. I am drawing up a list of those who must be invited, and Madame Elyse has already started on the bridal dress, a gorgeous thing of Brussels lace. I hope you will see it."

When she marries Lord Alving I shall be delighted to, Fiona thought. She stared pointedly at Annabel, who looked quickly away.

There was a lull in the conversation and Fiona again turned to Annabel and said very distinctly,

"Lady Annabel, is there not something you wish to say, an announcement you wish to make, something you spoke of to me earlier?"

The party looked from Fiona to Annabel, who for the first time publicly lost her composure and seemed on the point of tears. Fiona went to her and took her hand.

"Please," she said softly, "for the happiness of all of us."

Annabel took a deep breath, then, looking directly at her grandmother, she said defiantly, "I cannot marry Lord Chalmsforth."

"What!" the Dowager Marchioness exclaimed. "Are you quite well, Annabel? Pray tell me I did not hear you aright."

"You did, Grandmother. I cannot marry Lord Chalmsforth. He loves Miss Guthrie and she has told me that she loves him. For my part, I prefer to marry elsewhere."

There was a tomblike silence during which Chalmsforth fixed his eyes on Fiona's face. She caught his earnest gaze of relief and love and happiness and nodded to him almost imperceptibly.

Annabel was now in control of the situation.

"I wish tomorrow, Papa, as soon as we return to London, that you would place my retraction of the notice of my engagement, which you published earlier. And I would like your promise that you will never again publish anything on my behalf without consulting me first."

A furor broke out between the Dowager Marchioness and her son, recriminations, protestations, explanations. Lady Chalmsforth, who had caught her breath at the revelation, seeing the all-too-obvious embarrassment of Orbury's wife, hastened to draw her aside. Colonel Farendon and Mr. Vernon gazed in astonishment at the scene, and while the tumult showed no sign of abating, Fiona, finding herself in unexpected fear and confusion, turned to hurry from the room.

She was in tears by the time she reached the seclusion of

the library, her thoughts racing. How had she dared to bring such a thing about? Had she been right? Did he really love her?

Her answer came in the firm closing of the library door. Chalmsforth was there and, for the first time, she allowed him to see her tears, her vulnerability. He took her in his arms and she cried without shame in a place where all felt right and secure.

"Fiona! Fiona!" he whispered, holding her head close against his rapidly dampening shoulder. "How I love you, now more than ever. And it is true, then, that you love me?"

She pulled back to look into the face of the one she had so nearly lost and, taking his proffered handkerchief to wipe her eyes, she affirmed her love.

"I was afraid she would never speak," she concluded. "I was afraid we would forever be parted."

"So was I," he owned. "This past week has been a nightmare such as I have never known. But now it is over." Looking around the room, he added, "And we are here, where we first met, and you are in my arms, and everything is the same, yet so very different."

He kissed her then, as he had kissed her that first time, yet with a passion born of love rather than sudden infatuation, a passion so much deeper, so much more fulfilling.

"Everything is as it should be," she replied at last.

They sat together in front of the fire, clinging to one another as though, otherwise, it might all prove to be a dream.

"Does the fact that you are wearing my token obviate me from the necessity of asking for your hand in marriage?" he asked, his eyes twinkling.

"Indeed, no," she responded solemnly, "for what should I have to tell my grandchildren when they ask me about this moment?"

Gravely, he knelt down at her feet.

"My dear Miss Guthrie, may I ask you to do me the honour of conferring upon me your hand in marriage?"

Leaning down, she took his face fondly between those two hands.

"You may, sir, and with all my heart, I accept."

"I wonder if you have any idea of how happy you have made me?"

"If you feel as I do, then I believe I have," she responded, but anything else she might have wished to add was smothered by his kisses.

They stayed until the flames from the fire died down and only brightly gleaming embers filled the hearth. He told her everything that had occurred, not forgetting his encounter with Newlyn.

"I have discovered that you are most adept at piquet," he teased.

"Then Newlyn told you the truth, at last, of how I obtained that money."

He nodded, remembering his earlier recriminations.

"I apologize for believing otherwise, but the strangest part of all was to discover that it was no longer important what had or had not happened in the past. All I wanted was you, just as you are, for better or for worse. Nothing else made any difference. Having you at my side was all I cared about."

"Darling, darling Peter. I never dared hope that you would say that, though I cannot deny it was what I always wished for."

The red embers cast a burnished glow upon them meeting the glow coming from within to bathe them in happiness, peace, and serenity.

That happiness for Fiona seemed complete when he said, "Your school must continue—you are right in your assertion that girls should be allowed to receive an education worthy of the name; it must be so for our own girls as well as others. I hope, however, you won't find it necessary to spend all of your time there."

"I believe we might persuade Anne and Arthur Hadley to take it over if we can assure them a good living." She nestled against him, wondering whether she should yet mention her idea of an institution devoted to the higher education of women. No, perhaps that should wait for another time.

He kissed her, and it may have been that in that kiss were the seeds of Girton, the first college for women at Cambridge, though three generations were to pass before their great-granddaughter could enroll there.

About the Author

British-born Diana Brown has lived and worked throughout Europe and the Far East. Ms. Brown, a librarian, now lives in San Jose, California, with her husband and her two daughters, Pamela and Clarissa, who are named after Samuel Richardson's heroines.